W9-DBK-220

WISH UPON A COWBOY

"Kane blends folk legend and magic into a charming plot."
—*Publishers Weekly*

"Lots of ingenious situations, beautiful phrasing and a charming . . . hero . . . Ms. Kane's latest work is fresh and clever. Excellent entertainment . . . a must-read."
—*Old Book Barn Gazette*

"Ms. Kane tickles your funny bone and waves her magic wand to insure a good time is had by all. Bravo!"
—*Rendezvous*

"Kathleen Kane's remarkable story-telling talents shine once again in this captivating and wonderful tale . . . a rare and delicious treat to savor." —*Romantic Times*

SIMPLY MAGIC

"This historical romance by Ms. Kane is magic itself, with a wonderful blend of danger, love, and otherworldly magic. It is simply a must-read!" —*Old Book Barn Gazette*

"If you want to feel that tingle down to your toes, then rush out to get yourself a copy of *Simply Magic*."
—*Romantic Times*

"Simply wonderful. . . . Kane gifts her readers with stories that live long in the memory, and uplift the heart."
—*Affaire de Coeur*

"Anyone who reads a Kathleen Kane novel knows they are in for a thoroughly entertaining experience . . . a humorous but poignant storyline. As with all her superb novels, Kane has succeeded once again." —*Painted Rock Reviews*

DREAMWEAVER

"Kane incorporates tender and fantastic touches. True to her talent, Kane keeps the conflicts lively to the end and fills the plot with many surprises." —*Publishers Weekly*

"A . . . beautiful . . . love story . . . will warm your heart and leave you with a smile." —*Romantic Times*

"Kane just gets better and better with each one of her books." —*Interludes*

THIS TIME FOR KEEPS

"If you like your heroes tall, dark and sexy, and if laughter is your aphrodisiac, then rush to your nearest bookstore." —*Telegraph Herald*

"Wondrous romance that will leave you longing for more . . . Kane's extraordinary talents shine." —*Romantic Times*

"A lively plot of all-out seduction." —*Publishers Weekly*

"Peppered liberally with intrigue and humor. A wonderful story that everyone is sure to enjoy!" —*Old Book Barn Gazette*

"A fun-filled merry chase through history, bringing this reader to laughter and tears. Don't miss this one!" —*Bell, Book & Candle* (five bells)

"Kane has fashioned a likable heroine and a fast-paced plot . . . all with a gently humorous touch." —*Library Journal*

Just West of Heaven

KATHLEEN KANE

St. Martin's Paperbacks

JUST WEST OF HEAVEN

Copyright © 2001 by Kathleen Kane.

All rights reserved. No part of this book may be used or reproduced in any manner whatsoever without written permission except in the case of brief quotations embodied in critical articles or reviews. For information address St. Martin's Press, 175 Fifth Avenue, New York, NY 10010.

ISBN: 0-312-97766-2

Printed in the United States of America

St. Martin's Paperbacks edition / August 2001

St. Martin's Paperbacks are published by St. Martin's Press, 175 Fifth Avenue, New York, NY 10010.

10 9 8 7 6 5 4 3 2 1

To my husband Mark, for thirty years of love and laugh-ter. As steady as the Vega, you've always been there, ready to lend me a hand or provide a shoulder for me to cry on. You believe in me even when I don't believe in myself and make me laugh when I take myself or the world too seriously.

And now, thirty years and two kids later, you're still my best friend.

I love you.

CHAPTER ONE

"I won't let you take her from me," Sophie Dolan said, staring at the man seated behind a gleaming mahogany desk.

"Your mother's will says I can." Charles Vinson shrugged, tugged at the cuffs of his white linen shirt then adjusted the lapels of his black broadcloth coat. "But we don't have to be at odds, Sophie."

"Of course we do," she snapped, nodding her head so hard, her straw bonnet tipped precariously over one eye. "You're trying to steal my little sister."

"Steal?" he repeated and stood up. Adjusting the hang of his well-tailored coat, he walked around the edge of the desk and gave her a look usually reserved for a spoiled child. "I'm Jenna's legal guardian," he reminded her.

"I'm her *sister*," Sophie said and heard the strain in her voice. She wished she could swear at him. She wished she knew the right words to curl his toes and singe his eyebrows. She wished . . . it didn't matter what she wished. Wishing wouldn't change anything.

"And a spinster," he added, with a sympathetic shake of his head. "Hardly able to look after yourself, let alone a child."

She felt the jab hit home, but disregarded it. At

twenty-four years old, after all, she *was* a spinster. No point in fighting the obvious. Not when there were so many other things to be fought. Sophie reached up and pushed her hat back into place. "I'm perfectly able to take care of myself and Jenna—"

"However," Charles said, interrupting her as he let his gaze move up and down her body like a man considering whether or not to buy a particular horse. "Perhaps there's a way we could both have what we want."

She imagined that was just what the snake in the Garden of Eden's voice had sounded like. Smooth, slow, tempting.

"And what's that?" she forced herself to ask.

"Marry me and we can both have her."

So much for temptation. Sophie sucked in a breath. Just the thought of marrying Charles Vinson was enough to make her skin crawl. And not even for the sake of the little sister she loved, could Sophie imagine sleeping beside the man—not to mention doing *other* things.

"Don't you find me attractive?" he asked, giving her a smile that told her he knew exactly what she thought.

"Oh, you're handsome enough," she muttered, "but so's a diamondback, until it rattles."

"That razor-sharp tongue of yours is the reason you can't find a man," he said tightly, taking a step closer.

She wanted to move back, but she stood her ground, refusing to give him the satisfaction. "Spinsters are supposed to be outspoken," she said. "We're eccentric."

"You're crazy."

"Then why would you want to marry me?"

"It would make life easier for Jenna."

"And you're very concerned with Jenna, aren't you, Charles?" Sarcasm colored her words, but she doubted it would have any impact.

"As a matter of fact," he said, laying both hands on her shoulders, "I am."

The instant he touched her, Sophie's mind swam. Fog swirled across her brain and a familiar, throbbing ache settled behind her eyes. No, she thought, not now. She fought for air, fought to battle back the images before they could form, but it was too late and her mind spun with fragments, snatches of scenes. *Jenna, locked in a room, crying. Charles, counting his money and laughing. Jenna, forced to use her "gift" to fill this man's pockets. And finally, an image of Sophie herself, outside Charles's home, desperately beating on the door, trying to get in. To get to her sister.*

She dragged in an unsteady breath, and despite the numbing pain in her head that only worsened when she fought the visions that plagued the females in her family, Sophie shut them down. Blocked the mental spout that poured these and other unwanted images into her mind.

She didn't need a "gift" to know that Charles meant Jenna harm. She only needed eyes.

"I won't let you do this," she finally said, stepping out from under his touch.

"You can't stop me," he said, smiling. He'd worked too hard for this, Charles told himself. Spent months cozying up to the Widow Dolan. Insinuating himself into her good graces, playing on her fears for her youngest daughter, until at last, she'd given him guardianship over the child. And now that he had it, he wouldn't surrender the girl to a crazy old maid. Charles smiled inwardly. He'd been willing to marry her. After all, it would have made handling Jenna so much easier. But truth to tell, he wasn't anxious to tie himself to a redheaded viper with a tongue like barbed wire.

Especially when he knew her "sight" was only a fraction as strong as the child's.

But there was no point in alienating her completely. Not yet. "This is how your mother wanted it, Sophie. She named me Jenna's guardian. She trusted me. You should too."

"Trust a fox to look after the henhouse?" she laughed shortly and shook her head.

Gaze narrowed, he looked at her. "It's done, Sophie."

No. There was a way out of this. And she'd find it. Sophie wasn't about to leave Jenna to this man's tender mercies.

"I'll collect Jenna at the end of the month," he was saying and she forced herself to pay attention. "That should give you enough time to say goodbye to the girl. Naturally, since you've refused to marry me, I can't have you staying in my house with us. An unmarried woman . . ." He smiled. "Gossip. I'm sure you know how vicious it can be."

"Yes," she said, unwillingly remembering years of being the target of more gossip and rumors than anyone should be forced to endure. "I do."

"Then we understand each other," Charles said, walking back to the leather chair behind his desk. Taking a seat, he picked up a pencil and began going over the papers in front of him. "You know the way out, don't you, Sophie?"

A moment or two later, she was outside and drawing in deep gulps of the cool afternoon air in an effort to ease the anger bubbling inside her. It didn't help. Blast it! How had things come to this? Leaning back against the plank wall, she stared off down the street and only half listened to the train whistle echoing in the distance.

Pain still pulsed inside her head and she ignored it, as she was used to doing. Pain was a small price to pay for peace, after all. Yet, how much peace would she have if she lost her sister to a man who wanted nothing more than to use her for his own gain?

The train whistle sounded again, interrupting her thoughts with a long, mournful howl on the afternoon air. She and Jenna should be on that train right now, she thought. Going somewhere. *Anywhere.* And as that notion settled into her mind, she remembered the small ad she'd seen in the paper only that morning. Like leaves caught in a whirlwind, plans and ideas suddenly swept through her mind, tumbling over each other in their attempt to be recognized and acknowledged. *Of course,* she told herself as she straightened up from the wall and half turned in the direction of the station.

Like a light shining at the end of a long tunnel, Sophie saw a possible solution to her problems. All she needed to do was send a telegram—and wait for an answer. Determinedly, she started walking toward the station and the telegrapher's office, her steps quickening as hope bubbled inside. And slowly, Sophie smiled.

TANGLEWOOD, NEVADA
THREE WEEKS LATER ...

"It ain't right, Sheriff," Joe Markham complained from his jail cell.

"Maybe not, Joe," Ridge Hawkins said and turned the key in the lock, securing his prisoner in one of two small cells, "but it's the law."

And that was enough for Ridge. Hell, he didn't enjoy locking up his friends, but damn it, Joe shouldn't have gone after Parker Shoals that way. "If you'd come to me, I maybe could have talked to Parker for you."

"There's no talkin' to Parker and you damn well know it."

Ridge sighed, reached up and yanked off his hat. Warm for May, he told himself absently as he wiped his forehead with his sleeve. "Joe, just settle down and get comfortable. You're gonna be sitting there until Judge Stevens comes through town Monday next."

Jumping up from the narrow cot, Joe stalked to the iron door, grabbed a bar in each fist and shoved his face closer. "And while I'm here bein' comfortable, who the hell's gonna fix the hole in my roof? Maggie and the baby are out there all alone, and if it rains it's gonna get mighty damn cold in that house. Not to mention damp."

Ridge studied his friend's face for a long minute. No need to punish the man's wife and baby because he'd been a damn fool. "Don't worry about Maggie. I'll send Tall out there tomorrow. He'll have the roof fixed by nightfall."

Joe eased back, ran one hand over his face and nodded. " 'Preciate it. That deputy of yours is a fair hand with a hammer."

Ridge grinned. "Who do ya think keeps this place from fallin' down?"

"Not you," Joe said and turned back for the cot, clearly easier in his mind now that he knew his home and family would be taken care of. "Not unless you figure out a way to pound nails home with a six-gun."

Ridge shook his head and turned back for his office.

True enough, he reasoned. He didn't have much talent for anything besides wielding a gun. But then, that's all a sheriff really needed, wasn't it? That and a respect for the law.

He walked to the stove in the corner of the room, picked up a battered tin pot and poured himself a cup of coffee. The hot, black liquid was thick enough to plow and strong enough to fight back if you tried it. Taking a sip, he walked across the room to the dirty front window and stared out at *his* town.

Tanglewood wasn't much of a town, but it was his. The first real home he'd had in more years than he cared to count. He'd arrived three years before, walking into a hellhole of a place where cowboys and outlaws had free rein.

But within a few months of Ridge's arrival, things had changed. Locking up the real bad ones and running the rest out of the territory had been enough to ease Tanglewood into respectability. Now the little town at the foot of a range of snow-capped mountains was blossoming. They had a bank, a half-dozen new stores, a church, and come this afternoon, a new schoolteacher.

Yep, he thought, taking another sip of the powerful coffee. Tanglewood had become so damned civilized, pretty soon, he wouldn't belong here any more than the outlaws had.

Hell, he knew men who would laugh themselves sick at the thought of Ridge Hawkins being a pillar of respectability. He'd spent far more years on the wrong side of the law than he had on the right. And though he'd been honest with the town fathers when he'd applied for the job as sheriff, his past wasn't something he liked talking about. It was dead and gone as far as he was concerned.

Wisps of foglike memories drifted through his mind now and he saw himself just a few years back, riding at night, hiding from posses, until finally, he'd tried to steal from the wrong man.

Or the right one, he thought with a chuckle. It all depended on your point of view.

The front door stood open in hopes that a stray breeze might drift in, but instead Tall Slater raced through the doorway and, in his hurry, forgot to duck. He slammed his forehead into the door sash with a solid smack and instantly clapped one hand to his probably aching head.

Ridge winced in sympathy, took another sip, and walked toward his deputy, now bent over and shaking his head as if testing to see whether it would fall off his shoulders or not. There wasn't a doorway in town high enough to let the six-foot-five deputy enter in anything but a stooped-over crouch. You'd think the man would remember that. But more times than not, Tall had knocked himself near senseless and probably had a permanent knot dead center of his forehead.

"A couple more hits like that one," Ridge commented, "and we'll be sweeping what's left of your brains up off the floor."

Slowly, tentatively, six feet five inches of smile straightened up and, still wincing, shrugged. "Durn town was built for children."

Ridge shook his head and grinned. "What's your hurry, anyway?"

Tall frowned to himself, then suddenly he remembered. "The train. It's comin' in now."

"Three days a week it usually does, about this time."

"Yeah," Tall said and carefully let his hand drop from his aching forehead. "But today, the new schoolmarm's on it."

"So?"

"So, I figured if you didn't have anything else for me to do, I'd go down and meet her for you."

"Kind of you," Ridge said, noting the new shirt Tall was wearing, not to mention the shine on his boots and the crease in his new black pants. Apparently, his deputy'd been planning on making an impression on the new schoolteacher. Too bad.

Moving to put his coffee cup down on the corner of his desk, Ridge picked up his hat and put it on, settling the battered dirt-brown brim low over his eyes.

"Well," Tall was saying, "I am the deputy and I thought—"

"Sorry, 'Deputy,'" Ridge said, walking back to the door. "But you've got other duties. I want you to ride out to Joe Markham's place and let Maggie know he's locked up safe and sound."

"Ah, Sheriff—"

Ridge cut him off. "And then you can tell her you'll be back out there tomorrow to fix her roof."

Clearly disgusted, Tall ran one huge hand across his slicked-down, witch-hazeled hair and tossed an angry look in the direction of the cells. "Blast you, Joe!"

"I'll meet the schoolmarm and take her to the boardinghouse," Ridge said, acknowledging that he wasn't really looking forward to it. In his experience, schoolmarms were terrifying creatures. All sharp angles, beady eyes, and mean, straight-lipped mouths. Spinsters usually, they were the kind of women that men instinctively stayed clear of and children had nightmares about.

Nope, he was in no hurry to meet the woman, but Miss Hattie had asked him specifically to greet the new teacher and steer her toward the boardinghouse, so that's just what he'd do.

"Don't see why you can't ride out to Joe's place instead of me."

Ridge slapped the other man on the back as he passed him on his way out the door. " 'Cause I'm the sheriff and you're not."

Scowling, Tall grumbled something about the shame of being all slicked up with no one to appreciate it, then headed off to the livery to fetch his horse.

Through the train's dirty windows, Sophie took her first look at her new home and tried not to shudder. They'd really come to the back end of beyond, she thought.

Tanglewood.

What wood they were speaking of, she had no idea. There didn't seem to be a decent-sized tree anywhere. The tiny collection of sun- and wind-weathered buildings crouched at the foot of a range of mountains that seemed to be standing sentry even as it dwarfed the town she would now call home.

Home.

The word echoed inside her head and seemed to make Tanglewood just a bit more appealing. After more than two weeks of traveling on trains, laying down a purposely crooked trail, she was more than ready to take up her new job, under her assumed name, and begin the life she'd promised her sister.

Hard to believe that only three weeks ago, she had been in Albany, reading the answer to her telegram. She'd read the brief missive so many times, she knew it by heart. *You're hired,* it had said. *Room and board plus twenty dollars a month end See Hattie McCoy on arrival Tanglewood end*

The job of schoolteacher had come like a gift from God, she thought, and silently thanked her late mother again for insisting she get an education beyond painting decent watercolors. Thanks to her tutors, she was prepared to earn her own living. Right here in this squalid little town.

Here, in this place, she'd be simply Sophie Ryan, widow and mother of a four-year-old girl. They'd be safe. Even if Charles came searching for them, he would be looking for sisters. Not a widow with her only child.

Everything would be fine, she thought, fighting back another cringe as she looked out at the tiny Western town. Good Lord, what had she done?

The only thing she *could* do, she reminded herself sternly.

Turning to the little girl sleeping curled up on the seat beside her, Sophie whispered, "Jenna? Jenna, wake up, honey. We're here."

Eyelashes fluttered and two big green eyes opened and fixed on Sophie. Her long blond hair was only slightly tinged with red, giving her a golden look, and her pale skin didn't have a single freckle. Silently, Sophie admitted to envying the little girl that. Especially when she thought about all the hours over the years she'd spent rubbing lemon juice over her own freckle-dusted complexion. To no avail. Her freckles remained, just as did her wild tangle of deep red curls. Ah, well.

Jenna's coloring had been muted by her father's blond hair and fair complexion. While Sophie's father, her mother's first husband, had been as redheaded as his wife. For years, her mother had mourned the man Sophie barely remembered. Until she'd met the man who became Sophie's stepfather. Theirs was a happy house and when, after years of disappointment, her mother had discovered she was once again with child, their happiness was complete.

Hard to believe that so much could change in just a few short years. First a carriage accident had claimed her stepfather, and then her mother became ill. Now both of them were gone and Sophie was on the run with a little girl looking to her for protection. She found herself wishing again that things were different.

But, as her mother used to say, *If wishes were horses, beggars would ride.* No point in dwelling on what was past. Best now to simply focus on the future she would give the little sister she loved so dearly.

Smiling now, she pointed out the window. "Take a look," she said.

The child grinned and rubbed both hands over her eyes before scooting forward on her seat and peering out the window.

"Oh," she whispered, "it's nice, Sophie . . ."

Wincing slightly, she leaned down and reminded the little girl, "Mommy. Remember, honey? You're going to call me 'Mommy' from now on."

Jenna glanced at her. "I 'member, but it's silly."

"I know," Sophie said, forcing a smile she wasn't really sure of. "But it'll be easier if everyone here thinks you're my little girl."

It would be easy to fool everyone, if Jenna could only remember. After all, she supposed it was fairly unusual for two sisters to be so far apart in age.

"But—"

"Please, honey."

Slowly, the girl nodded, and turned back to look out the window. One small problem solved, Sophie stood up and shook out the fall of her skirt, trying to get as many wrinkles as possible out of the fabric. Then reaching up, she adjusted the tilt of her hat, ran one hand across the rat's nest that was her hair, and told herself that first impressions weren't all that important anyway.

"You and the girl getting off here?" the man behind her asked.

Sophie shot him a quick look. "Yes, we are."

The florid-faced man gave her a quick nod. "Can't say as I'm sorry any."

For heaven's sake, Sophie thought. Jenna had saved his life. One would think he'd be a *little* grateful.

"Still don't know how that young'un knew I'd choke on a piece of apple, and I got to say, it ain't natural."

Sophie flushed and reached into the overhead shelf to pull down their bags. She'd tried to keep Jenna quiet, but the little girl was just too young to know that people didn't *want* to know the future. That they feared anything they couldn't understand.

She herself had learned that lesson at too young an age and had been trying ever since to simply be normal. But, she wondered, what was normal? Charles Vinson? This man who should have been grateful that thanks to Jenna's warning, there had been time to slap him on the back and dislodge the bite of apple stuck in his throat?

Or was normal the little girl looking up at her with trusting eyes?

Setting her bags on the seat, Sophie glared at the big man and said, "It was a simple enough prediction to make. Someone who eats as much and as quickly as yourself must expect to choke on food at one time or another."

"Now see here, missy," he began.

"Come, Jenna," she said, ignoring the blustering man, and as she took up her bags in one hand, she reached out with the other to her sister.

The little girl slipped her hand into Sophie's, gave the big man a smile and a wave, then scooted out of the seat.

As they made their way down the narrow aisle, Sophie felt the other passengers staring at them and she knew she and Jenna wouldn't be missed. The little girl had seen too much, picked up on too many secrets. The woman who drank whiskey in secret. The man who stole money from his employer. The woman whose husband was going to die. The man who set fire to the train's water closet with a discarded cigar.

Secrets, she thought. Everyone had secrets. She knew that better than most.

At the end of the car, Sophie paused and looked back at their fellow travelers. She hoped no one else from their car was getting off in Tanglewood. She didn't want stories about what Jenna had said and done on the trip rippling through town. They needed a fresh start, with as little gossip as possible. Because every piece of gossip was a potential clue laid down for Charles to follow.

And Sophie knew Charles would try to find them.

Straightening her shoulders, she lifted her chin, tightened her hold on Jenna's hand, and turned for the doorway. The conductor was already there, waiting for them. Plainly, he was as anxious as the passengers to see her and Jenna leave the train.

"Mrs. Ryan," the man said, nodding, yet keeping what he obviously considered a safe distance from her and Jenna. He took the iron steps down to the platform, then reluctantly held up one hand to help her alight. He let her go as quickly as possible, then turned to help Jenna.

The little girl took his hand and stopped, one foot poised in mid-air over the step. Looking up at him, she smiled and said, "Your baby wants to be named James."

The man stiffened as though he'd been shot and stared at the girl as though he feared she might sprout wings and fly. "Baby?" he asked. "Uh . . . my wife and I don't have children."

Sophie groaned tightly and made a grab for her sister. But Jenna wouldn't be stopped.

"Yes you do," she crowed happily. "He's in his mommy's tummy."

The conductor straightened up and looked from Jenna to Sophie and back again. "But . . ." he stammered. "That's impossible . . ."

Tugging at the little girl's hand, Sophie helped her down from the steps then turned, determined to leave the conductor and this whole train trip firmly behind her. But a hand came down on her arm, and when she turned, expecting to be met with accusing eyes, she looked instead into the conductor's hopeful expression.

"Does she mean it?" he whispered, ignoring the interested stares of the passengers staring down at them from the train. "Can she really see what she claims to?"

A cold, sharp wind swept along the train platform, fluttering the hem of her dress and sending icy fingers up her calves. A rush of steam burst from beneath the train and rose up like a small, private fog, enveloping her, Jenna, and the conductor in a temporary world of white.

She should just leave. Turn and pretend Jenna had said nothing. Pretend the conductor wasn't now staring at them as though they were a cross between heaven and hell. But she couldn't. There was too much hope in the man's eyes.

"Yes," she said softly, staring directly into his gaze. "She really sees it."

A slow, proud smile creased his face as he went down on one knee in front of Jenna. "My son," and he said the words with awe, "likes the name James, does he?"

"Uh-huh," she said, reaching out to pat his cheek. "And he wants to ride the train with you too."

That grin of his broadened even further and as he stood up again he looked down at Jenna and said, "Then he will. I promise."

The little girl frowned suddenly and said, "But his sister is afraid of the train so don't make her ride it, all right?"

"A girl too?" The conductor nearly hooted in delight.

Oh, for heaven's sake. This was *not* how their new life was supposed to start. They needed to blend in. To become a part of the town. To slip seamlessly into the life of Tanglewood. Instead, they were beginning to draw an interested crowd.

"Come on, Jenna," Sophie said and turned quickly away, drawing her sister after her. Hurrying her steps, she looked back at the conductor still standing where she'd left him, looking as though he'd been struck by lightning.

And since she wasn't watching where she was going, she ran smack into a man tall enough and broad enough and strong enough to have passed for a brick wall.

She bounced off him like a rock skipping on the surface of a still lake, and before she could find her balance again fell to the platform at his feet, pulling Jenna down on top of her. Her dropped bags plopped open, spilling her clothes onto the dirty wood planks. The hem of her skirt was hiked indecently high, and even as she reached down to cover herself, she looked up at him. Her gaze traveled from the toes of his dusty brown boots, up the length of his denim-clad legs, and across his broad chest. She noted his square, clean-shaven jaw, a nose that looked as though it had been broken more than once, and a pair of pale, ice-blue eyes looking at her from beneath lowered black eyebrows. Too-long dark hair scraped the collar of his long-sleeved white shirt, and when he folded his arms across his chest, Sophie's throat closed up as her gaze locked on the star pinned to his black vest.

CHAPTER TWO

Several slow seconds ticked past as Ridge stared down into a pair of the greenest eyes he'd ever seen. Green like spring meadows and soft shadows in lush valleys. Green that was deep enough to stir a man's soul and cause him to forget his own name. A hard, swift rush of attraction slammed into him as he looked into those eyes—even with the flicker of temper and then wariness flashing in them.

She made quite a picture, sprawled out on the platform. The skirt of her simple blue dress was hiked up to her knees, giving him a good look at a pair of trim ankles and shapely calves, encased in black cotton stockings. With her hands braced on the floor behind her, she pushed herself into a sitting position and shook her head. The movement tilted a silly straw hat dotted with yellow and white daisies sitting precariously atop a wild tangle of red curls that strained against the knot she'd tried to confine them in. A part of Ridge wanted to see those curls hanging long and free and he imagined she'd look something like a redheaded lion.

A scatter of golden freckles dusted her cheeks and the bridge of her nose, and her chin had a defiant tilt to it. Her mouth was wide and generous, even though at the moment it was twisted into a disgusted frown.

Well, whatever else was going on with her, she certainly had the temper to go with that red hair. Prickly as all get out, he told himself. And one thing he didn't need right now was to be dealing with any more cranky women than he absolutely had to. He flicked a casual glance up and down the length of the train, searching the platform for the schoolmarm he was supposed to be meeting. Five or six people stepped off one of the other cars and headed for town, but there was just no sign of a razor-lipped, beady-eyed, mean-looking spinster lady. So much for a new school-teacher. Well, she could have missed the train, he supposed, and shifted his gaze back to the woman still collecting her spilled clothes.

Remnants of a chivalrous streak he hadn't been sure he possessed shot through him and he bent down beside the cantankerous female. After all, he had no real reason to suspect she was anything but what she appeared to be. A good woman. Until he knew different, he'd treat her as such.

"At least let me give you a hand with that," Ridge said, reaching for a white cotton petticoat edged in a wide lace border.

"No, thank you."

He reached for it anyway and his fingertips just brushed the fabric when a stray wind shot from under the train, lifted that petticoat and ran with it along the length of the platform.

He stood up and watched as the delicate material billowed in the breeze like the full sails on a clipper ship.

"Oh, my stars," the woman snapped.

The little girl laughed and her soft giggle floated

on the same breeze that was even now taking that slip of lace off toward the open desert.

"Wait here," she told her daughter and, after giving him one last, scathing look, pushed past him, running after her petticoat.

Ridge was right behind her, listening to the clatter of her heels on the plank floors and the catcalls and whistles from the crowd. "Lady," he called out, but she paid no attention.

"Look at it go," someone shouted as the wind gusted again, tossing that petticoat into a dip and dance on the air.

"There you go, lady. Almost got it!"

"Pretty thing, ain't it?" someone else asked of no one in particular.

Damn it. She was putting on a helluva show here, but he couldn't enjoy it. Images flashed in his mind. Visions of that train starting up, rolling forward, and this crazy redhead falling beneath the steel wheels just because she'd been too stubborn to let him help her gather her things. What had she thought? That he waited on train platforms for the chance to rifle through ladies' undergarments?

His gaze narrowed as she jumped, made a grab at the damn thing, and came up short.

"Whooee!" someone shouted. "You was close that time, for sure!"

Ridge grumbled and ran faster, outdistancing her in a few easy lopes. Reaching up, he snatched the petticoat from the wind's grasp, then turned around to face her.

"Ah hell, Sheriff," one of the men yelled, "it was just getting good!"

Shooting a frown at the man, Ridge asked, "Don't you have somewhere to be, Ben?"

"Nope," the man replied with a grin. His friends laughed and Ridge tried to ignore him as the redhead approached.

Out of breath, cheeks flushed, eyes shining with temper and embarrassment, she glared first at the men slouching against the wall. "You all should be ashamed of yourselves," she snapped and had the satisfaction of watching at least one of them duck his head.

Then she turned back to him, and before he could offer her the damn petticoat, she grabbed at it, and they both heard the fine lawn material tear.

She smacked his hand and he scowled at her. "Look what you've done now," she muttered thickly, wadding up the petticoat between two clenched hands.

Her hat was tipped over one eye and she blinked up at him with the other. Some of her hair had worked its way loose and a cloud of red curls lay across her shoulders to tumble down her back. Damn, but she was a sight. When she wasn't talking. "*You* tore it," he said, "I just caught it for you."

"I didn't ask for your help."

"You're welcome."

"You expect to be *thanked*?" she asked, clearly astonished. "If it weren't for you, none of this would have happened."

"I'm beginnin' to like her," one of the men said, from his spot along the wall.

Both of them glared at him and the speaker suddenly felt the need to study the scuffed toes of his boots. Finally, Sophie wadded what was left of her best petticoat into a ball and stuffed it under her arm.

She reached up, tipped her hat back into place, and blew a stray red curl out of her eyes.

Blast and damnation. She'd hoped to start off on the right foot here in Deadwood ... er, Tanglewood. She'd hoped to make a good first impression and settle into life as quietly and unassumingly as possible.

Instead, she would probably be the subject of town gossip for weeks. Imagine, she thought with an inward groan, the new schoolteacher treating her audience to the sight of her underwear flying across the train station. And not only that, but she'd fought the sheriff for possession of her petticoat and come off the loser.

The *sheriff*, of all people. The one man she should have avoided like the veritable plague. After all, if one were to be nitpicky about it, she was, technically, a kidnapper. As that word rumbled through her mind, she fought it down. She'd done nothing wrong, after all. Jenna was her sister. It was Sophie's duty to look after her. To protect her from harm. And if that harm just happened to be the child's legal guardian ... well, so be it.

Although she didn't expect this small-town sheriff to see things that way.

Oh, for pity's sake.

And it didn't help her temper any to look up into his blue eyes and see the flash of humor sparkling there. Not only had he humiliated her in public, but he'd *enjoyed* it!

The first day of her brand-new life was not off to a good start.

Best to salvage what she could of her dignity and go about her business. And first things first. What she had to do was find Hattie McCoy, the woman who'd hired Sophie as the new schoolteacher, and then get settled. With that thought firmly in mind, she lifted her chin, ignored the group of men still whispering and laughing over her antics, and faced the sheriff.

"If you've quite finished 'helping' me, I'll be going now," she said and left him standing there while she marched back to Jenna's side. Stuffing her ruined petticoat into her still open bag, she picked up both bags in one hand and, with her free hand, took hold of the little girl.

"So—Mama—" the girl began.

"Not now, Jenna," she said and walked back down the length of the platform with determined strides. She passed the sheriff and ignored the small knot of men with nothing better to do in the middle of the day than laugh at women they didn't know. Holding her chin high and keeping a firm grasp of Jenna's hand, Sophie kept her gaze straight ahead and kept walking until she was clear of the train station and headed down the town's one and only Main Street.

She wasn't running away, she reassured herself. She was simply doing what she had to do. Getting started on the life she was going to build for herself and Jenna. Feeling a bit better, Sophie let her gaze slide over the town that would now be home.

A far cry from Albany, she thought with a silent sigh. There were no neat, tree-lined streets crowded with polished carriages and high-stepping horses. Nor any finely dressed women scurrying in and out of well-tended shops.

Here, the heart of Tanglewood looked as though it might blow down during a decent-sized windstorm. The buildings had a temporary, ramshackle look to them, though here and there, she spotted a pot of wilted flowers or a hopeful splash of paint. Most of the businesses boasted two-story false fronts in an effort to make the places look bigger and perhaps more prosperous than they were. An illusion which might have worked if their painted signs hadn't been flaking and peeling in the sun.

She felt a twinge of worry scatter through her. It was all so different, she thought. So wild. So . . . untamed and uncivilized. Even the sky looked bigger here, she thought with a glance heavenward. Oh, the books she'd read about the West simply hadn't prepared her for the reality.

Maybe, Sophie thought, she wasn't up to the challenge. Maybe she'd finally—as her stepfather used to say—bitten off more than she could chew. On the other hand, she told herself, what choice did she really have? She was here now. She would have to make the best of the situation or cry defeat. Slink back to New York like a beaten hound, give in to Charles Vinson, hand over her sister to a man Sophie knew would mistreat her, and spend the rest of her own life wondering what might have happened if she'd had just a bit more courage.

Besides, she thought, choosing to look at the brighter side, in a place as wide open and undefined as this, she could become anyone she chose. Here, she might find the "normalcy" that had always eluded her back in Albany . . . where everyone knew the Dolans and just how far from normal they really were. A slight smile curved her mouth, despite the lingering hesitancy inside. Tanglewood might actually turn out to be the answer to her prayers.

She glanced at the buildings she passed, trying to look at them with a kinder eye, noting the barber shop, a millinery, the mercantile, a gun shop. Women in bonnets shopped with baskets over their arms and a heavy farm wagon rolled down the middle of the street as if daring anyone to challenge it. An old yellow dog snoozed in the shade of a porch and, somewhere in the distance, a blacksmith's hammer rang out on an anvil. Two little boys darted past her, their feet kicking up small clouds of dust in the street, and Sophie looked after them with a smile. Some things, after all, remained constant.

Then the glorious aroma of fresh-baked bread snaked along the air and teased her until Sophie's stomach rumbled noisily. She turned to cast one longing glance at a tiny restaurant with shining window-panes.

"I'm hungry, Sophie," Jenna whined.

"I am too, honey," she said, giving the restaurant a last, wistful look before smiling at the little girl beside her. "But first we'll get settled, all right? Then some supper?"

Jenna looked back over her shoulder at the train station. "Can that man have supper with us?"

A quick knot of worry tightened in her stomach. "Which man, honey?"

"That one," she said. "The man you were playing with."

Sophie sneaked a look over her shoulder. The sheriff stood in a patch of shade cast by the train depot's porch roof. But some stray slash of sunlight managed to hit the star on his vest to wink at Sophie as if issuing a silent warning. She swallowed hard and turned her head back to the front. "We weren't *playing*," Sophie corrected her. "And no, he can't."

"But Sophie, he—"

"Mama, remember?"

"Mama—"

"Look, honey." Sophie interrupted the girl before she could get going again. Lifting the carpetbags to wave at a sign she'd just spotted, she said, "There's the boardinghouse. See now? We'll find Mrs. McCoy, get settled in our room, and then we'll have supper, all right?"

"All right," Jenna muttered and kicked her shoe against a pebble in the dirt.

Just a half block farther along, Sophie found their destination.

"McCoy Boardinghouse, Rooms for Rent, Daily or Weekly." The sign hung crookedly from a post in what she supposed was considered the front yard. Sparse tufts of grass dotted the dirt and a row of neatly aligned rocks bordered a path leading directly to the wide front porch. Sitting on that porch were a few whitewashed chairs and tables and a pot holding what looked to be a struggling rosebush.

But the porch was freshly swept and the windows facing onto the street fairly sparkled in the afternoon sun. And truth to tell, Sophie was suddenly so weary, she wouldn't have cared if Mrs. McCoy rented rooms in a stable. Weeks of traveling with a child and running from a man determined to find them were taking their toll and all she really wanted now was to lie down and close her eyes.

The minute she walked into the boardinghouse, Sophie wanted to weep in relief. The outside of the place might have needed work, but inside, it was a different story altogether. Every inch of the place spoke of constant attention. Afternoon sunlight poured in through shining windowpanes to dance across the brightly colored rag rugs dotting the gleaming wood floor. White lace curtains, stiff with starch, rattled in the breeze drifting beneath the window sashes.

A long hallway stretched out directly in front of her, probably leading to the kitchen. On her left was a staircase, its steps and banister polished to a high sheen, despite the worn spots made by countless pairs of feet. Not a speck of dust could be found anywhere, Sophie thought, turning her head to take in the small front parlor, noting the overstuffed furniture, the whitewashed walls, and the fire burning in the hearth.

It was a small, cozy haven, she thought, and felt every tense muscle in her body slowly uncoil and relax. Like an outpost of civilization in a raw, windswept world, Hattie McCoy's boardinghouse welcomed guests with warmth and charm.

Tightening her grip on the handles of her bags, Sophie fought the fatigue beginning to sweep through her. A few more minutes, she told herself, and before she could call out, she heard the sound of quick footsteps tapping against the floor. A small, round woman bustled down the length of the hallway, smoothing a freshly pressed white apron down over her expansive middle. She was several inches shorter than Sophie's five feet eight, and weighed at least a hundred pounds more. Her face was round and wrinkle-free, her soft blond hair was pulled up into a loose knot on top of her head, and a spray of fine lines fanned out from the corners of her blue eyes. This was a face used to smiling, Sophie thought, and immediately warmed to her.

"Well, my goodness," the woman said, stepping forward to take Sophie's bags from her. "You look beat down to the ground, child." Bending low, she tipped Jenna's chin up with one meaty forefinger and clucked her tongue. "Poor little mite, you look about done in."

"You're nice," the little girl said.

"Why, thank you," the woman said, "I think you're mighty sweet too."

"Hattie McCoy?" Sophie asked, hoping she was correct.

"That's right," the woman said and straightened up to meet her gaze.

"I'm Sophie Ryan," she said, the false name falling neatly off her tongue. Should she be worried that lying was becoming easier? No. Later, she thought. She'd worry about that later. "I'm the new schoolteacher."

Surprise flashed across the woman's features briefly then gave way to an expression of concern. She reached out, took Sophie's hand in hers, and gave it a hearty shake. "Well, isn't this a pleasure? I've got your room all ready for you," she continued, then paused and gave Jenna a quick smile. "But you didn't tell me you had a child."

Jenna leaned into Sophie's leg and she dropped a reassuring hand onto the girl's shoulder. "Is it a problem?" she whispered, hoping it wouldn't be. She hadn't mentioned Jenna in the telegram she'd sent accepting this job for fear the town of Tanglewood would change its mind about hiring her. Now, though, that seemed a foolish decision. What if she'd traveled all the way here only to be told no? What would she do then? Where would she go?

Speaking quickly now, despite the fog of weariness beginning to blur her vision, she said, "I assure you, Jenna's no trouble at all. She can stay in my room and of course I'll pay extra for her meals and—"

"Here now." Hattie interrupted the flow of words

with a shake of her head and sent another smile at the girl. "No need to get into a stew about this. Don't you worry about a thing, honey. Why, I've never known any child to be any real trouble. Spunky is all and I purely love spunky in a child."

Relief swept through her and Sophie's knees trembled with the force of it.

Hattie must have noticed because she stepped alongside her, dropped one meaty arm over her shoulder, and guided her to the staircase. "You come along with Hattie, honey. We'll get you all settled in and you can have a nice lie-down before supper, how's that sound?"

"Wonderful," Sophie admitted, giving in to the glorious feeling of being taken care of. For too long now, she'd had to be the strong one. It was nice to take a mental step back, however briefly, and let someone else do the worrying.

"And I don't want to hear another word about paying extra for that sweet-faced child." Hattie looked over her shoulder at Jenna and said, "You come along now, sweetie, so your mama and you can have a nap." Then to Sophie, she added, "Why, that little thing couldn't eat enough to fill a teacup."

The flow of conversation washed over her and through her and Sophie moved like a sleepwalker. She hardly noticed the upstairs climb or the long hallway running the length of the second floor. Absently, she noted the doors she passed but paid little attention until Hattie stopped, opened one, and ushered her into a lovely room.

Sunshine rippled through the windows that overlooked the street. Yellow and white gingham curtains rippled in the breeze, casting dancing shadows across the writing table, chest of drawers, and the two chairs drawn up in front of a potbellied stove. A round mirror hung above a mahogany washbasin, reflecting the bed against the opposite wall. The wrought-iron bedstead held a thick, comfortable-looking mattress covered by a gaily patterned quilt and a mound of pillows. Here, too, bright rag rugs on the shining wood floor provided splashes of color.

Later, she would appreciate the warmth and beauty of the room. At the moment, it was all she could do to tear her gaze away from that bed to thank her hostess.

"It's very nice, Mrs. McCoy, thank you."

"Piffle," the woman said with a wave of her hand, even as she moved to wipe a nonexistent spot of dust from the bedside table with the corner of her apron. "Nothin' to thank me for, hon. And as to the other, you just call me Hattie. Everybody does."

"Hattie," she repeated with a nod. Odd, she couldn't imagine anyone in Albany being so familiar with a complete stranger. Back home, she knew married couples who still addressed each other as Mr. and Mrs. even after years of marriage. But she supposed that here, in the rough-and-tumble West, society's rules seemed foolish at best and a waste of precious time. Besides, she thought with an inward smile, she rather liked the informality.

"Why, you poor thing, you're asleep on your feet." Hattie clucked her tongue again, drew Sophie to the bed and practically pushed her down onto it.

A soft sigh escaped her as her body seemed to melt into the bed's downy comfort.

"You too, little miss," Hattie told Jenna and helped the girl up onto the high bed. Then without another word, she picked up the extra folded quilt at the foot of the mattress, snapped it open and let it fall gently down atop them. "Both of you get some sleep now, y'hear? I'll come wake you in plenty of time for supper."

Then she slipped out of the room, closing the door quietly behind her.

Sophie curled onto her side and drew Jenna in close. The little girl snuggled against her, sighed heavily, and was asleep within minutes. Sophie, though, lay awake a bit longer, watching the curtains dip and sway to the dance of the wind and listening to the sounds of her new home drifting through the window.

Safe, she thought, as her eyes slid closed, they were safe. For now.

CHAPTER THREE

Ridge smiled to himself and closed the door on Tall's grumbling. Every night, without fail, his deputy muttered darkly about the dangers of going without food. Ridge supposed a man Tall's size must get hungrier than most, but waiting an hour or so until Ridge finished his supper hadn't killed him yet.

It was the same story every night.

Routine, he thought. He'd slipped into a routine that was comfortable even as it chafed at him. Frowning, he reached up, rubbed one hand across the back of his neck and told himself it was pointless to struggle against the very thing he'd spent the last three years building.

Ridge glanced into the last splash of color trailing behind the dying sun, crossed the boardwalk and paused at the edge. Bracing one shoulder against the porch post, he shoved his hands into his pockets and let his gaze drift across the familiar scene.

Kerosene lamps flickered gently behind curtained windows. Doors were closed against the coming night and the scents of wood smoke and suppers cooking swirled on the slight breeze dusting across the desert. Farther down the street, the saloon was just kicking up its heels. The first stars were already winking into life in a purple sky and somewhere in the distance a lone coyote howled.

The sound rippled through him and brought an eerie sense of recognition to the wild streak that still lay buried deep within him. Shifting his gaze to the darkening desert, he briefly imagined jumping onto his horse and riding off into the night. Losing himself in the wild country and traveling the lost paths that wound up into the mountains. A part of him hungered for it, the solitude, the quiet.

A child cried, a door slammed, and Ridge shook off his thoughts. He pushed away from the post and started down the boardwalk toward Hattie's. The old days were long gone, he told himself and remembering them didn't do a damn bit of good.

"Evenin', Sheriff," Ike Swanson called as he stepped out of his barbershop and closed up for the night. "Off to supper, are you?"

"About that time," Ridge said with a nod and kept walking, unwilling to be drawn into one of Ike's notoriously long stories. Things'd be bad enough once he hit Hattie's place. Not for the first time, he realized he should have moved out of that boardinghouse years ago. But again, it had become comfortable, and living in someone else's house made this time in Tanglewood less permanent somehow.

He turned into the rock-lined walkway and took the front steps in two long strides. Yanking off his hat, he opened the door and stepped inside. He hung his hat on the same peg he used every night and walked down the hall, following the sound of voices.

The dining room pulsed with activity. Kerosene wall lamps threw softly shifting shadows over the faces of the people gathered at the well-set table.

The Reverend Elias Kendrick had gray tufts of hair sprouting out from the sides of his mostly bald head and blue eyes that sometimes saw too much. A kind man, he'd given up fire-and-brimstone preaching when he was old enough to learn the road to hell was never clearly marked and that the Lord was more interested in saving sinners than praising saints.

The whiskey drummer, Henry Tuttle, just passing through town on his sales route, was a talkative little man with quick dark eyes and a sly smile.

Hester Appleby, a seamstress, was as jumpy as a rabbit. Her pale gray eyes, magnified behind a pair of thick spectacles, darted around the room as if she were constantly looking for a place to hide.

But Ridge wasn't paying much attention to the regulars. Instead, his gaze shifted to the redhead from the train station. He shouldn't have been surprised to see her; after all, Tanglewood wasn't big enough to boast a hotel and the only other rooms to let were above the saloon. Still, he'd spent the last couple of hours forgetting about those green eyes of hers and wasn't entirely sure he was ready to look into them again.

Another quick, hard jolt of awareness hit him low and dangerous as he watched her. She looked up then, as if sensing his presence, meeting his gaze with hers. A brief frown flickered across her features and was gone again in the next instant. Ridge laughed shortly under his breath. Apparently, she wasn't any happier to see him than he was her.

"Hello, Ridge," the reverend said, "have you met the widow Ryan?"

Widow? Ridge's gaze flicked back to her with renewed interest.

Movement caught the corner of his eye and he looked to her daughter, kneeling on a chair and gazing at him. A wide, brilliant smile lit up her small face and her eyes went round as saucers as she patted the chair back beside her. "Sit by me, Daddy," she said.

His breath caught in his throat.

Like a stray bullet, her words stopped everything in the room.

So much for routine, he thought even as he managed to expel that breath and take another. What in the hell was going on here? he wondered. But before he could get the question asked, everyone else piped up with their two cents' worth.

"Daddy?" Henry repeated gleefully.

"What's this?" the reverend said.

"Oh, my," Hester whispered, ducking her head until Ridge thought she might plop her forehead into her soup.

Slowly, thoughtfully, he shifted his gaze to the redhead. A flush of color rode high on her cheeks as she said quickly, "Jenna, honey, that's not your daddy."

The little girl nodded so hard, her soft hair flew about her face. Pushing it back out of her eyes with both tiny hands, she pouted and told her mother, "Yes he is, too." The imp gave him a heartbreaker's smile and something inside Ridge tightened when she added, "I *know* it."

"Whooee, this just keeps getting better," Henry chortled, rubbing his hands together and settling in for what looked to be an entertaining evening.

"Just hold on a minute here, Henry," Ridge said tightly, narrowing his gaze at the little salesman until he swallowed hard. "The child's made a mistake, is all."

"Has she?" the Reverend Kendrick asked quietly, his watchful gaze darting back and forth between the redhead and Ridge.

"Jesus, Elias," Ridge nearly shouted, then remembered who he was talking to and lowered his voice. "Of course she has."

"Oh dear, oh dear, oh dear," Hester muttered, her head still drooped over the soup bowl. "This is all so distressing."

"Damn right it is," Ridge snapped, wondering what in tarnation *she* had to be so upset about. It wasn't her being called "daddy." Then he glanced at the little girl who'd started all this. He winced to see her big green eyes fill with a sheen of tears. Good job, he told himself, shifting uncomfortably. Made a child cry.

Before he could try to make it right, though, the redhead stood up and looked at all of them in turn before saying, "This is all an unfortunate misunderstanding."

A misunderstanding or some sort of half-assed blackmail scheme, he thought, and determined that he'd find out which. Damn fast.

"Scandalous," Hester whispered.

"Now, now," Elias said absently, obviously aware that he should be the one to comfort the poor woman, but plainly more interested in what was going on around him.

Hattie chose just that moment to stride into the dining room, carrying a platter of steaks that sizzled and popped and gave off a scent that normally would have had Ridge's mouth watering.

Seeing all of them up and shouting, she stopped dead and her seven-year-old son Travis, only a step or two behind her, ran right into her wide backside. He carried a heavy, still steaming bowl of mashed potatoes that slammed into Hattie's behind, and she yelped, tossing the platter high. Well-done steaks took flight, spinning and tumbling in mid-air before slamming down onto the table and the people watching it all happen in stunned silence.

"What in the name of all that's holy, and them that's not, is going on around here?" Hattie shouted as the last of the steaks hit the floor.

"That's what I'd like to know," Ridge told her, his gaze locked with a redhead who'd been nothing but trouble since she stepped off that damn train. Maybe the kid had made a simple mistake. And maybe it was something else entirely.

Just a few hours ago, Sophie had thought this cozy front parlor a warm, welcoming room. Now it felt like a courtroom crowded with four curious judges.

Four because the children had been hustled off to bed and that poor simpering fool of a woman, Hester, had also gone off, swearing that she simply couldn't bear to discuss such "intimate" things.

Intimate, indeed, Sophie fumed and paced the length of the room one more time. She might have expected a bit of solidarity from a fellow spinster. But then, she reminded herself, as far as Hester knew, Sophie was a man-hunting widow on the prowl for her next husband and using her child as bait.

Oh, good heavens, she thought and reached up to rub the pounding throb that had nestled between her eyebrows. She'd been worried about keeping Jenna's visions quiet. And here she was about to be done in by nothing more than a little girl's wistful imaginings. At least she *hoped* it was her imagination. Although why Jenna had chosen Ridge Hawkins as her fantasy papa, Sophie had no idea. All she'd been able to get out of the girl was one simple statement, over and over again.

"He *is* my daddy."

That little voice seemed to be echoing inside Sophie's head and only increased the throbbing there. Ridge Hawkins. She'd known the moment she'd run into him at the train station that he was going to be trouble.

But he'd certainly been aptly named, she thought with a covert glance at his chiseled-in-rock features. His expression was as stony as his name. Hattie, on the other hand, fairly vibrated with excitement, while the reverend, bless him, might be suspicious, but was withholding judgment. The little man with the twitchy nose and inquisitive eyes looked as though he were hoping for more ribald confessions.

Sophie wanted to smack him.

"Well?" Ridge blurted. "Just what is it you're trying to pull here, lady?"

She stopped, half turned and glared at him. "I *beg* your pardon?"

"Now, Sheriff," the reverend started. "You've said yourself the child made a mistake."

Ridge shook his head and took a step closer to her. "No, Reverend, I've been thinkin' about that and I believe I've been a lawman long enough to know a con when I see one."

Henry chuckled, shaking his head when the others glared at him.

"A *con*?" Sophie repeated, outraged at his tone and the look on his face. But just to be sure she'd been insulted, she asked, "What exactly is a con?"

"A confidence game, Red," he said, moving closer again. "And if you're thinking to blackmail me by having that little girl claim me as her daddy, you've got another think coming." He paused, reached up and dusted the palm of one hand across the star on his shirtfront. "In case you hadn't noticed, I'm the sheriff here. And in this town, I lock up *whoever* breaks the law. And that includes pretty women."

"True, true," Henry muttered. "Ridge here'd lock up his own mama if she stepped over the line."

What a lovely trait in a person.

Sophie looked at the sheriff for a long moment, telling herself all the while that it was important to remain calm. Important to ease into her life in Tanglewood. But even as she thought it, her brain refused to listen. After all, hadn't her dignified entrance into town life pretty much ended when she and this . . . *sheriff* had chased her petticoat down the length of a train station? Besides, she told herself, surrendering to the bubbling anger within, there were times when it was simply *impossible* to be rational. And this was one of them. Lord knew, she'd dealt with officious men before this. Perhaps it was just as well that Sheriff Ridge Hawkins learn right from the start that she was *not* a woman to be trifled with.

She couldn't afford to have him think she was afraid of him, could she?

"You've been *thinking*?" she said, her tone making it clear that she found the concept astonishing.

"Now, don't you get all het up," he started, shaking his head.

" 'Het up'?" she repeated. "What an excellent description. 'Het up' is just what I am."

"Here we go," Henry muttered from the sidelines.

"So," Sophie went on, closing the short distance between them. Hands at her hips, she tilted her head back and glared at him as she said, "All of your *thinking* has led you to the conclusion that a four-year-old girl has criminal intentions toward you."

"I didn't say that."

"Oh!" She threw both hands high. "Of course not," she corrected, giving him a smile that had nothing to do with good humor. "You must have meant that *I* am the mastermind behind this ingenious plot."

"Stranger things have happened, Red."

"In your world, probably," she interrupted him again, and ignored the muffled laughter coming from their audience. "But not in mine."

He inhaled sharply.

"What you're saying is," she went on, as if trying to understand just what he'd been thinking, "that I and my daughter traveled by stage and by train for more than two weeks to reach this tiny spot in Nevada for the sole purpose of blackmailing *you*."

"Now, just wait a minute," he said, and rubbed one hand across his face.

"You must be quite well off," Sophie went on, warming to her theme. "Are you a secret millionaire, simply working as a small-town sheriff to avoid the boredom of everyday life?"

His eyes narrowed dangerously.

Henry Tuttle laughed outright and even the reverend snorted a chuckle.

"It's no wonder, then, that word about you has spread as far as Albany, New York," she continued, hardly pausing for breath. "Why, Tanglewood must be ankle-deep in women vying for your attentions!" Planting her hands on her hips again, she walked a slow circle around him. "After all, there's more than your millions to consider. There's your gentlemanly behavior. Your warm smile. Your trusting nature."

The sarcasm hit him hard and he said, "All right, I think you've had your say now."

"Thinking again?" Sophie asked, eyes wide in mock innocence. "Are you sure that's wise?"

"She sure enough got you, boy," Henry said, wiping his streaming eyes.

Ridge ignored him and muttered, "Now, you just hold on a minute here, Red. If you'll remember, it was *your* daughter calling me 'daddy' that started all this."

"Well, for heaven's sake," Sophie countered with a huff, "lock the child up! What are you waiting for, *Sheriff,* there's a dangerous criminal on the loose! Of course, you'd better post a guard on her. She's small enough to slip through the bars of your cell."

Hattie snorted and Ridge narrowed his gaze.

"All right, that's enough of that," he said tightly.

"Oh, I agree," she snapped. "It's *quite* enough!"

"She's a regular firecracker, ain't she?" Henry muttered, then shrank back nervously when she sent him a scathing look.

Ridge had been in gun battles and come out feeling less used up. That woman could tear the flesh off a man's bones in less time than it took to draw a breath. She'd made him feel foolish, and even while he resented it, a part of him admired her for it. Gumption, he thought. She had it in spades. Not afraid to stand up for herself or her child, she'd faced him down and forced him to back up.

His gaze swept over her again. She might look like some soft city female, but underneath those nice clothes and fine airs, there was a damn desert bobcat waiting to pounce. And he had the claw marks to prove it.

"You made your case, Red," he told her quietly.

"My *name*," she said, "is Sophie Ryan, not Red."

He smiled and shrugged. If calling her "Red" bothered her, then that's just what he'd do. Lord knew, it wasn't much, but it looked like it was the only hit he'd score in their little battle. Then her name struck him as familiar and he gaped at her. "*You're* the new teacher?"

She sniffed. "That's right. Why?"

Well, this sure as hell explained why he hadn't been able to find the damned teacher at the train station. He'd been looking for someone pinch-faced and scrawny. He never would have pegged *this* woman for a schoolmarm.

However, there was a glint in her eyes at the moment that brought back vivid memories of razor strops and rulers. His gaze swept her up and down before settling back at her eyes again. "You don't look like any teacher I ever had," he said honestly.

One red eyebrow lifted. "Is that an actual *compliment*?"

He thought so, but before he could answer, Hattie clapped her hands together suddenly and both of them looked at her.

Shaking her head, the woman pushed herself up from the settee and crossed the room to glare up at Ridge.

Now he liked Hattie as much as anyone else, but he wasn't blind to her faults either. Somewhere in her forties, she was nosy, hardheaded, and bossy. She was just as likely to mother a man as she was to give him a swift kick in the backside if she thought he needed it. The woman had already outlived three perfectly good husbands and, as everybody knew, was on the prowl for number four. Every single man in town between the ages of forty and sixty kept a wary eye on her at all times.

"Ridge Hawkins," she said and stepped up to within an inch of him. "You leave off bothering her right this minute."

"Bothering her?" he repeated, stunned. Hadn't she just been sitting there chuckling along with the rest of his "friends" while this female chewed on his hide? "Hattie, I didn't start this, remember?"

"Sent all the way to New York to get us a decent teacher and I don't aim to start that hunt again"—she paused to wag one fat finger in his face—"just because you couldn't keep quiet when you ought."

Inhaling sharply, Ridge opened his mouth to fight that little speech, but Hattie didn't give him time.

"Now, I grant you," she said, with a nodding smile to the rest of the room, "what the child said was a bit of a surprise . . ."

"Yeah," Ridge agreed wryly, "just a bit."

Sophie glared at him.

"But the plain truth is," Hattie went sailing on, "we all know children are as like as not to make up stories. Now, as much as I'd love to sink my teeth into a juicy bit of gos—" She caught herself, smiled apologetically to Sophie and changed her choice of words. "*News,* the fact is, this ain't it."

She jerked a nod at every man in the room before looking at Sophie again. "Now, don't you worry, hon. Not a word of this leaves this house or *some* folks'll be mighty damn sorry."

Ridge gritted his teeth. He wasn't finished. Not by

a long shot. He had lots more questions he figured he wouldn't be getting any answers to. Especially so since Hattie was guarding the woman like an old hen with her last chick. But Tanglewood was a small town and the new schoolmarm wasn't going anywhere. He'd have his answers. Eventually.

"Thank you, Hattie," Sophie said and fixed her gaze on Ridge. "And as for you," she said stiffly, "I'll accept your apology whenever it's ready."

He choked on a snort of laughter. Whoever she was, he told himself with another brief stab of admiration, she had sand. Somehow, she'd turned this whole thing around until she'd made it seem he was at fault. "*My* apology? That'll be the day."

She stared at him with what he figured she considered to be a withering gaze. Well, he'd looked down into the black barrels of too many guns to be bothered by a redhead's icy glare. No matter how pretty she was or how she affected him.

"Somehow," she said tightly, "that doesn't surprise me."

His back teeth ground together. There was only so much of this he was willing to take in one night. Bending his head toward her, he lowered his voice and said, "Lady, you've already said I'm no gentleman. So don't you push me."

Her green eyes narrowed dangerously and he watched the full rush of temper color her cheeks again. Her jaw worked and he could see that she dearly wanted to let loose with a screech. But to give her her due, she held her tongue, satisfying herself instead with giving him another scorching look. Then she nodded politely at Hattie and the rest of them before turning and deliberately stomping her pretty little heel down onto the toe of his boot.

Ridge winced at the sharp stab of pain and watched her walk out of the room with all the aplomb of a queen. When she was gone, conversation buzzed around him while the others in the room talked about what had just happened.

He paid them no mind and instead walked to the foot of the staircase and stared up after her into the shadows. His toes throbbed and his mind raced.

Sophie Ryan, he thought, had managed to do what few people ever had. Set him on his ear. And damned if he hadn't almost enjoyed it. As he remembered the fire in her eyes, he found himself wondering if that fire burned just as hot with passion as it did with anger.

And he knew he was in serious trouble.

CHAPTER FOUR

Images, visions, flashed across the surface of her mind, chasing each other through wisps of uncertainty, shrouding the pictures in a mist, making it all so strange, so out of focus. The sheriff's face appeared, stern, eyes accusing, then skittering into a smile as he reached for her.

Before he touched her, though, the scene shifted, swirling wild colors and shapes until she saw Jenna, crying, hiding in the desert, racing across the hot sand until she was swallowed by the fog, leaving only the shattering echo of her cries behind.

Sophie twisted in her sleep, moaning, trying to escape the images she was able to block during the day. It was only here, at night, that her "gift" sometimes asserted itself, refusing to be put aside, refusing to be ignored.

And the colors in her dream shifted, curving and coiling into shades of gray and black, and out of the shadows came Charles's face, smiling.

A sharp kick in her side shattered the spell that held her and Sophie's eyes flew open. Gasping in air like a fish tossed onto a riverbank, she shot into a sitting position and stared into the moonlit darkness of her room. Her heartbeat thudded like a well-beaten drum as the remnants of the visions faded away slowly. Seconds ticked past and at last her heart left her throat and slipped back into her chest where it belonged.

Another hard kick shook the last of the fog away and she glanced down at her sleeping sister. Long, strawberry-blond hair swept across the white pillowcase and her face looked nearly angelic in the soft light. Sophie reached over and smoothed one hand along that silky cheek before swinging her legs off the mattress and slipping out of bed.

"Why now?" she muttered to herself as she wrapped her arms around her middle. It had been weeks since the visions had crowded her dreams. Weeks when she'd almost begun to hope that after years of quashing the images that flashed into her mind at the most inopportune moments, she'd finally beaten them into submission.

"Apparently not, though," she whispered, walking across the room toward the slash of moonlight that sliced through the darkness. Her knees trembled slightly and the throb in her forehead warned her that the visions were still with her, just hovering at the edges of her mind, waiting for a chance to come back and be recognized. But she wouldn't allow that. Wouldn't acknowledge what her mother had always called her "gift."

It wasn't a gift. It was a curse. The worst kind. The kind that set you apart from everything you wanted. That set you apart from the world.

She'd seen enough evidence of that back home. Rubbing her hands up and down her arms, Sophie remembered the house where she'd grown up and the family that everyone in town had considered just a "bubble off plumb."

As far back as anyone could remember, the Dolan women had been "different." They knew things no one else did. Saw danger before it pounced. Saw love flower where no one expected it. They could look at a person and instantly recognize the secrets buried deep within. It was said they could read souls. And most people didn't appreciate that.

By day, their neighbors kept a safe distance, being polite, but offering no real friendship. But by night, they all came to the Dolan house, looking for direction or advice or a peek into a future that frightened them. And during the years Sophie's mother had been a widow, the coins those people paid for a glimpse beyond the veil were all that kept her and her mother going.

They all wanted to know what the Dolans could see . . . but at the same time, they resented Sophie and her mother for being able to see what they couldn't. By the time Sophie was ten, she'd resigned herself to the fact that she would never really be accepted. By anyone but the family she loved.

But accepting it and being happy about it were two different things.

At the window, Sophie sank to the floor, lifted the sash, and propped her arms on the sill. A soft, cool breeze dusted across her face, lifting her hair and teasing her skin until a ripple of gooseflesh raced along her spine. But she welcomed it. Awake and chilly was better than asleep and running from her own mind. Leaning into the moonlight, she stared down at the street below.

Most of the windows were dark, as Tanglewood slept. But at the far end of the street, the brightly lit saloon tossed patches of yellow lamplight into the dirt. Piano music, slightly out of tune, drifted on the night air and the low rumble of voices and laughter carried just as easily in the stillness.

A lone rider steered his horse down the middle of the street and Sophie's gaze followed him. Alone, she thought. He looked so alone and just for a moment she wondered what that would be like. To answer to no one. To have no responsibilities. No one wondering who you are or what you want. No one counting on you.

"Sophie?" Jenna's voice whispered, curious.

Instantly, she shifted her gaze to the shadows crowding around the wide bed. "Go back to sleep, honey," she said quietly.

The little girl sighed and shifted, making the mattress creak just a bit under her faint weight. "You're here."

"Of course I'm here, honey," she assured her gently. "I'll always be here."

"Good."

In seconds, Jenna's easy breathing told Sophie the girl was sleeping again. Smiling to herself, she turned back to the window, and watched the solitary horseman move off down the street to be swallowed by darkness.

There was something else she hadn't considered before. Being alone, having no one to answer to or worry about, also meant having no one to love.

And loving Jenna was worth everything.

By morning, Sophie was more than willing to get started on their brand-new life. To put aside the ugly episode with the sheriff and the visions that had continued to haunt her throughout the night. Jenna, on the other hand, wasn't so easily dissuaded.

She shifted a look at her sister and noted the short arms crossed over the narrow chest and the disgusted huff of breath escaping her. Four years old or not, the child had no trouble expressing her fury.

"But he *is* my daddy," the little girl insisted as Sophie deftly worked a buttonhook on the little shoes.

Morning sunshine drifted through the partially opened window and a sigh of a breeze swished into the room.

It would have been a perfect beginning to their first day in Tanglewood . . . if she hadn't spent the last half hour arguing with a certain little girl.

"Honey." She glanced up again and said, as patiently as possible, "You have to stop saying that."

Jenna swung her free foot, kicking at the bed she sat on. "Don't have to," she said, despite managing to keep her bottom lip thrust out in a magnificent pout.

Sighing, Sophie finished her task, came up on her knees, set the buttonhook aside, and placed her hands on the mattress at either side of her little sister. Staring into the soft green eyes, so like their mother's, she bit back a sigh. How could she explain to a little girl that the things she saw in her head weren't things that everyone *else* saw?

And for pity's sake, how could she convince her that seeing Ridge Hawkins as her daddy was a huge mistake? And it *was* a mistake, she assured herself, remembering the flash of suspicion in his blue eyes. All she needed was the local sheriff getting nosy enough about her to make inquiries.

From what everyone had said about him the night before, Sophie had the distinct impression that he wouldn't think twice about throwing her into a jail cell and turning the key.

"Jenna, honey," she began and paused as the child's mutinous expression only darkened further. In reaction, her voice became sterner. "We both know he's not your daddy, so you can't call him that."

"But you want me to call *you* 'mommy' and you're not."

"That's different."

"No's not," she insisted, shaking her head.

"Yes," Sophie snapped right back, "it is. First of all, I *asked* you to call me 'mommy,' remember? The sheriff doesn't want you to call him 'daddy.' "

Scrunching up her face, Jenna thought about that one for a minute, then her expression cleared and she smiled. Throwing her hands up, she shrugged and said, "He has to like me first, huh?"

All right, Sophie thought. She'd take whatever she could get. "Yes, honey. It'd be better if you waited a while to call him 'daddy.' "

"I'll wait."

"Good." Five or ten years ought to do it.

"Till tomorrow."

Sophie closed her eyes and shook her head. And people thought *she* was hardheaded. Conceding the argument for the moment, she stood up, put the buttonhook away, then helped her sister down.

Turning for the mirror, she picked up her one and only hat, set it at just the right angle and slid the hatpin home. It was important to make the right first impression on these people. After all, they'd be entrusting their children to her.

She straightened the hang of her short, bottle-green jacket, then smoothed her hands over the matching skirt. Her face was a bit pale, making her freckles stand out like a white fence that had been splattered with gold paint, and there were shadows under her eyes. But then a night of sleeplessness was bound to affect a body one way or the other.

Still, all things considered, it could have been worse. She caught Jenna's eye in the glass and asked, "So. How do I look?"

"Pretty," the little girl said with a sharp nod.

"Thank you."

"Daddy likes it when you wear green."

She groaned. "Jenna . . ."

"And he likes your hair too," the child continued, then tilted her head to one side and asked, "What's a lion look like?"

"Sweetie—*what*?"

"A lion." Jenna pulled at her hair ribbon and looked at the end of it as though she'd never seen one before. Amazing how quickly a child could get distracted.

"What about a lion?" Sophie prompted.

"Daddy thinks you look like one if your hair's down and all over you."

"He does, does he?" Sophie muttered, shifting her gaze back to her own reflection. Meeting her own gaze, she wondered if that was supposed to have been a compliment or not. Thinking she looked like a lion, after all, was hardly poetry. Especially since the lion with a lot of hair was the *male*.

But then, she reminded herself sternly, she didn't want poetry from Sheriff Ridge Hawkins. She wanted to be left alone.

Didn't she?

"Daddy thinks you have pretty eyes too," Jenna added belatedly. "Do I have pretty eyes?"

"You have beautiful eyes," Sophie assured her.

"Daddy likes yours."

A flicker of pleasure darted through her before she could stop it.

"That's very nice of Daddy—" She caught herself and gritted her teeth. "I *mean* Sheriff Hawkins."

Jenna smiled.

Sophie inhaled slowly, deeply, and counted to ten, then twenty. It really wasn't the girl's fault. She simply said what she saw. She was too young to know any better. Too young to know that what went on in people's minds and hearts was no one else's business.

But she would teach her. She would teach her how to block the images. How to keep stray thoughts from sliding into her own mind. And, most especially, how to keep from repeating everything she learned.

She could do it. After all, she *was* the new teacher, wasn't she?

"Well," she asked, looking at Jenna's reflection, "are you ready to go and look at our new town?"

"Uh-huh," the girl said, already headed for the bedroom door.

Sophie snatched up her purse, slipped it onto her wrist, and caught up with Jenna before she could scoot into the hall. "Now, remember the rules?" she asked, tipping that stubborn little chin up with the tips of her fingers.

The girl sighed heavily and nodded. "I 'member."

"Tell me," Sophie said.

Scowling, she went on in a singsong, "we've been through this before" kind of voice. "Don't tell people what I see inside my head."

"Good," Sophie said with a smile. "And why?"

Another sigh, louder than the first. " 'Cause it's scary sometimes and people won't unnerstand."

"That's right."

Rubbing beneath her nose with her closed fist, Jenna added, "I don't unnerstand either, Soph—Mommy," she corrected quickly. "How come I can't tell 'em?"

How come indeed. She was a bit young to be told stories about witch trials and the tendency of people to want to destroy something they didn't understand. Sophie didn't want her sister scared . . . she just wanted her safe. So for right now, she decided to do nothing more than a "because I say so" kind of thing.

"I don't *unnerstand* either," she said, deliberately pronouncing the word just as Jenna did. "It's just better this way."

"You don't know either? Really?" the girl asked, clearly astonished. "I thought big people knowed everything."

Shaking her head, Sophie guided her sister into the hall, then closed the door behind her. Taking one small hand into hers, she muttered, "You'd be surprised, honey. Sometimes big people don't know *anything*."

Ridge watched her making her way down the boardwalk and scowled to himself. Hell, he was still bleeding from the barbs she'd shot at him the night before. Woman had a tongue like a bowie knife. Sharp and deadly on both sides. Half the night, he'd lain awake remembering everything she'd said and—since it was too late—coming up with some real clever answers too. But mostly, he'd remembered her eyes and flush of color on her cheeks and the defiant way she'd faced him down.

Hell, he couldn't name more than three or four people who'd stood up to him like that. Most folks walked a wide circle around him. But not Sophie Ryan. She'd stood toe to toe with him and backed him right into a corner. In front of witnesses. He'd be lucky if his reputation as a bad man to cross would stand up under the gossip that was sure to spread.

Walking to the porch post, he leaned one shoulder against the sturdy beam, folded his arms over his chest and narrowed his gaze as he watched her go. Quick, efficient steps, he told himself. She walked like a woman who knew where she was going. Naturally, in a town the size of Tanglewood, she could hardly take three steps without someone stepping out of their door to strike up a conversation. Everyone in town wanted to meet the new schoolteacher.

Especially since Henry Tuttle was doing all he could to spread the tale of how Sophie had bested the sheriff.

Ridge frowned again and saw Davey Sams step out of his gun shop long enough to shake Sophie's hand, then bend down to get acquainted with her daughter. But that didn't last long. Davey straightened abruptly, turned around and disappeared into his shop, closing the door behind him.

Hmm. A worm of suspicion uncoiled inside him. Ridge tugged the brim of his hat down lower over his eyes and noticed that Sophie was walking a bit quicker now, her heels tapping against the boardwalk loud enough for him to hear the staccato beat clean across the street.

"That's her, huh?"

He didn't even glance at Tall as the deputy came up behind him. "Yeah, that's her."

"She's a real looker, ain't she?" the other man mused thoughtfully.

Ridge frowned and crossed his arms over his chest.

"You can't even see her face from here. How would you know?"

"A man knows these things, boss."

"Is that right?"

"Sure," Tall went on, apparently oblivious to the tightness in Ridge's voice. "Hell, just look at her figure for a minute. Now, no God in His right mind'd make a woman's body look like that without givin' her a face to match."

Uneasiness crawled through Ridge's body, but he told himself it had nothing to do with Tall's wandering eye. Hell, everybody in town knew that the man was always on the scout for a pretty face. Still . . .

" 'Course," Tall mused, "I could see why you'd not think much of her."

"Is that right?"

"Well . . ." The deputy paused as if searching for a safe way of bringing up what had happened between Ridge and Sophie the night before. Apparently, though, he couldn't find one since his voice faded off.

Ridge's back teeth ground together. "Aren't you supposed to be out at Maggie Markham's place fixin' the damn roof?" he asked tightly, angling his deputy a hard look.

"Hell, boss. Why don't you just cut him loose and let him fix his own damn roof?"

Ridge's lips thinned. "Because he broke the law."

"Aw, he didn't mean nothin' by it."

"Then he shouldn't have broken Parker's jaw."

Tall kicked at a board. "Parker shouldn'ta cheated at cards."

"We don't know that he did."

"Joe says he did."

"Well now, Joe would, wouldn't he?" Ridge didn't

have much liking for Parker Shoals, the banker. And Joe Markham was a friend of his. But damn it, the law was the law. Joe hit Parker, so Joe'd face the judge. It was that simple.

In the time he'd been sheriff, Ridge had lived by one rule. There was a reason for the laws we live by. And no excuse in the world was good enough for breaking 'em.

He'd done enough of that in his past to know it for a fact. And if it hadn't been for running into Marshal J. T. Thorne one dark, cold night, he might still be hiding from posses and skipping just out of the reach of a rope.

"So go fix that roof," Ridge said abruptly, tired of talking about it.

Tall grimaced and hunched that too-long body as if trying to go unnoticed. It didn't work. Finally, he nodded and said, "I'm goin'."

When he shambled off, Ridge flicked his gaze back to Sophie. Damned if she didn't stir something inside him he hadn't known existed. He'd known plenty of women in his time, but not one of them stirred up both his juices and his brain. This one was different. She not only kept a man's interest, but she forced him to stay on his toes just to be able to spar with her.

It'd probably be a good idea, he told himself, to stay clear of her. At least until he knew more about her. But, he thought as he stepped off the boardwalk into the street, he never had been a man to turn away from a challenge. Or a risk.

Casting quick looks each way, he loped across the dirt road, dodging in between horses and wagons. Making his way through the morning shoppers, he headed after Sophie, not really sure what he'd say when he caught up to her.

The crashing blow of metal on metal drowned out Sophie's voice as she shouted a greeting to the blacksmith. Frustrated, she shot a quick look at Jenna, kneeling behind the bottom rail of the fence that surrounded a small paddock to one side of the smithy. Several horses wandered around the hard-packed earth and Jenna seemed completely entranced by them.

Which would give Sophie a minute or two to get directions to the schoolhouse. Supposing of course, she could get the blacksmith's attention. True, she could have asked Hattie but she'd thought to simply find it on her own. Yet here she was, nearly at the end of the street, and there was no sign of it.

The smithy's hammer slammed down again onto the red-hot horseshoe he had positioned on a massive anvil. Turning the iron shoe with a pair of tongs, he worked with a rhythm that throbbed in the air. Sound echoed around her and the heat pouring from the interior of the shop made her long for a breeze that didn't come.

She watched and was quickly caught up in the almost graceful movements he made as he worked. A huge man, the smithy's coffee-colored skin rippled with muscles beneath the leather apron he wore over a soiled blue shirt. His face and arms shone with perspiration as he toiled directly in front of the fully stoked forge. Firelight flickered against the back wall, and magnified the big man's shadow into that of a giant.

Mesmerized, she watched, not even trying to catch his attention now as he walked from the anvil to the forge and back again until the horseshoe was just as he wanted it. When it was finished, he dropped it into a barrel of water and the red-hot metal hissed and sizzled angrily.

Only then did he look up and spot her just at the edge of the shop. Wiping his forehead on his shirtsleeve, he set his hammer carefully to one side, dipped his head and asked, "Can I help you, ma'am?"

The rumble of his voice echoed the size and strength of him and Sophie smiled to think how well suited this man was to his job. She glanced quickly around the smithy and noted that every tool had its place and that the floor was neatly swept. A man after her own heart, it seemed. Tidy. Organized.

"Yes," she said and took a step closer, still keeping an eye on Jenna. Holding out her right hand, she said, "I'm Sophie Ryan."

He glanced at her hand as if unsure what to do about it for a long minute. Then he smiled and his features eased into warmth. There was a gentleness in his deep brown eyes that belied his great size and obvious strength. Still watching her, he wiped his big hands on his apron front, then folded his fingers around hers carefully.

A moment later, he released her and said, "Toby Crow, Miz Ryan, but you just call me Toby."

"Pleased to meet you, Toby," she said. "I'm—"

"The new schoolteacher," he said, smiling. "I know."

"Really?" She hadn't even made her way all the way down the street and the news had beaten her?

"Small town, ma'am," he said, glancing briefly toward Jenna, where she was attempting to pet one of the horses. "Not got much else to do, 'cept talk about each other."

"I suppose so," she said, and wondered how long it would be before the inevitable talk about Jenna would begin.

"What can I do for you?"

"Actually," she said, with another look at the child, "could you tell me where the school is?"

A brief frown scuttled across his wide face and it was like watching a wave slowly move toward shore. "Well . . ."

"Is there a problem?" she asked.

"No problem," another voice piped up from directly behind her.

She knew that voice all too well and had to force herself to turn around and face Ridge Hawkins. It didn't help matters to realize that the moment she looked into those too-knowing blue eyes of his, something inside her jumped in recognition. And remembering what Jenna had told her only made it worse. He thought she had pretty eyes.

Of course, he'd also accused her of being a blackmailer, for heaven's sake. He was only too ready to judge her a criminal. Her spine stiffened as she gave him one quick, dismissive look.

He smiled at her, grinned at Toby, then shifted his gaze back to her.

"Toby just doesn't want to be the one to show you the schoolhouse." He leaned one elbow on the top rail of the fence. "Apparently, no one else did either, or you'd have seen it by now."

She inhaled sharply, lifted her chin and said, "If you don't mind, *Sheriff,* I was speaking to Mr. Crow."

"Don't mind at all," the man said. "Just trying to help, is all."

She doubted that very much. "I don't want your help," she said tightly. "Or your conversation for that matter."

"You don't have to climb up on your high horse again—"

"I'm not climbing anything," she said tightly, feeling the beginnings of another headache coming on. "And I'll thank you to mind your own business." Glaring at him, she asked, "Shouldn't you be off arresting someone?"

"Who'd you have in mind?" he asked.

"You are the most insuf—"

"Ridge," Toby interrupted, "you stop it now. Don't you be givin' Miz Ryan reason to regret comin' here."

"Me? It's her. I only came over to—" he started to say.

Jenna's yelp caught their attention and in an instant, Sophie was hurrying around the edge of the enclosure, berating herself for not paying closer attention. But the girl was all right. She'd only fallen through the bottom rung of the fence, and by the time the adults got to her side, she was already up and dusting off her behind.

"I slipped," she said unnecessarily.

"So I see," Sophie said as her heart slid back into her chest.

"That horse try to eat you, little miss?" Toby asked with a smile.

Jenna shook her head and very seriously said, "Oh no, sir. Misty wouldn't do that. She likes me."

"Is that a fact?" Scratching his chin, Toby looked back and forth between child and horse a few times.

"Uh-huh," Jenna continued, tugging at her bedraggled hair ribbon. "She likes you too, though."

"Hmmm . . ." The sound groaned from deep inside his chest and sounded like the steel wheels of a train rolling along the tracks.

Giving both men a forced smile and fighting past the headache trying to drag her down into pain, Sophie laughed tightly and said, "Children . . ." as if that explained why a horse was having a conversation with a little girl.

When neither of the men smiled back, she grabbed Jenna's hand and speaking up into the silence, said, "If one of you will please point me toward the schoolhouse, we'll be going."

Ridge tipped his hat back farther on his head and after a long moment answered quietly, "It's just around the bend there." He pointed to the end of the street. "A bit past Hurley's Feed and Grain."

Nodding, she said stiffly, "Thank you." Then, turning her daughter around, marched off.

In the silence, both men heard the little girl as she walked by the horses gathered at the rail—just as though the animals were saying goodbye to her. "Misty and Moonlight and Martha and Maverick and Fred." She said the last name on a giggle that seemed to hang in the air long after they'd crossed the street and hurried on.

Ridge glanced at his friend and saw the same confusion in Toby's eyes that he knew was in his own.

"Did you tell her the names of the horses?"

"Nope," Toby said, reaching out to stroke Moonlight's muzzle, while keeping his gaze fixed on the woman and child.

Ridge nodded thoughtfully. Somehow, he'd known Toby was going to say that. And being right about it didn't make him feel a damn sight better. "Then how d'ya suppose she knew 'em?"

CHAPTER FIVE

"Don't see why we need no durn schoolteacher any-how," Travis McCoy grumbled. "Heckfire, this's gonna ruin everything."

Ever since that last teacher, Mr. Avery, left town, things had been real nice. Oh, sure, every once in a while, his ma made him read or do some ciphering, but she usually got too busy to pay much mind to schoolin'. He figured that wouldn't be happenin' now though. Not with the durn teacher livin' in the same durn house as him.

He scowled to himself and looked up at the mountains towering over Tanglewood. Sunlight poked through a couple of lazy clouds and threw pieces of shadow on the mighty pretty tree-lined slopes. But not pretty enough to get his mind off what was goin' on.

Yep. The days of a fella bein' able to go fishin' when he wanted was over.

Seven years old and he was a beaten man.

"It surely is," his best friend, Luke Jones, said, hurling a fist-sized stone at a small cairn of rocks they'd set up for target practice. He missed. "Shoot. Why, my ma's already talkin' 'bout me getting a haircut and wearin' socks."

Travis jerked his head, tossing his too-long brown hair out of his eyes, and took his turn. His stone missed too, and disgusted, he kicked at the dirt, looking for new ammunition. "I ain't getting no haircut," he muttered darkly. "And ya don't need socks if you're wearin' shoes. What's the sense in coverin' up your feet two times at once?" Womenfolks had the durnedest notions sometimes. Seemed all they did was think up ways to make a man's life miserable.

"My ma says the new teacher's stayin' at your place."

"Yeah," Travis said and pried a likely lookin' stone loose of the dried earth it was stuck in. "Till she gets that schoolhouse and the rooms behind it all cleaned out, I guess."

He threw his stone and when it smacked the stack of rocks he grinned. Looking at Luke, he saw his friend smiling too, and there was the same look in his eyes as there was the time they sneaked those cigars out of the mercantile and had them a nice quiet smoke in the alley. Travis smiled in memory of that fine time . . . well, it was fine until they got sick and their mas took a strip of hide off of each of 'em.

"What're you thinkin'?" Travis asked.

"I'm thinkin' we should figure a way to get rid of that new schoolteacher 'fore she gets set."

Hmm. "You figure she'll scare as easy as Mr. Avery?"

"Heckfire," Luke said with a snort of laughter. "She'll be easier'n he was. All womenfolks scare easy."

Yeah, Travis thought, that was true. But there was her little girl to think about too. She'd followed him all over the kitchen this morning, asking him to play and what all. 'Course, she was too young to play with and she was a girl on top of it, so he couldn't, but still, he didn't want to see her all scared and cryin'.

"All right," he said, "but we don't scare the little one. She's just a baby."

"Deal," Luke said and the two of them wandered out to set up their target again.

Maybe she shouldn't have spent so many years squashing her "gift." If she'd had the ability to draw on visions at will, she might have been prepared. But the moment that thought popped into her head, she dismissed it. *Nothing* could have prepared her.

Not even the bedraggled state of Tanglewood itself compared to what the citizens laughingly referred to as a schoolhouse.

Sophie dropped Jenna's hand, shook her head in disbelief, and simply stared at the monstrosity looming directly ahead of her. Small, it stood alone behind a short cluster of boulders as if trying to hide itself away. And she didn't blame it one bit. The rough plank walls had at one time been whitewashed, but the wind and sand and rain and whatever else happened around here had taken its toll. Splotches of white paint freckled the building, making it look like a survivor of some horrible disease. The shutters hung at drunken angles alongside windows whose panes had been shattered. One of the two front steps was missing, and as she stared blankly, a tumbleweed rolled along in front of the place, topping off its abandoned look.

The ever-present wind kicked up, dragged several shingles from the drooping roof and plopped them onto the ground. And even from here, Sophie could see a bird's nest in the top of the chimney.

"Well, perfect," she muttered and walked forward as if drawn by some unseen hand.

Jenna skipped alongside her, oblivious to the shack in front of her.

"No," Sophie said aloud to herself, "it's not even a shack. This is a disgrace."

"I like it," Jenna said. "It'll be pretty."

"Perhaps," Sophie answered, "if we set fire to it and start over."

The little girl laughed, bent down and picked up a stick. Swinging it in a wide arc, she whirled around and around, singing to herself as she played.

Sophie, though, was in no mood for singing. How did the people of Tanglewood expect a teacher to actually teach in a building that looked as though it were being held together by the dirt caked on its walls?

A quick, sharp pain stabbed her forehead and Sophie gulped, closing her eyes against it, knowing what it meant and fighting desperately to turn the tide of a coming vision.

Honestly. She hadn't had so much trouble stifling these blasted things in years. What was it about this place that stirred things up so? Squeezing her eyes more tightly shut, she told herself not to look. Not to notice what her mind was trying to show her.

She didn't *want* these images. Didn't want to see beyond the present. But despite her wants, despite her efforts, a wavering, fog-shrouded picture rose up in her mind of the schoolhouse, painted a soft yellow with dark green trim and a blue door. Flowers dotted the porch rails and a cluster of children played in the dirt in front.

Determined, she tried to close the vision off, to push it all aside, but before she could, she watched storm clouds descend on the schoolhouse and lightning crack in a dangerous sky. A man stepped out of the shadows and walked toward her. Lightning flashed and winked off the star on his chest. Face grim, tight, he reached for her . . .

A strong hand closed around her upper arm and she jumped, startled out of the vision.

"Red?" The voice came from right beside her. "Hey," he said, his grip on her upper arm tightening. "Are you all right?"

Sophie staggered slightly, her mind still swimming with images that both fascinated and terrified her. She lifted one hand to her forehead as if somehow she might be able to force the pictures away. It was happening too often now. The visions, the images, crowding in one on top of the other. What had happened to her control?

"Red?" that voice came again and Sophie blinked, shook her head, and looked up into deep blue eyes as dark and mysterious as the waters of a still lake. This close to him, she noticed little things for the first time: the tiny squint lines at the corners of his eyes; the fact that his dark hair was too long, curling just at the edge of his frayed shirt collar. The scent of bay rum clung to him and she breathed it in, felt surrounded by it, *calmed* by it.

The steely grip he had on her upper arm tightened slightly as he looked at her with concern. And Sophie didn't want to admit, even to herself, that she was grateful for both. The hold he had on her arm kept her trembling knees from giving out, and as to the other . . . well, it had been too long since anyone had worried about her.

An unexpected sheen of tears filled her eyes at the thought and she ducked her head to keep him from noticing the effect he had on her. She concentrated on the firm, warm grip of his hand on her arm. His touch was like a lifeline, an anchor to this world, and it had drawn her back from a place she tried never to go.

"You don't look so good," he said, then added, "maybe I should get you back to Hattie's."

"I'm fine," she said and, to prove it, pulled free of his grip. Without the warmth of his touch, she felt shakier, more *alone* somehow, but she ignored that sensation, cast a quick glance at Jenna then turned back to him. "Thank you," she said and told herself that her voice probably didn't sound as trembly to him as it did to her.

"One look at the place and you keel over?" he asked, a tight smile on his face as he shifted his gaze briefly to the ramshackle schoolhouse.

"Do you blame me?" she asked, grateful to be on safe ground. At least while they talked about the school, she wouldn't be thinking about the concern in his eyes or the strange heat that seemed to still simmer on the spot where he'd touched her.

"Guess not," he said, shoving his hands into his pockets. Staring at the dilapidated building, he shook his head and muttered, "Looks pretty pitiful at that."

" 'Pitiful' would be a step up, Sheriff," she countered, waving one hand at the place. Good, she thought with an inward smile. Arguing would keep them both on solid footing. There was no reason to think about the deep, beautiful color of his eyes, the strength of his hands, or the odd effect he seemed to have on her. Life would be much easier all the way around if she kept the sheriff as a friendly adversary.

"Still," he said, as if defending himself and his town for letting the place get into such sad shape. "Shouldn't be too much trouble to fix it up."

"Do you have a match with you?" she muttered, heading closer to the building.

He laughed shortly. "I heard that, and you should know, arson's against the law."

Last night's argument leaped into the forefront of her mind and Sophie shot him a quick look. "You already think I'm a criminal. Why not an arsonist as well?"

"Now, I never said that—"

"You most certainly did," she countered, whirling around to face him, keeping that hideous schoolhouse to her back. "You accused me of being a con . . ." She frowned, trying to remember, then gave up and said, "Something."

"Artist," he provided.

"Exactly." She nodded at him as though he were a student who'd just gotten a spelling word correct.

" 'Accuse' is a harsh word," he said, pulling his hands free of his pockets only to fold his arms across his chest.

"But fair," she snapped, watching his features tighten. Maybe a part of her couldn't blame him for the things he'd said the night before. After all, it wasn't every day a strange child stepped up to you and called you "daddy." But then again, should a sheriff, of all people, be so willing to jump to conclusions?

As if reading her mind, he said quietly, "About last night . . . maybe I was a little quick to—"

"Accuse?" she provided.

"Suggest," he corrected.

Sophie snorted at the term.

"All right," he said, holding both hands up in mock surrender. "I'm, uh . . ."

"Sorry?"

He frowned and changed course. "Let's just say I wish I hadn't been so quick on the trigger."

Not much of an apology, she told herself. But still, it was better than nothing, she supposed. And it would be pointless to rehash last night's entire argument. Besides, she had other things to think about now. Drawing in a deep breath, she called up every ounce of patience she possessed and said calmly, "Apology accepted."

He opened his mouth to argue, apparently thought better of it and slammed his mouth shut again.

She smiled to herself. It's a wise man who knows when he's beaten. "Sheriff Hawkins."

"Ridge," he corrected, staring into her eyes with a kind of heated stare she'd never seen directed at herself before. The kind a man might give to a woman he was *interested* in.

But that was ridiculous. The only interest he had in her was in his professional capacity. And that thought was enough to give her cold chills. And no matter how he might affect her, she had no business even contemplating a relationship with this man. For heaven's sake, he was the one person who had the power to lock her up and take Jenna away from her.

"Sheriff Hawkins," she said again, more firmly this time, letting him know in no uncertain terms that she wasn't interested in his interest. At least she had the satisfaction of seeing his full lips thin into a grim line of frustration. "I'd rather not redress last night's . . . *conversation*."

"If that means you don't want to argue anymore, I'm glad to hear it," he said and gave her a slight smile that produced a small dimple in his left cheek.

A fluttering sensation rippled through her and,

caught off guard, she swallowed hard and tried to explain it. When she couldn't, Sophie put it down to not having had any breakfast this morning. She'd been in such a hurry to examine her school and get ready for classes.

Classes. There wouldn't be any classes held here until she could be sure the building wouldn't fall down on her students. And no classes meant no teaching, meant no pay. A dark hole opened up inside her as she briefly considered the small stash of money she had to live on until she was paid.

Oh, she'd better inquire about the financial situation right away. Hattie, she thought. Hattie would know. But first, she was going into that death trap to see everything there was to see. If she was going to fix it, she needed to know exactly how much fixing was going to be required.

The fluttering disappeared, to be replaced by a hollow feeling in the pit of her stomach.

She looked the schoolhouse over again as she mentally prepared a list of supplies. Thinking out loud, she murmured, "A little elbow grease, a broom, paint . . . *lumber*."

"So," the man beside her said suddenly, "where do we start?"

We? She looked up at him and saw that he was serious. He meant to stay and work with her on this place. Though she was tempted by his offer of help, Sophie couldn't afford to become any more closely acquainted with the town sheriff. Despite that dimple in his cheek and the gleam in his eye when he looked at her, he wore a badge pinned to his chest. A badge that put her at odds with him. How infuriating, that she, a woman who'd done nothing wrong, would find herself in the position of having to go into hiding.

Charles should have been the one forced to give up the familiar, the comfortable. He should have had to change his name and look over his shoulder. But, she thought with an inward sigh, what should have been was a far cry from what was. And the simple truth was, Sophie Dolan—*Ryan*—was a woman on the run from a law that would hand an innocent child over to a man who sought only to use her.

And the man standing in front of her now was a representative of the very law she was trying to avoid. She needed to keep a polite distance between them— which shouldn't be difficult. After all, hadn't she been told time and time again that her razor-sharp tongue sent every man for miles around into a dead run?

So, all she had to do to be rid of the man was to be herself. Simple enough. And no time like the present to start.

She looked directly at him so there would be no mistake when she said, "*I* start by inspecting my school. *You* start by leaving."

He blinked, and in that second she called out to the little girl drawing pictures in the dirt. "Jenna, do not move from that spot. I'll be right inside."

"But I wanna see," the child said.

"No, honey," she answered, "it's not safe."

"Damn right," Ridge said and reached out to grab the darn woman before she could take a single step. "Don't you be foolish about this," he told her. "Just a minute or two ago, you looked like you were gonna faint."

Her eyes went wide. "I do not faint," she assured him.

"Whatever you say, Red," he said with a sharp nod.

"But either way, you're not goin' in there."

"Let go of my arm," she told him and gave him a look that would have sent a lesser man running for cover.

"Not likely," Ridge told her with a shake of his head.

What was it about this female, anyway? One minute she was flaying him alive and the next, she was dismissing him as if he didn't exist.

Now, standing there in her fine dress and ridiculous hat, she tells him she's planning a stroll into a building that looked as if it were about to fall down. All right, so it was a shameful thing to admit. The town had let their schoolhouse fall to hell, but he'd be damned if he'd let the schoolteacher fall along with it. He'd keep her out of that place if he had to lock her up to do it.

And judging by the stubborn look in her eyes, he just might have to. "What kind of a man would I be if I let a woman go into that building?"

She stared up at him, and just for a moment Ridge was almost positive he actually *saw* sparks flash in her eyes.

"If you *let* me, did you say?" she asked in that quiet, purely female tone that every man recognized as dangerous.

Sophie Ryan was turning into a real piece of work. Hell, he hadn't had to work this hard just to talk to a woman in years. She was more prickly than ten porcupines sittin' in a cactus and damned if he wasn't enjoying it. He kind of liked never knowing which way Sophie's wind would blow. And the fact that her red hair shone in the sun and the wash of freckles across her nose looked like gold dust in a pail of cream was just a bonus. Females like this one were few and far between and she could get as snippy as she damn well pleased, he told himself. No way in hell was he going to stand here and watch her get crushed by a falling-down schoolhouse.

"Red," he said, "you aren't going in there until it's safe."

She straightened up to her full height, which put her frown just below kiss level, narrowed her gaze, and said flatly, "Sheriff Hawkins."

"Ridge," he said, more to irritate her than anything else. Damned if he didn't enjoy watching those green eyes narrow into battle slits.

She skimmed right past it.

"I am a grown woman."

"Amen to that," he said, letting his gaze slide over her, noting her rounded hips, the lush curve of her breasts, her narrow waist.

Her frown deepened. "I make my own decisions."

"I can see that."

"And no one *lets* me do anything."

"That's just what I said, Sophie," Ridge told her, bending down so that their locked gazes were only inches apart. "I'm not *letting* you into that schoolhouse, so get used to it."

The toe of her shoe tapped against the dirt in a brisk, no-nonsense rhythm. A chill wind swept in off the desert, tugging at the full skirt of her dress and loosening a few stray curls to dance about the sides of her face. Impatiently, she pushed them back behind her ears.

"Don't you have work to do somewhere?" she asked.

"Nothin' that can't wait."

"I can wait too, Sheriff."

And she would too, he told himself with an inward smile. She was just stubborn enough to plant herself right here and wait until he'd left before going into that blasted school. Why in the hell hadn't they fixed that place up? How had they expected her to teach classes in a room that most folks wouldn't consider a fit stable?

"Sophie," he warned, "don't you push me into doing something I don't want to do."

"Such as?"

"Such as," he said, pushing his face even closer to hers, "plopping you into a jail cell and closing the door on you."

Just hearing him threaten the thing she feared most was enough to dry up her mouth and send her heart into a quick-step beat that pumped her blood through her veins at a ridiculous rate. Fear, pure and simple, washed over her and Sophie had to fight to keep her voice even. Calm.

"You wouldn't."

"You just try me," he said with a slow smile.

A battle of wills simmered in the air between them. Green eyes locked with blue, neither of them blinking, neither of them willing to give an inch. They might have stayed like that for hours if a sudden crash and a small, terrified yelp hadn't broken the spell.

Sophie turned to the spot where Jenna had been only a moment or two ago. The child was gone.

"Oh, my God," she said slowly, quietly, as she swiveled to look at the school. "Jenna?"

Ridge was already moving. He shouted, "Stay there!" over his shoulder as he raced for the building and the little girl inside.

CHAPTER SIX

In a few long strides, Ridge was at the foot of the steps, and though he wanted nothing more than to rush inside and grab that kid, his instincts forced him to go slow.

He could hear her crying, so he knew she was all right. At least for the moment. His gaze swept across the rotted-out planks that served as a porch and he muttered another vicious curse. The damn town council should have fixed this place up long ago. But they hadn't wanted to spend the money on it until they were sure they actually had found a teacher.

Sophie came up behind him and tried to push past. He held out one arm to keep her back. Turning his head to glance at her, he muttered, "We both go charging in there and we're liable to bring the whole damn place down."

That stopped her cold, and though he saw fear tighten her features and glitter in her eyes, she nodded and quit trying to muscle him out of the way.

Satisfied, he called out, "Jenna? Can you hear me, honey?"

"Yes," she said and sniffed pitifully.

"Good, that's good," Ridge said, then added, "you stay right where you are, all right? Don't move."

"I won't," the little girl said quietly, her voice wavering. "Daddy," she added a heartbeat later, "I'm stuck."

"Stuck?" Sophie repeated, her voice rising.

"It's all right, honey," he said, grinding his back teeth together at the fear in the child's voice. "We'll get you out."

Sophie's fingers tightened on his forearm, each of her short, rounded nails digging through the fabric of his shirt to tear at his skin. And he didn't blame her one damn bit. He felt her fear and shared it. Hell, there was more than just the dilapidated state of the place to worry about. He hadn't said so before, but with the weather so cool lately, there was a good chance that snakes had moved into the schoolhouse, looking for a nice warm spot to curl up in.

And now wasn't a good time to mention that. He glanced over his shoulder at Sophie again. Those freckles of hers stood out starkly against the pallor of her cheeks. The wind had tipped her hat to the back of her head and a riot of red curls had escaped her tidy knot to fly about her face. But her gaze was locked on the darkened doorway to the schoolhouse. She saw nothing, felt nothing but the fear for her daughter.

His heart twisted in his chest and in a few quickly passing seconds he wondered what it must be like to be loved so much—to know that no matter what else happened in your life, love would always be there. And a part of him envied the lost child.

He'd never known a love like that and Ridge felt the emptiness of that thought echo inside him like a single shout in a canyon. A hell of a thing for a man his age to admit to. That he had no one and nothing beyond a tin star and a fast horse.

He covered her hand with his and squeezed hard. Sophie's gaze flicked to his and Ridge said, "I'm going in after her. You stay put."

She opened her mouth but he spoke again quickly to cut her off.

"Arguing will only waste time."

Her gaze locked with his, her jaw worked, she swallowed hard, then nodded. "Go. Just, go," she muttered thickly.

Prying her hand off his arm, he turned back for the schoolhouse and, taking one long step, skipped over the missing pieces of wood before carefully easing his weight down onto the remaining planks. The floor groaned beneath him but held, and he kept going, wanting to get that child and get out while his luck held.

He stepped through the doorway and gave himself a moment to let his eyes adjust to the shadowy interior. Though he ached to find the girl and ease her fears, blundering around in the dark could do more harm than good.

Upended desks and benches lay scattered around the room as if tossed aside by a bored giant. Cobwebs hung in ghostly tatters from the ceiling and twisted and danced in the wind darting through the shattered, grimy window glass. Sunshine fought its way through the dirty panes, struggling to bring light into the tiny building, but it was like trying to illuminate a cavern with a single match.

And from somewhere in the shadows came the soft sniffling sound of a child crying.

Sophie practically vibrated in her impatience as she watched Ridge ease carefully into the building. Logically, she knew he had to go slowly. But logic had no part in what she was feeling at the moment. All she wanted was for Jenna to be safe. And in her arms. *Now.* She bit down hard on her bottom lip to keep from shouting, "Hurry."

The wind kicked up again, blowing a long, red curl across her eyes and distractedly she plucked it free. She heard the plop of shingles as several more fell from the roof and dropped to the dirt. She shivered and sent up a prayer that nothing else would tumble down.

Half turning toward the town just behind her, she wondered if she should go for help, then discounted it. By the time she got back, Ridge would be out with Jenna and it would all be over.

Blast and damnation, why hadn't she been watching? How could she have become so involved with talking and arguing with the sheriff that she failed to notice the girl wandering into that building?

A watery film blurred her vision and she viciously rubbed at her eyes. Tears were useless. As useless as she felt at the moment. She could hear Jenna crying and everything inside her screamed to go inside. To find her. Instead, she stood here, *waiting,* depending on a stranger, a man she hardly knew, to rescue the child who meant everything to her. Stuck, Jenna'd said. What if Ridge needed help to free her? What if by waiting where he'd told her to, she was wasting time Jenna needed?

Brain racing, heart pounding, she wondered why she wasn't getting one of those blasted visions now. When she could actually *use* it. Closing her eyes, she tried, for the first time in years, to summon the images she usually tried to bury. But there was nothing. No mind-numbing headache. No swirling pictures twisting through her brain.

A huge, heavy hand came down on her shoulder and Sophie jumped, whirled around, and eyes wide, stared up at Toby Crow. She hadn't even heard him approach, but now she grabbed at him as if he were a life rope tossed to her in an angry sea.

"Somethin' wrong?" he asked, his gaze already sliding past her to the darkened interior of the schoolhouse.

"Jenna," Sophie managed to say, curling her fingers around the big man's forearm. "She's hurt. Ridge went in to get her."

"Then he will," Toby assured her.

"I have to help," Sophie said, knowing she had to do something. *Anything*.

He patted her shoulder heavily. "You will, when she comes out."

"Everything all right?" someone shouted and they both turned to look.

A small crowd of people were hurrying toward the school, answering a call for help that hadn't even been sounded.

Scowling to himself again over the town council's stupidity, Ridge narrowed his gaze and swept the interior of the school slowly, looking for a flash of blond hair or a snatch of color from her little red dress. "Jenna?" he called quietly, treating the place as gingerly as he would a snowbound mountainside in danger of avalanche. "Where are ya, honey?"

"Here," the little voice came softly on a choked off sob.

Instantly, Ridge moved off to his right, toward a

darkened corner. Stepping gingerly, carefully, he winced at every creak and groan of wood as he crossed the room, keeping one wary eye open for snakes.

Then she was there, such a tiny thing, lying on the dirty floor, her soft blond hair haloed out around her head, a tipped-over desk lying atop her legs. She looked up at him and gave him a teary smile. A stray beam of sunlight crossed her face, making the solitary tear on her cheek glitter like a diamond. And when she held her arms up to him, something inside Ridge tightened painfully.

Such trust was a thing not given lightly and the fact that she looked at him like he was some sort of dime-novel hero hit him unexpectedly hard. As did her insistence on calling him "daddy." Lord knew, he'd never really expected to hear that word applied to him and it humbled him to admit how terrifying that one little word was. And how much a long-buried part of him enjoyed hearing her say it.

"Daddy, I hurt myself," she said around a quivering bottom lip.

"You'll be all right, darlin'," he said softly.

"I knowed you'd come."

He smiled, took one of her little hands in his and curled his fingers around hers to give her a brief squeeze.

Squatting beside her, he forced a grin and asked, "Well now, how'd you manage to do this?"

She gulped a breath and wiped her nose with the back of her free hand. "I was sitting on it and it falled over and knocked me down," she said, her voice thick with unshed tears.

"Can't have that, can we?" he asked. Reaching across her, he grabbed hold of the bench with one hand and gently lifted it just high enough for her to scoot her feet from beneath it.

She sighed and sat up so that she could rub her shin. Her black cotton stockings were torn and he saw a small patch of scraped flesh. Once she was free, he set the bench back down again and releasing her hand, lifted her off the floor. He'd check for sprains and broken bones once they were safely outside. For right now, all he wanted to do was get her clear of this place before a good stiff wind shot in off the desert and brought the whole building down.

Cradling her against his chest, he supported her slight weight with one forearm under her behind. He moved to head for the door, but stopped when she placed both hands on his cheeks and turned his face toward hers.

Her soft green eyes were on the same level as his, and staring into them now, he felt something inside him shift. Beneath her hands, his face grew warm and she smiled as her gaze seemed to look deep within him.

"I knowed you'd come, Daddy," she said softly, her little fingers moving on his skin like tiny feather strokes.

Ridge smiled at her, despite the "daddy" thing. Now wasn't the time to remind her she wasn't supposed to be calling him that. "Sure you did, honey," he said quietly. "I wouldn't leave you in here."

She gave a little sigh and shook her head and he couldn't help thinking that her eyes suddenly looked as old as time. In that tiny, heart-shaped face, those green eyes of hers shone with ancient knowledge.

"No," she said softly, "I knowed you were coming to be my daddy."

"Jenna, honey . . ."

She laid her palms flat against his cheeks and locked her gaze with his. Several long seconds ticked past and Ridge felt a small, niggling push at his mind. As if something was trying to make itself known. To make him see what he couldn't.

But that was foolishness.

The little girl in his arms smiled again and said, "Not foolish, Daddy."

Drawing his head back, he stared at her and wondered at the coincidence of her statement and his thoughts. But he didn't wonder long. The odd moment passed and Jenna was just a scared little girl again. Smiling, she wrapped her arms around his neck and laid her head on his shoulder, silently putting her trust in him.

And Ridge set that one strange moment aside, telling himself that he was getting fanciful in his old age. Then he headed for the door and the slash of sunlight beyond.

Sophie felt as though she'd been holding her breath since the moment Ridge had stepped inside the schoolhouse. Her mouth was dry, her chest felt as though it were being squeezed by an invisible iron band. Arms folded across her middle, she held on tight.

The small knot of people surrounding her talked and argued about the sad state of the building, but she wasn't listening. Every ounce of her concentration was focused on that shadowy rectangle that was the open doorway.

At last, he appeared, his tiny burden clasped close to his chest. Sophie'd never seen anything as beautiful as Jenna's dirt-streaked face. She pulled in her first easy breath, and the voices around her faded into the background, becoming nothing more than a low murmur of sound. As soon as Ridge stepped off the porch, she snatched the little girl from his arms and ran anxious hands up and down her arms and legs, checking for injuries. But beyond a tear in her stocking and a small scrape on her shin, Jenna seemed in better shape than Sophie felt.

"Are you hurt?" she asked finally, setting the girl on her own two feet.

"No, Mama," she said, flashing a wide smile at Ridge. "Daddy found me, just like I knew he would."

"Daddy?" someone in the interested crowd repeated.

"What's this?" another voice asked.

"All of you hush," Hattie snapped, then added, "Haven't you ever heard a child play pretend before?"

That question quieted the crowd of people who now clustered around them, but Sophie still winced at the implications and the no-doubt already-blossoming seeds of gossip.

Jenna, however, was oblivious. Delighted by the attention, she looked up into the faces watching her and grinned, showing her dirty hands, palms out. "I falled down."

"You sure did," Hattie said on a chuckle. "Got your dress all dirty too, didn't ya?"

The little girl inspected the damages, then noticed the tear in her stocking and the slight smear of blood. Her eyes went round and wide and her bottom lip quivered like a plucked bow string.

"Oh, honey," Sophie said quickly, "it's all right."

"Surely is." Hattie bent down, planted both hands on her knees, and looked the child directly in the eye.

"How about I take you on home and get you cleaned up?"

"Oh, that's not necessary," Sophie said quickly. "I'll take care of her."

The older woman smiled and shook her head. Then, leaning in closer, whispered, "Honey, you got all these menfolks standing around feeling terrible about this child getting hurt. Don't waste it."

"What?" Sophie tossed a quick look at the men now standing to one side and arguing among themselves. She hadn't given them a thought before this. Now, though, since Hattie'd mentioned it, she did notice the uncomfortable expressions mingled with guilt-ridden tones.

"Darlin'," the woman whispered as she unnecessarily smoothed her hair, "when a man's feelin' guilty about not doin' what he ought to have done, it's the best time to get him to do it."

Hmm. She took another, longer look at the men and thought about it. She needed this schoolhouse rebuilt as quickly as possible. So maybe Hattie was right. Now that she knew Jenna was fine, it might be wise to make the most of this situation.

"The town council has to vote on spending the money," one man said loud enough to be heard over the others.

How could they *not* vote to spend money on a schoolhouse for their own children? she wondered, her temper beginning to boil deep within.

"Well," a man with two long strands of hair combed over a bald pate said, "two of us are here. Let's vote."

Sophie smiled at him.

"That ain't legal," the first man countered.

She scowled and opened her mouth to argue, but was cut off.

"It is if we say it is."

Ridge spoke up and Sophie's gaze shifted to him. His features were closed and tight and anger sparked in his cool blue eyes. Well, good, she thought and waited a minute to hear what he had to say.

"That damn place is ready to fall down, George," he said, facing the man arguing against spending the money.

George ducked his head, hunched his shoulders, and took a step back. Almost as if he was *afraid* of the sheriff.

"Not to mention snakes," Toby put in quietly.

"Snakes?" Sophie nearly shouted, staring at Toby in wild disbelief.

A couple of the men shifted, their feet shuffling in the dirt.

"Yes'm," the blacksmith said. "Sometimes in winter and spring, the rattlers go lookin' for somewhere warm."

"That's true enough," one of the men in the crowd muttered.

"Rattlers," she muttered under her breath and took another long look at Jenna, as if checking for any unnoticed fang marks. Good Lord. Rattlesnakes. Falling-down buildings. In trying to keep her sister safe from Charles, she might have gotten her killed by bringing her to this raw, unkempt place in the middle of nowhere.

Glaring at Ridge, she said flatly, "You knew."

"Yeah," he admitted.

"And you didn't tell me."

"Not much point in telling you," he said.

"Point?" she repeated, giving in to the fear and anger pulsing through her. "Jenna's my sis—*daughter,*" she reminded him. "Doesn't that give me the right to know?"

"You know now," he said, shooting his friend a "why'd you open your mouth?" glare. "Does it help?"

No. It didn't. All it did was serve to feed her already overwhelming fury. Was this godforsaken town in the middle of hell?

She should have gone to a big city, where she and Jenna would have been just two people out of thousands. At least she wouldn't have been faced with things like rattlesnakes and sharp-eyed sheriffs.

But it was too late to change anything now, she reminded herself. Tanglewood was now their home and it was high time she stopped trying to make it something it wasn't and dealt with it on its own terms. After all, as her mother used to say, there was never a quitter in the Dolan family.

And she wouldn't be the first. Straightening her spine and lifting her chin, she looked from Ridge Hawkins to the rest of the men, pausing briefly to lock gazes with each of them. She'd always believed in speaking her mind and had long since stopped caring what others thought of what she had to say. After all, there were some benefits to being an "on the shelf" spinster. One of them being that you no longer had to dance attendance around a man's feelings.

Planting her hands on her hips, she took a long, deep breath and lit into them. "You should be ashamed of yourselves," she started and the nearly bald man flinched as if slapped. "You hired me to teach and expected me to do my job in *that*?" She waved one hand behind her. Surrendering to the words pouring from her throat, she went on, stalking back and forth in front of the men watching her with wary gazes.

She didn't even notice the slight smile on Ridge's face as he watched her.

Tipping her hat back out of her eyes, she glared at the first man. "I shall need lumber." She moved to the next man. "And paint." She kept moving. "And windows." In front of the last man, she added, "And help. This is not just a schoolhouse but *my* house. And my daughter and I are *not* going to fight the rattlesnakes for living space."

She nodded her head so abruptly her hat tipped all the way over her forehead and across one eye. Reaching up, she plucked it free, held her hatpin in one fist and shook it at her startled audience.

"Now, I want you all to get busy and start doing what you *should* have done long before I got here!"

Hattie clapped her hands together loudly and one of the men glared at her since he was far too leery of Sophie at the moment.

"Nicely said, Red," Ridge muttered.

She turned on him like a snake. "As for you," she said, advancing on him, still waving that hatpin dangerously. "You're no better than the rest of them. You're the *sheriff*," she said. "You should have burned this place to the ground to make sure people would be safe!"

"Now, hold on a minute," he said, features tight and gaze narrowed.

"I don't have time to hold on," she muttered, pushing past him and marching toward the schoolhouse. "It appears that like everything else that needs doing in this world, it will take a *woman* to get it done."

In stunned silence, the men watched her hike up the

hem of her skirt and climb the rickety steps. Then, apparently too angry to be worried about any danger, she walked directly into the schoolhouse and began to drag the first of the battered desks out onto the porch.

"I purely do like that girl," Hattie murmured as she took Jenna's hand and turned for home.

CHAPTER SEVEN

ONE WEEK LATER ...

"That female is hell in petticoats," Ridge muttered, not for the first time in the last few days.

Across the street, Sophie Ryan marched along the uneven boardwalk like a soldier on parade. Spine stiff, shoulders straight, she nodded to the people she passed and hardly seemed to notice the men scurrying to get out of her way.

All week she'd been at it. Going from store to store, gathering "donations" from the merchants. She'd attended the town council meeting and had decided that the money they'd allotted for rebuilding the school should instead go toward buying books and papers and who the hell knew what else. The building supplies, she was demanding—and getting—from the storekeepers.

He'd never really seen a tornado, but Ridge had a feeling they looked something like Sophie. Just spinning into town, setting down and sending everything in reach into turmoil.

That red hair of hers bound neatly at the top of her head, skirts flapping with her brisk strides, heels clicking against the wood planks, she was a force of nature. And most folks in town had already discovered there was nowhere to hide once she had up a full head of steam.

And the sheriff's office hadn't escaped her notice either. Joe Markham had been pleased as punch when the judge had cut him loose with nothing more than a ten-dollar fine and an order to stay out of trouble. Apparently Joe figured there'd be less work to do out on his farm than there was in town. Wasn't Tall right now over at the school tearing the old roof off to get ready for the new? Hell, he told himself with a scowl. Before he knew it, Sophie Ryan would be the damn mayor.

"And first thing she'll do is fire me," he muttered with a shake of his head. All week, he'd watched her as she took up her life in Tanglewood. He'd sat across from her at Hattie's table, slept down the hall from her, and even caught her once leaving the water closet.

He shifted uneasily remembering how she'd looked, all flushed and warm from her bath, small, pale hands grabbing at the edges of her faded green robe. Ridge never would have suspected a plain white cotton nightgown that covered a woman from neck to toes could be so blasted seductive.

But damned if the image of her in that nightgown hadn't kept him lying awake in his bed all night. Shaking his head now, he sucked in a deep breath to steady himself and deliberately pushed that memory of her to the back of his mind. Even lush curves and warm skin couldn't lure him close enough to have to deal with her prickly temperament.

Not to mention the fact that he still didn't quite trust her. There was just something about her that set little alarms off in his head.

From somewhere down the street, a dog barked furiously. Ridge stepped off the porch and into the street to take a look, grateful to have something else to think about besides Sophie Ryan. A freight wagon rolled past him, its empty bed jouncing in the ruts of the street and kicking up a cloud of dust that almost blinded him.

Waving one hand in front of his face, Ridge pulled the brim of his hat down low to shade his eyes from the glare of the sun and stared off toward the edge of town. He saw a man alone, riding slow down the middle of the street. He held the reins in his left hand and kept his right on his thigh, close to the pistol holstered there. Even from where he stood, Ridge saw the tell-tale rawhide strips tying that gun down and he knew there was going to be trouble.

He cast a quick look around the busy street and wished to hell it wasn't Saturday. Everyone from the outlying ranches came to town on a Saturday morning to do the shopping and to see some fresh faces. Got mighty damn lonely sitting on a ranch away from town all week. The merchants were doing a brisk business and he noted all the women and children bustling about the boardwalks.

One thing he didn't need was a gunbattle with careless bullets flying all over everywhere, doing damage and hurting innocent folks. And he didn't have a single idea how to avoid it.

"Damn it," he grumbled as he hitched his own gun belt a bit higher on his hips and started walking down the street toward the horseman.

Sunlight beat down onto Tanglewood, giving the town its first taste of the coming summer. A clear blue sky shimmered with the reflected heat, and as he walked, Ridge felt a drop or two of sweat roll along his spine. It was always like that, he remembered absently. Just before trouble started, all of his senses quickened.

He could taste the dust in the air, smell the bread baking in the restaurant, and hear the high-pitched shouts of children playing somewhere to his left. But even as his senses went on alert, his gaze never strayed from the man still moving toward him on a slow-stepping horse.

It was all too damn familiar. How many times had he walked into trouble? How many times over the years had he actually *courted* it? Until he'd come here. To this town. And this life.

"Mr. Simpson," Sophie said, placing both hands on the polished wood counter and leaning toward the little man staring at her as though she might start foaming at the mouth. "I've already received a donation of all the lumber we'll need from the mill at Ford Creek. All I'm asking you to do is donate the paint and window glass required to complete the job on the school-house."

"Now, ma'am," the man said, after clearing his throat loudly, "it ain't that I don't *want* to give ya the paint . . ."

Sophie just looked at him, waiting. She'd been dealing with the merchants of Tanglewood long enough now to recognize the dance of delaying tactics. Though they all eventually capitulated, it seemed to make them feel better to fight her for a while first.

"But that window glass comes all the way from St. Joe and," he added, apparently finding a backbone briefly, "it costs a pretty penny, I don't mind telling you."

"I'm sure it does," she said sympathetically, then

asked, "Mr. Simpson, Hattie tells me that you and your wife have *five* daughters?"

He ran one finger around the inside of his collar as if looking for more breathing room. Then, rubbing his whiskery jaw with one hand, he admitted to the truth. "Yes'm. Be six come August."

Sophie smiled triumphantly. He was beaten and they both knew it. Honestly, this was all so much easier with Hattie's help. The woman knew everything about everyone in town and wasn't the least bit shy about sharing what she knew.

"Well, then," she said, easing back a bit from the counter, "my congratulations. And I know you certainly want to do what's best for your children's education, don't you?"

"I s'pose," he murmured and rolled his eyes, already adding up the cost of donated paint and glass.

"That's fine, then," she said and made a quick notation on the paper she drew from her bag. "Now," Sophie said, tucking the paper away again. "As to the color of the paint . . ."

"You're killin' me here, ma'am," the man whined, giving her a pitiful look that froze and shifted as his gaze slid past her to the window facing the street.

"What is it?" Sophie asked, half turning to see what could possibly have turned Morton Simpson such an appalling shade of green.

But there was nothing unusual out there. The too-bright sun shone down on a town bustling with life. Her first Saturday in Tanglewood had been a surprise. It was such a quiet little place during the week and to see so many strange faces wandering through it was a bit of a shock. But at the same time, it was exciting.

Made her feel a bit less like she'd moved to the ends of the earth.

As she watched the people through the wide front window, her gaze seemed to be drawn to one man. Ridge Hawkins. Something inside her tightened, but she fought against it. Silly to be so affected by the mere sight of a man. Particularly, she told herself, *that* man.

Argumentative, bossy, arrogant, he was all the things she'd never admired in a man.

And yet, a corner of her mind whispered traitorously, he was also strong and brave and frankly had the broadest shoulders and the bluest eyes she'd ever seen. And then there were his hands. Long-fingered and callused, they had strength and gentleness too, she thought as she remembered the way he'd held Jenna and comforted her after her accident at the school.

Then too, she thought, remembering a certain night in the hallway at the boarding house, there was the look in his eyes when he'd seen her in her robe and nightgown. A rush of heat swept through her with a wild stirring of sensation and she only hoped Mr. Simpson put her flushed face down to the heat of the day.

"This don't look good," Mr. Simpson muttered.

She swallowed hard, then noticed he was still looking out the window.

Clearing her throat, she looked through the glass at Ridge and asked, "What do you mean? What are you talking about?"

The little man scuttled out from around his counter, hurried to the window, and leaning in close, looked off down the street in the direction Ridge was headed. "Yep. Just like I thought."

Blowing out an exasperated breath, Sophie walked to his side and demanded, "What are you talking about?"

"You best come away from that window, ma'am," he said, taking hold of her arm and pulling her backward.

She shook him off with a quick move and a look that should have put hair back on his head. "Explain yourself, Mr. Simpson."

Scowling, he pointed off down the street. "See that young fella headed this way?"

There were several "young fellas" but Sophie knew instinctively which one he was talking about. "The one with the dirty hat?"

"Yeah," he said tightly.

"What about him?" She spared him a quick look. "Really, Mr. Simpson, get on with it, if you please."

"He's a gunfighter," the man said shortly.

"Really?" she asked, turning back to look at the young man with the stringy hair and rumpled clothing in a new light. So this was a gunfighter. Hardly seemed as frightening as one might expect, judging from the sometimes lurid dime novels to be found on any street corner. Not that she actually *read* them, mind you. But she had been known to idly flip through their pages on occasion.

"You see Ridge?"

"Yes," she said, shifting her gaze back to the man who now had his back to her.

"He's heading over to send that fella packing and it might be wise to get out of range."

Out of range? Of *bullets*?

"Do you mean they might actually *shoot* at each other?" she asked.

"Yes, ma'am," he told her solemnly. "I'd say there's a good chance." He took another step back from the window for good measure. " 'Course, Ridge's pretty good at his job, so maybe not."

"For heaven's sake," she muttered, more to herself than the skittish storekeeper. "They can't shoot guns at each other. There are women and children out there. Someone will be hurt."

But even as she said the words, she noticed that the crowds had thinned remarkably. People scurried for cover, ducking into the shops and alleys lining the street. Apparently, this wasn't an unusual situation. In just a few short moments, Ridge Hawkins was practically alone with the oncoming gunfighter.

Sophie's breath caught in her throat. This wasn't fair. Not fair at all. True, he might be the sheriff, but this was *their* town. Should they really all stand by and watch a single man meet trouble alone?

Back home in Albany, there were dozens of constables, ready to help the citizens and each other in times of trouble. Here, there was this one man standing between the people of Tanglewood and danger.

She shot a look at the little man beside her and frowned to herself. How could these people look themselves in the mirror? What kind of example was this to set for their children?

"Aren't you going to offer your assistance?"

He looked at her like she was speaking Greek. "That ain't my job, ma'am."

"It's your job to protect your home. Your business."

He snorted. "Now, that's why we pay Ridge, ain't it?"

Good Lord, she thought. If everyone else in town felt as Mr. Simpson did, Ridge Hawkins would be alone on that street in a matter of minutes. He's a sheriff, she told herself, and no doubt used to danger. But at the same time, she knew it wasn't right. Not right at all to leave him to deal with a potentially dangerous situation all alone.

And was she expected to simply stand here and watch? No, Sophie thought firmly. Before she could think better of it, she marched to the door, yanked it open, and drove the bell above it into a wild dance that pierced the still air with a jangling, discordant sound.

"Ma'am," Mr. Simpson said, "come on back here, ma'am."

She ignored him as any sensible woman would. For heaven's sake, would the people here allow young thugs to scatter them like frightened birds? Were they willing to let gunfights take place on the very street where their children played? This was their *home*. *Her* home now too. Well, Sophie Dolan—*Ryan*—wouldn't be among those seeking shelter from a storm.

Marching along the boardwalk at a brisk pace, she ignored the whispered warnings hushed at her from those she passed. Her gaze darted from Ridge to the gunman and back again. A flutter of something warm and dangerous started low in her stomach and spread to her nether regions as she watched Ridge lift his right hand to set it atop his pistol butt.

He looked so sure of himself. So confident. So . . . He suddenly noticed her presence. She gave him a smile of solidarity and he reacted with a brief scowl before turning his attention back to the man almost abreast of him.

* * *

Damn woman!

But Ridge couldn't think about Sophie now. He didn't dare take his eyes off the young man sitting atop a worn-out chestnut gelding. It had been a while since he'd seen the gunfighter. But he really hadn't changed all that much.

The Kid smiled broadly, reached up to tip his hat farther back on his head, then resettled his right hand even closer to the butt of his pistol. "Hey, Ridge," he said. "Been a while."

"Yeah, it has," Ridge said, keeping far enough back that he couldn't be kicked and stepping to one side so that the sun was to his back, giving him a slight, but welcome edge. "Heard you were down in Mexico."

"Yeah?" the Kid asked, leaning forward on the pommel of his saddle. "And where'd you hear that?"

"Around." Go into any saloon west of St. Louis and the talk would eventually roll around to gunfighters, and once that conversation started, most folks ended up talking about William H. Bonney. Billy the Kid. "What're you doin' here, Billy?"

"Nothin'," the younger man said with a casual shrug that didn't fool Ridge in the least. It was said that Billy did everything with an easy smile—talk, laugh, kill. Since the Lincoln County war three years before, Billy'd been riding a rough trail. The Kid glanced around the now nearly empty street, paused to smile and tip his hat at Sophie, then looked back to Ridge. "Pretty lady over there."

Ridge's jaw tightened. Damn it, why didn't she disappear like everybody else had? "She ain't lookin' for a new friend."

Billy's lips thinned slightly and he stiffened in the saddle. "I'm not lookin' for trouble, Ridge. Just want to lay low for a couple days. Get my horse rested up."

"I don't think so, Billy," he said, letting his fingers curl around the butt of his pistol. You just never knew how Billy Bonney was going to react. Some days, he'd be as nice as all get out. Others, he'd just as soon shoot you as look your way.

The gunman's gaze flicked to the badge on Ridge's chest. "You know, Dirtwater Dave told me you was a lawman now. I didn't believe him."

"Been a couple years now," he answered softly.

A fly buzzed near Ridge's ear and the low droning sound was just another irritation. Everything inside him was keyed up for possible battle. And now he had to worry not only about Billy's unpredictable temper, but Sophie's unpredictable nature. Hell, for all he knew, she could step off that boardwalk at any minute and tell Billy the Kid to wipe his boots before coming into town.

As if his thought prompted her actions, Sophie came down the three short steps in front of the barbershop, walked to his side and stood staring up at the young gunfighter.

"Sophie," Ridge said tightly, taking one step in front of her, "go inside."

"I will not," she said, sparing him a quick glance before stepping out from behind him and returning her sharp gaze to the man on the horse. "I won't run from trouble, Ridge Hawkins. I've read about situations like this."

"Ma'am," the Kid said, interrupting her flow of words and receiving a frown for his trouble. "It might be best if you just do like the sheriff says."

"And if I don't," she asked, tilting her chin up at a mutinous angle, "are you planning to shoot me?"

Inwardly groaning, Ridge could hardly keep himself from tossing her over his shoulder and carting her to the closest store. Where he would lock her in.

Billy reared back in his saddle and stared at her, shock evident in his wide eyes. "Ma'am, I ain't *never* shot a lady yet and don't aim to start now."

"I might," Ridge murmured just loud enough for her to hear, but she disregarded it.

"That's hardly commendable," Sophie said sternly. "Since it means that you have no compunctions about shooting men."

"If that means I'll shoot back when shot at, yes, ma'am, I will." Billy's left hand tightened on the saddle pommel. Tearing his gaze from her, he said simply, "Ridge . . ."

"That's enough, Sophie," Ridge said and put himself squarely between her and Billy again. And this time, he'd keep her behind him if he had to hog-tie her.

Naturally, though, his move didn't stop her from talking.

"As I said," Sophie continued, taking advantage of their silence, "I've read about these situations, and if you're going to have a 'shoot-out,' I believe the accepted form would be for you to dismount and stand with your back to the sheriff's."

"Sophie . . ."

"Or is that for dueling?" she wondered aloud, then waved a hand in dismissal. "Doesn't matter, the result would be the same, wouldn't it?" Without waiting for an answer, she plunged ahead. "Bloodshed."

"Ma'am," Billy said quickly when she paused for breath, "you got no cause for worry from me."

"No?" She didn't sound convinced and Ridge

flexed his fingers to keep from throttling her. What did she think she was doing, egging on a man like Billy? Couldn't she see the wildness in his eyes? The eagerness in the fingertips that danced ever so closely to his pistol?

"No, ma'am," he said, nodding at the sheriff. "I reckon I know better than to try something fast and loose in Ridge Hawkins's town."

"Is that right?" she whispered and Ridge felt her stare on the back of his neck.

Ordinarily, he might be willing to take Billy at his word, but since Sophie was standing right in the line of possible fire, he kept his gaze fixed on the Kid as he offered, "You can take your horse down to the livery. Toby may make you a trade for your animal. It looks about done in."

Billy gave him a sheepish smile. "Been doin' a lot of runnin' lately. I 'preciate it."

Ridge nodded and stepped back, holding one arm out to ease Sophie back as well. She was stiff as stone and about as easy to move. "You'll be leavin' soon."

The Kid nodded slowly. "Reckon so." Then he tipped his hat to Sophie and said, "Pleased to make your acquaintance, ma'am." Then he leaned down and held his right hand out. "Ridge, good to see you again. Looks like takin' root agrees with you."

Ridge shook his hand and said only, "You watch your back, Billy."

"Always do, Sheriff," the Kid assured him and nudged his horse into a walk again. "Always do."

Well, things were calm. For now. But that didn't mean the danger was over. Nothing was assured until Billy was on his way out of Tanglewood and back to Mexico. And Ridge would be there at the livery to be damn sure the Kid got on his way quick.

But before he did that . . . he grabbed Sophie's upper arm, turned her around, and steered her in a fast walk toward the sheriff's office. Around them, the town slowly chugged back into life, with people straggling out of the shops and gathering in small knots to talk about what they'd just seen. After all, it wasn't every day Billy the Kid rode into your town and out again without a shooting.

"What are you doing?" she demanded.

He didn't answer. Didn't pay her any more attention than he did the other people they passed. His brain seethed with fury and every step he took only fed the flames. Sophie skipped alongside him, her feet getting tangled in her skirt, despite her efforts to hike it out of her way.

He paused at the edge of the boardwalk, grabbed her by the waist and swung her up the short set of steps. Setting her onto her feet again, he heard her teeth click together.

Then he grabbed her hand, and dragged her into the sheriff's office, slamming the door behind them.

Once inside, she yanked free of his grasp, swiped her fallen hair out of her eyes, and glared at him. "I have *never* been dragged through a street before, Sheriff Hawkins. Would you mind telling me why you decided to treat me to such an experience?"

He stepped up close to her and grabbed her upper arms, jerking her close enough that she had to tilt her head way back on her neck just to meet his gaze. "Because, Mrs. Ryan, it was either that or strangle you out there in front of witnesses."

Sophie stared up into his eyes and swore she actually saw flames of fury dancing in those blue depths.

His grip on her arms was strong, but not bruising, so she didn't believe his threat of physical violence for one moment. And despite the fact that she could almost feel his anger rippling off him in waves, she was feeling something else as well.

A strange, not altogether unpleasant warmth skittered unevenly throughout her body. From the top of her head to the tips of her toes, she suddenly seemed to be tingling in a very unusual fashion. Mouth dry, she licked her lips and watched as his gaze fixed on her mouth, following her tongue like a hungry man looking at a steak.

Her throat closed up.

She coughed, swallowed hard, and fought past the hardship to say plainly, "I was only trying to help."

"Help?" he repeated and let her go so quickly that she stumbled back a step or two before she caught her balance. "You could have gotten us both killed."

"Oh, I don't think so," she said, and made a half-hearted attempt to fix her hair. When yet another lock fell down across her eyes, she gave it up. "He was very young, after all."

"Yeah," Ridge told her flatly as he pulled off his hat to slap it against his thighs. "He *is* young. That's why they call him Billy the *Kid*."

"Billy the—"

"Ah," Ridge said, an evil little smile curving his mouth as he watched her shock set in. "I see you've read about him too."

Stunned, Sophie dropped into the closest chair and didn't even speak when Ridge glared at her and said, "Now I'm going down to Toby's to make sure Billy gets out of town. You stay put, Sophie, or so help me God I'll lock you in one of the cells for your own protection!"

CHAPTER EIGHT

True to his word, at least today, Billy changed horses at the livery, trading his gelding to Toby in exchange for a mare with fast feet and a wild disposition. Then he was gone, with nothing more than a small swirl of dust to mark his passing.

Ridge stood in the shade of the livery stable's overhang and squinted into the sun. Snatching off his hat, he wiped his forehead with the sleeve of his shirt, then slapped the hat back on. They'd all dodged a bullet today, he thought, breathing easier as Billy's silhouette faded into the heat-induced haze in the distance. Could have been real trouble, he told himself, especially since Sophie had decided to take a hand in things.

"What in the hell was she thinking?" he muttered.

"Seems to me," Toby said from right beside him, "she was tryin' to help."

Ridge swiveled his head to look at his friend. "By getting herself—or both of us—killed?"

Toby chuckled. "You look pretty much alive to me."

"No thanks to her," he said, recalling the flash of pure, outright *fear* he'd felt when the damn woman stepped off that boardwalk to confront the gunfighter. It had been years since he'd actually been afraid of anything.

Came from staring down the barrels of too many

guns to count. Once you'd faced the doorway to hell, there wasn't much left that could bring a scare to your soul. Or at least that's what he'd thought until today. Still scowling, Ridge tried to understand it. He'd stood between danger and the innocent before without feeling that sick pit of dread open up in his guts.

What was it about this Eastern woman that put her apart from the crowd? he wondered. Surely not her disposition. Cranky as all get out and a tongue made for shaving the flesh off a man's bones. Not her flashy way of dressing, certainly. Dresses buttoned to her chin and her hair tightly bound, she wasn't exactly *trying* to seduce a man.

But damned if she wasn't doing just that.

Toby laughed again and slapped Ridge on the back with a friendly pat strong enough to crush a smaller man.

"You got it bad, don't you, son?"

"What?" he asked, shifting his stance to brace his feet wide apart and fold his arms across his chest.

"For the new teacher," Toby said, with a shake of his head. "Didn't figure I'd ever see it. Ridge Hawkins goin' soft for a woman."

"Toby," Ridge said, frowning at his friend, "when it's this hot out, you shouldn't be standing so close to your forge. Between the heat and the fire, you're havin' your brain fried."

Toby's wide face split in a grin that was echoed in his dark brown eyes. "You say what you will, Ridge. That woman's gotten to you."

All right, that was way too close to what he'd been thinking. He didn't need his friends noticing him acting strange. It was hard enough noticing himself.

"Damn near gotten me killed, if that's what you mean."

"It ain't and you know it."

"You're crazy," Ridge said with a forced laugh.

"I may be crazy," Toby told him. "But I ain't stupid. Or blind."

"I hardly know her." And what he didn't know still worried him. Though he wasn't about to say so.

"Don't seem to matter none," the blacksmith said, moving back into the smithy, near the shimmering heat of the forge. Grabbing up a horseshoe, he tossed it onto the fire, then picked up the bellows and pumped them, driving air into the flames.

Ridge didn't know how he stood it. Sweat rolled down the big man's face and chest, glistening like raindrops in the glow of the fire. Winter or summer, rain or shine, the blacksmith was here, wielding a hammer so heavy that most men couldn't lift it, let alone swing it with an almost easy grace.

In the years that Ridge had been in Tanglewood, he and Toby had become friends, each sensing the aloneness of the other. They were both outsiders and in that they shared a common bond. Even fifteen years after the war, a black man didn't find many places to fit in. And as for Ridge, well, most God-fearing Christians didn't have much use for a man who until recently had lived his life on the wrong side of the law.

Ridge had never had many friends, and though he valued Toby, he wasn't about to let the man get away with saying something like that.

"You don't know what you're talkin' about."

Toby laughed again, picked up the hammer and rested it on one muscled shoulder. "I'd say the look on your face pretty much says I do."

"Damn it, Tob," Ridge said, stalking toward his friend, "she's the most annoying, stubborn, pushy . . ." His voice trailed off as he shook his head, trying to dislodge the picture of her in his mind. But it didn't work. There she stayed, that silly hat of hers perched high on her head, her chin tilted and those green eyes narrowed as she stared down Billy the Kid.

By damn, if he hadn't been so scared for her, he would have admired the hell out of her. That was some woman.

Even if she hadn't known just who she was sassing.

"She is all that," Toby agreed and picked up a pair of tongs. Using them to pluck the horseshoe from the fire, he laid it on the anvil, positioned it just right, then slammed the hammer down onto it. Sparks flew and the white-hot metal gleamed and pulsed in the shadows. "But," he added, turning the shoe slightly, "she's also the only soul in this town who walked out there to back your play with Billy."

"Yeah," Ridge muttered. But then he hadn't expected any help. Townspeople hired sheriffs so they wouldn't *have* to face down trouble themselves. Oh, not that most of them wouldn't fight if pushed. But they damn well expected their lawman to take most of the risks. And that's as it should be, he thought, trying to imagine Morton Simpson facing down Billy or someone like him.

Of course, he wouldn't have thought Sophie would do it either, yet there she'd stood, "Armed only with her mouth," he said aloud.

Chuckling, Toby said, "The way folks around here jump when she talks, I'd say that's a pretty good weapon."

"It damn sure is," Ridge admitted, having been on

the receiving end of that mouth a time or two himself. Bracing one shoulder against the plank wall, he glanced at Toby and said, "She was something, wasn't she?" Shaking his head, he said on a laugh, "I swear, Billy didn't know what the hell to do with her."

"Sound like somebody else you know?" Toby asked with a knowing look.

"Yeah," Ridge said, nodding, "it does."

And that was the problem, he thought. He just didn't know whether to grab her and kiss her hard enough to straighten her hair—or to strangle her and call it justifiable.

Although, he thought with a resigned sigh, he was leaning more toward the kissing.

Damn it.

ALBANY

"Any word, Mr. Finney?" Charles Vinson looked up from the stack of papers on his desk and met the hard, flat stare of the man across from him.

"Yes, sir," the man said and pulled a notebook from the inside pocket of his brown and gray–striped suit.

Ah well, Charles told himself, the fact that the man obviously preferred hideous suits didn't necessarily mean he wasn't a decent detective. After all, the Pinkertons had a reputation for accomplishing their tasks no matter what.

"Here it is," Finney said, nodding to himself as he read his own notes. "A widow and her child seen on a westbound train. The child apparently caused quite a stir with some shenanigans."

"Such as?" Charles's ears perked up. This might be

it, he told himself. Of course Sophie would try to hide her trail by posing as Jenna's mother. As if that would throw him off the scent for long.

The detective snorted derisively. "Apparently, the child was telling fortunes. Frightened a few passengers."

Judging from the man's expression, he didn't believe in any such nonsense himself. But Charles could tell him differently—if he'd been so inclined, which he wasn't. He'd seen Jenna's gift. He knew it to be real and powerful. And he wanted it for himself.

At any cost.

"I see. Well." Charles's features took on a mask of cool indifference. Wouldn't do to let the hired help see how excited he was by this news. Steepling his fingers, he said only, "That's very interesting, Mr. Finney. Have you discovered their final destination yet?"

"Not yet."

A quick, sharp stab of disappointment hit him low, but he concealed it. "Pity."

Flipping the notebook closed and slipping it into his pocket again, the detective stood almost at attention and said, "If I may suggest . . ."

"Yes?"

"Perhaps you might consider offering a reward?" Finney shrugged slightly, and the movement barely registered. "People are often more willing to help someone else when they benefit as well."

"An interesting suggestion, Detective," Charles said, leaning back in his maroon leather chair. Bracing his elbow on the arm, he tapped one manicured fingertip against his chin. "And how do we advertise this reward?"

Another shrug. "Newspapers, wanted posters distributed to local law enforcement."

He thought about it for a long moment. Another expense added to the money already spent on hiring the Pinks in the first place. However, he thought, mentally calculating the riches to be had once Jenna was in his control, with the child's gift of "sight," he would be able to master the stock market within a few weeks. And that was just the beginning. There were fortunes to be made in shipping and importing and farming and mining and—well, the possibilities were endless.

Smiling, he told himself that any monies spent in the search to find the girl were nothing more than an investment in his future.

Shifting his gaze to meet the dark, stony eyes of the man patiently awaiting further instructions, he said simply, "Do it."

TANGLEWOOD

Sophie cupped her face in her palms and forced herself to draw several long, deep breaths. Billy the Kid. Good heavens, she'd been standing in the middle of the road, giving Billy the Kid a lecture on the manners of good gunfighting.

Her head felt light. Her stomach did a quick somersault and she swallowed hard. What a fool Ridge must think her. She'd gone marching off to help him when in reality . . . She paused, let her hands drop to her lap and tilted her head to one side as she thought about this. In reality, he hadn't needed help at all. Pushing up from her chair, Sophie walked to the front window and looked out at Main Street.

It was as if none of it had happened. People were streaming from the shops to continue on about their market-day errands. As if a near gunbattle on a pretty Saturday morning were nothing more exciting than a new hat. Which led her to suppose that this wasn't the first time it had—or rather *hadn't*—happened.

"Just exactly who is Ridge Hawkins?" she wondered aloud, her fingers lightly tapping against the windowsill. A man Billy the Kid avoided having trouble with. A man who stood up to a notorious gunfighter—single-handed, mind you—with no trouble at all.

Yet, if he was a famous lawman, surely she would have heard of him, as she'd read of so many others, such as the Earps, or Bat Masterson, or Wild Bill Hickok. But then, she could say the same about his being a gunfighter, couldn't she?

"So what *do* I know about this man?" Brain racing, she turned around to face the office, letting her gaze sweep the cluttered room. Dust gathered in the corners, a cobweb swung lazily from the ceiling, and a veritable mountain of papers lay stacked haphazardly on the desk.

Well. Her eyebrows lifted slightly. She knew he was a man and therefore a stranger to a broom. Otherwise, there was nothing remarkable about the room, short of the impressive weapons rack hanging on the wall nearest the door. Three shotguns and four rifles stood on that rack and their brass fittings gleamed in the indirect sunlight. Sophie would have been willing to bet that the guns were the only things in the office that were dusted with any kind of regularity. Of course, she admitted silently, a man living among people like Billy the Kid had better keep his weapons in good working order.

On the far wall at least ten different wanted posters hung, the ink drawings of hard-faced men watching her as if silently daring her to look away. A cold chill ran along her spine as she stared into those eyes. Slowly, she crossed the room, drawn to those faces like lead shavings to a magnet.

Her gaze drifted from one face to the next as she drew closer, her heels clicking in the emptiness, sounding like a faint heartbeat. Inch-high black print screamed out from the cream-colored notices: Wanted. Reward. Robbery. Murder. Horse stealing.

A sharp jolt of mind-numbing pain staggered her suddenly. Clapping one hand to her forehead, Sophie closed her eyes and saw . . . her *own* face on a poster not unlike these. The vision quickened, fluttering past her mind's eye, dazzling her with its clarity. She watched, helpless, as her face was added to the motley collection of criminals hanging on sheriffs' walls throughout the West.

And then the images were gone, leaving her shaken and terrified, trying to decide if it had been an actual vision or if her own fears had created it.

"That's it," she murmured, instantly grabbing at the second explanation in favor of the first. "It has to be." She'd been suppressing her visions for so long now, they were completely unreliable, so it must have been her own imagination causing the headache and the images. Besides, if it had been a true vision . . . what could she do? There would be nowhere to hide. She'd be running from lawmen, bounty hunters, and even ordinary people who might recognize her face and turn her in for the reward.

For heaven's sake, she'd just finished irritating a man with the power to send her to prison.

Would Charles actually do something like offer a reward for her return? she wondered and immediately told herself, Of course he would. Though he would be loath to spend any money, she thought wryly, he'd consider it an investment in his future. A future that he wanted Jenna to help him plan. Sophie's own "gift" had always been sporadic—until recently. So Charles had no interest in her. But in order to get Jenna, he would have to find Sophie. And if that meant offering a reward for her capture, he'd do it.

He'd have nothing to lose and everything to gain. Why hadn't she thought of this before?

"And what can I do about it now?"

"Do about what?" Ridge's voice came from right behind her and Sophie jumped, startled. She hadn't even heard the door open.

"Still a little skittish?" he asked, reaching out to take hold of her upper arm.

A flash of heat shot from her arm through her chest and rocketed right down to the soles of her feet. Really, this had to stop. Nothing good could come of this attraction she felt for the sheriff. He was a potential enemy. One whom she should keep at a distance. And in another moment or two, she'd step back and away from him.

"I suppose I am," she said, silently relishing the sensations his touch brought to the surface.

"Yeah," he countered, tightening his grip on her arm slightly. One dark eyebrow arched as he added, "Most folks feel that way after their first gunfight."

Apparently, he was still a bit perturbed.

She glanced down at his hand on her arm, then up

into his eyes again before reminding him, "No one fired a gun."

"You were lucky," he said, bending his head until they were eye to eye. "*We* were lucky."

Sophie cleared her throat and met his gaze. Perhaps she'd been a bit precipitate, but her intent had been pure enough. She'd only wanted to help and, despite how it had turned out, she didn't regret the impulse. "If you're waiting for me to apologize, you might want to sit down."

He let her go, shook his head, and threw his hands wide in obvious exasperation. "Damn it, Sophie!"

She frowned at him. "There's no reason to swear at me."

"I can't shoot you, so cussing you's all I've got."

"I only wanted to help," she said, now sincerely beginning to rethink her impulsive behavior. It certainly wouldn't do her a spot of good to have the one man who might conceivably lock her away in a jail cell mad at her all the time.

And come to think of it, maybe she should try being a bit nicer to the sheriff. However, she looked into those glowering eyes of his and told herself that that was easier said than done. He might do strange things to her equilibrium, but he also had the capacity to stoke her temper faster than anyone she'd ever known.

Then he surprised her again by sighing heavily and shaking his head. "I guess I know that," he said, shooting her a long look. "But standing up to people like Billy is *my* job. Not yours."

It was his job. She knew that. But there'd been something more in his tone when he'd faced the young tough. She looked at him as something else occurred to her for the first time. "Why didn't you arrest him?"

"Billy?"

"Yes. Isn't that your job too?"

Ridge viciously rubbed the back of his neck. "Because he's not wanted in Nevada, that's why."

"But if he had been?"

His gaze narrowed on her. "Then he'd be in a cell right now."

And she didn't doubt it for a moment. Even facing the dangers of dealing with a gunman, he would have done what he thought right. He would have upheld the law. She could see it in his eyes. And in response, a flicker of worry sputtered into life in the pit of her stomach. To this man, the law meant *everything*.

And that put him at direct odds with her. Because for the first time in her life, she was, technically, a criminal. It didn't matter that the law was wrong in her case. He wouldn't care.

"Sophie," he said, dragging her back from her thoughts. "If you're gonna be livin' here, then I have to know that you're not going to be stepping into the middle of every brawl, shootout, and knife fight that comes my way."

Brawls. Shootouts. He said it all so matter-of-factly. This was his way of life and he was completely suited to it. She'd never forget the surge of something raw and wild that had swept through her when she'd seen him striding toward the mounted gunman. With the hot sun slashing at him, his eyes squinted and his jaw set, he'd looked powerful. And confident.

And alone.

Which was why she'd gone out there in the first place. What kind of man was it, she wondered, who accepted such things as a part of his life and thought no more about it? What kind of man believed so firmly in the law that he would risk his own life daily to uphold it?

A dangerous man.

"Knife fights," she muttered, thinking instantly of the bowie knife. She'd read several stories in which the legendary and lethal knife had played a prominent role.

Strange how much more entertaining tales of the West were when you were back East, sitting safely at home on a tidy street in a *civilized* city. How much harder it was to imagine such things as shootouts and knife fights happening to someone she *knew*. Someone she . . . what? Cared about?

Oh, God help her. She couldn't care for him. Not at the risk of Jenna's future. Not at the risk of her own freedom.

"What're you thinking?" he asked quietly. "I can almost see your brain working. And to tell you the truth, that worries me some."

She blinked, smiled, and shook her head. "It's nothing," she said. "Only that somehow . . ."

"What?" He moved closer. Close enough that she could smell the telltale scent of the bay rum he must have applied after shaving.

"This is all so different from what I've re—"

One corner of his mouth twitched. "What you've read."

"Well," she said. "Yes."

He moved even closer and she thought briefly about backing up, then decided that would look cowardly.

"Books can't teach you everything, Sophie," he said.

"Of course not, but—"

"You scared the hell out of me today," he told her quietly.

"I did?"

"Yeah," he admitted and reached out to tuck a stray red curl behind her right ear.

She shivered slightly at the touch of his fingertip against her skin.

"Surprised me too," he said.

Honestly, Sophie thought absently, he had the most amazingly beautiful eyes.

"You surprise me a lot, Sophie," he continued.

"Really?" Her heart crept out of her chest and up her throat. She felt his gaze slide across her features and she held her breath in anticipation. Of what, she wasn't sure.

"Yeah," he said, nodding thoughtfully. "You do. And you know something?"

"What?"

He tilted her chin up with the tips of his fingers. "I never liked surprises."

Stung, she came right out of the pleasant little haze he'd woven. A rush of color swamped her cheeks, she felt the heat of it pulsing through her. What on earth had come over her? Had she really been standing in front of a man, hoping he'd kiss her? Oh, good Lord.

She inhaled sharply, gave him a brief, stiff nod and moved back and away from him. Turning slightly to move around the man who at the moment she desperately wanted to kick, she said, "Well, forgive me for being unpredictable." Gripping a fistful of skirt, she hiked the dusty hem free of the floor, straightened her spine, frowned at him and added, "I assure you, if you're ever in a knife fight, you needn't worry that I'll leap to your defense." Stabbing her index finger at his broad chest, she added, "On the contrary, *Sheriff,* I just might be tempted to find a knife and join your opponent!"

And she'd actually considered being *nicer* to the man, she fumed silently. Sophie'd taken only a couple of steps toward the office door before Ridge grabbed her arm again, turned her around to face him and said, "You didn't let me finish."

"Oh," she said quickly, eager now to get away from him. "I think you've already said quite enough."

He shook his head and gave her a slow, easy smile that a few minutes ago might have affected her. Now, thank heaven, she was impervious to his charm.

"I said," he whispered, bending low enough that his breath brushed her cheeks, "I never liked surprises. Until *now.*"

Then *he* surprised *her* by planting a quick, hard kiss square on her mouth. Her stomach whirled, her mind raced, and her heart nearly flew from her chest. She'd read about kisses as she'd read about so many other things. What young woman hadn't read her share of politely written romances? But in all of those stories, the hero gave the heroine a sweet, chaste kiss that left her nearly as untouched as she'd been before. Not once had she read about the sort of peculiar, nearly overwhelming heat that rippled through her like the echoes from a stone tossed into a pond.

Apparently the authors of those books had been kissing the wrong men.

Sophie barely had time to enjoy the liquid sensation pooling in her knees before the whole experience was over. He released her and she struggled to remain upright, locking her knees and fumbling behind her to grip the edge of his desk.

"Your hat's falling off," he said, then chuckled before strolling out of the office, leaving her staring after him.

CHAPTER NINE

"Sophie's not scared of frogs," Jenna said quietly.

Travis McCoy jumped, startled at the sound of the child's voice, and took a step back and away from the schoolteacher's bed. Tightening his hold on the squirming frog he held in his right hand, he shot a look at the little girl standing in the open doorway.

Wouldn't you know the kid would see him putting the frog in her mama's bed? Heck, if she told *his* ma what he was up to, he'd get a lickin' for sure.

"Can I see him?" Jenna asked, walking farther into the room.

"I reckon," Travis grudgingly offered and tossed his hair back out of his eyes. As she came closer, he held the frog out and Jenna stretched out one hand to pet its head.

"He ain't a dog," he said, disgusted.

"He's soft, though."

"Yeah, I caught him myself. Down by the creek a couple weeks ago." And he'd hated the idea of giving the frog up, but had considered it a small price to pay if it scared the teacher into leaving town. But now, he guessed he'd get to keep it.

"Sophie's not gonna leave, y'know," Jenna said.

He glanced at her. "How come you call your ma by her rightful name?"

Jenna bit at her bottom lip, then lifted her shoulders

into an exaggerated shrug. " 'Cause I keep forgetting."

"Forgetting what?"

"To remember."

He frowned at her. Served him right for trying to talk to a girl. "You don't make no sense a'tall."

"I do too," she said, and her bottom lip jutted out in a perfect pout. "And I know stuff too."

"Yeah?" Travis asked, not really interested, as he stuffed his frog back into his pocket. "Like what?"

"Like you stole some cigars from the store and you put 'em in the pantry."

Travis shot a look at the empty doorway, half expecting to see his mother standing there glaring at him. Slapping one hand across the little girl's mouth, he bent down and said, "Hush now, don't talk so loud."

She pried his fingers off.

"You been following me around?" he demanded in a harsh whisper.

"Nope, but I saw you."

"How'd you see me if you wasn't followin' me?"

"I just did."

"You are the strangest girl," he muttered even while telling himself that he'd better find a new hiding place for his cigars.

"Am not."

"Are too."

"Am not," Jenna said, then added, "And Sophie— Mama's not scared of snakes either, 'cept for the bad ones, so you should take yours back from the closet."

Travis drew his head back and stared at her through narrowed eyes. Now he knew darn well that child hadn't been around when he'd put the garter snake in the teacher's hatbox. So how'd she know about it?

"You *saw* me do that too, did ya?"

"Uh-huh." She leaned on the edge of the bed and idly swung her right leg back and forth. "You wanna play?"

Thoughtfully, he said, "I reckon we could play for a while. Then maybe you could tell me the other stuff you see."

Three days later, Ridge was wondering if he'd taken leave of what little sense he'd started life out with. He couldn't seem to stop thinking about the woman who was taking Tanglewood like Grant took Richmond. Unstoppable, Sophie Ryan was bound and determined to get this schoolhouse up and running and wasn't about to take no for an answer from anyone.

She had the menfolk taking turns, working in shifts, damn near from sunup to sundown. And the ladies of Tanglewood weren't much help to their husbands either. They kept bringing food over so the men wouldn't have to leave work to eat and damned if they didn't side with Sophie every blasted time there was an argument. Ridge wouldn't have been a bit surprised to find a genuine war—men against the women—had broken out. Except for the fact that most of the husbands wouldn't dare go against their wives.

Humiliating, really, to watch these women riding roughshod over the men. But he was in no position to say anything. Grimacing tightly, he glanced down at the hammer in his hand. Hell, she even had *him* pounding nails. And he wasn't a damn carpenter. Ridge was more comfortable with a pistol than a hammer, yet here he stood, hip deep in sawdust and nails and planks and God knew what else littering the floor of the schoolhouse.

But even Ridge had to admit . . . silently, of course

. . . that she did get things done. The new roof was finished, the plank walls were almost ready to be painted, the floors and steps had been braced and repaired, and the rooms at the back of the building for her and Jenna were about ready to be moved into.

She was a wonder, all right. Never still for a minute, she poked her nose into everyone's work, offered her opinions—whether they were asked for or not— and, to give her her due, wasn't afraid to swing a hammer herself.

"That woman should have been a general," he muttered as his gaze followed her across the room.

"Hell, the army don't work this hard," Tall whispered from just behind him.

Ridge shot him a quick, unsympathetic look. He had his own problems and didn't care to hear about his deputy's. "Aren't you supposed to be hanging the new windows?"

Tall's features twisted into a pitiful mask. Holding up one hand to display the line of blood seeping from a nasty-looking cut, he said, "I broke one of 'em."

Ridge shook his head. "God help you if she finds out."

"Well, don't tell her," the younger man said and the tone of his voice should have been funny—if it wasn't so damned pathetic.

A sorry state of affairs, Ridge told himself, scowling. And it was all Sophie's doing. She'd marched into Tanglewood and snatched the reins of leadership right out of the mayor's—and *his*—hands.

"I won't say anything," Ridge said. "But if I was you, I'd get over to the mercantile and have Simpson cut you another one. Fast."

"I'm bleedin' here," Tall whined.

"Don't think that'll matter much to some folks," Ridge said, shifting his gaze back to Sophie.

"No, sir," the deputy said on a tired sigh. "I don't suppose it will."

Tall slipped out the open window frame, and Ridge noticed the slanting rays of the dying sun slash across the floorboards. Day's over, he told himself and tossed the hammer onto the nearest desk. The clatter of sound caught everyone's attention and Ridge said loudly, "That's it for today, fellas."

Mike Thorn, Dick Whittles, and George Fenwick set their tools down, threw him a smile of thanks, and headed for the door.

"Just a moment," Sophie said quickly, and moved to head the men off before they could leave. Waving one hand at the far wall where the new blackboard hung at a drunken angle, she said, "We can't leave things half finished, can we?"

"Now, ma'am—" George started, but she interrupted him.

"It wouldn't take long," she said.

"It'll be dark here in another minute or two," Mike said, inching his way toward escape.

"I brought a lamp," Sophie said brightly.

"My missus'll have dinner waitin'," Dick said and Ridge thought he detected just a bit of a whine in the other man's tone that set his own teeth on edge.

"*We're* tired," he said, his voice drowning out all the others.

Sophie turned toward him. "Sheriff Hawkins," she said with an exaggerated sigh, "this wouldn't take long."

Mike had made it to the door and George was just a step or two behind him. Ridge kept her focused on him so the others could make their escape. Dick saluted him silently as he followed his friends.

"It'll get done tomorrow," he said, locking his gaze with Sophie's.

"What's wrong with today?" she countered.

"Tonight," he corrected. "*Today* is over."

"Piffle," she snapped.

"Piffle?" One dark eyebrow lifted.

"The sun hasn't gone down yet."

"You should know by now, the minute she's down, it's blacker than pitch around here."

"My lamp—"

"Wouldn't throw enough light."

"You're wasting time," she told him. "The work would have been finished by now."

Hardest-headed female he'd ever met. "Sophie, the men have gone home," he said quietly.

She whipped around, stamped her foot, then whirled back to face him. "You did that purposely."

"What?" he asked, innocence coloring his tone.

"Argued with me so I wouldn't notice them leaving."

"Sophie, every time we talk, we argue."

"That's not true," she said.

"See?"

He shook his head and in the soft, golden light of sunset watched a frown scuttle across her features briefly.

"Very well," she said after a long moment, "I'll do it myself."

"Don't you be foolish," he told her, but it was too late. She was already snatching up a hammer and heading for the blackboard.

Muttering curses under his breath, he crossed the

room quickly and stopped alongside her. While she rummaged through a box of nails looking for just the right one, he dropped to one knee behind her.

"I'm perfectly capable, you know," she said, paying no attention to him at all.

"Yeah," he muttered, and positioned two nails, holding them in place with his fingers. "So I noticed."

"All this needs is a bit of straightening."

"Uh-huh." A couple of swift, sure strokes of the hammer drove the nails home and Ridge smiled to himself as he set the hammer down again and stood up. Crossing his arms over his chest, he watched her.

"You'll see," she told him and took a step. She stopped short, tried to step again and was stopped just as surely as the first time. Scowling fiercely now, she glanced back over her shoulder, first at him, then down, to where he'd nailed the hem of her skirt to the floor. Lifting her gaze to his, she said, "I can't believe you did that."

"You are the movingest woman I've ever known," he said bluntly. "It was the only way I could think of to stop you."

"For heaven's sake," she muttered darkly and tugged at her skirt. The material pulled but didn't give and she yanked at it again a couple of times before giving up. "Release me this minute."

"I don't think so," he said, with a shake of his head.

"Sheriff Hawkins—"

"It's Ridge."

"You can't just nail people to the floor."

"Sophie," he said, tipping his hat to the back of his head. "You've been riding roughshod over me and everybody else in town for days."

"I have not, I've only . . ." She paused and tugged at her skirt again.

A small shred of guilt unwound inside him. All right, maybe he shouldn't have nailed her skirt to the floor. But damn it, a man could only take so much. And when up against a woman like Sophie, Ridge figured, all's fair. Besides, she hadn't been this still in days.

"Been working us and yourself near around the clock. What's your big hurry, anyway?"

The light in the room had gone a pale orange. Through the open window frames, Sophie saw the last of the sunset's brilliant colors bleeding into a lavender sky that would all too soon become the warm black velvet of a desert night.

She looked up into the shadowy depths of Ridge Hawkins's blue eyes and knew she couldn't tell him the truth. That she was desperate to get the school up and running. That she needed to be at work, teaching the children in Tanglewood as quickly as possible. She *had* to show the people of this town how much they needed her. How much their children needed her.

Then, if Charles Vinson did show up, demanding that she be thrown in jail and that Jenna be handed over to him, the townspeople would be on her side. It was the driving force behind everything she did now. She had to make her place here. She had to become one of them so that they would all stand beside her against an outsider.

And she had a feeling that time was running out.

Every night, her dreams were filled with broken shards of visions. Splintered images of Charles's face. Of Jenna's tears. Of Ridge's hard, chiseled features. Every night, she chased through the shadows of her own dreams seeking some sort of comfort. Yet every morning, she woke to the fear that her new world would soon come crashing down around her.

She couldn't—*wouldn't*—let that happen.

Swallowing hard, she turned her back to the man watching her and fumbled at the waistband of her simple black skirt.

"What are you doing?" he asked.

"What I have to," she said, as her fingers worked the buttons free.

"Sophie . . ."

She sucked in a long, deep gulp of air, prayed for courage, then let her skirt drop.

"Jesus, woman!" he said. "You can't do that."

Stepping out of the material puddled at her feet, Sophie risked a quick glance at his stunned expression before saying tartly, "You left me no choice."

"Damn it, Sophie."

Still clutching her hammer and the nails she'd selected, she walked stiffly to the blackboard, uncomfortably aware of the draft whipping beneath the hem of her petticoat. Chills raced along her calves, thighs, and even higher, creating a wicked sensation that made her feel weak in the knees.

He grabbed her arm and spun her around to face him. In the dying light of the sun, his features looked ferocious. Jaw tight, eyes narrowed to slits, he stared down at her and asked, "Are you tryin' to make me loco?"

"I'm *trying* to fix this blackboard," she managed to say, despite the knot in her throat.

"If you aren't the stubbornest, most pigheaded—"

"I believe that's redundant."

"What?" he asked, then shook his head. "Never

mind." Tossing a glance over his shoulder at the doorway, he looked back at her and said tightly, "You can't walk around in your petticoat."

"You didn't leave me much choice," she pointed out and felt the cold fingers of the wind play along her legs again.

His grip on her arms tightened as he drew her closer to him. "Sophie Ryan," he muttered, his gaze moving over her face with a fierceness she felt. "Why in the hell did you have to come to *my* town?"

Heaven knew, she'd asked herself that question countless times in the last week or so. It was as if fate had played a nasty joke on her—sending her to the one man who not only turned her blood into liquid fire, but who had the authority to ruin her life. Yet, right now, at this very moment, she couldn't imagine being anywhere else. Her stomach spun and her head felt light. His touch sent warmth spiraling to the very center of her, and with a certainty she'd never known before, she said, "You're going to kiss me again, aren't you?"

A muscle in his jaw twitched and she thought for a moment he might try to deny what she'd already seen in his mind. But then that moment passed and he drew her even closer against him.

"God help us both, Sophie," he whispered, his breath dusting across her face as he bent his head lower, "but you're damn right I am."

Then his mouth came down on hers and Sophie's mind went blissfully blank. His lips met hers and she went up onto her toes to meet him. Reaching up, she wrapped her arms around his neck and felt him slide his own arms around her waist. He held her tightly, so tightly, she wasn't sure she'd be able to breathe and a part of her didn't care.

This is what she'd waited for most of her life. This flash of heat. Of wonder. He parted her lips with his tongue and she gasped in astonishment at the gentle invasion. But surprise quickly faded to be replaced by a wild, quickening hunger that tore at her insides and sent wicked ripples of anticipation to every inch of her body.

His tongue stroked hers, building a fire that threatened what was left of her composure. Her body trembled, her mind raced. Hesitantly at first, and then more boldly, she returned his intimate caress, exploring his mouth with her lips and tongue and wondering why it was that books never explained *everything*.

She'd never guessed, never dreamed, that anything could be as magical, as completely overwhelming, as this small intimacy. And as he claimed her, his hands roving up and down her back, she let her mind dissolve, let fears of the future fade into nothingness and gave herself instead to the wonder of this moment.

He tore his mouth from hers and trailed his lips along the column of her throat. She felt every damp kiss. Every tendril of heat that quickened inside her. And she trembled with the force of the sensations ricocheting through her.

His hands moved again and she felt the slightest brush of his fingers across the swell of her breast and Sophie inhaled sharply and pushed free of his grasp.

"You touched my—my—" She couldn't even *say* it.

"I surely did," he said, then dragged in air like a drowning man coming up for the third time. "Not nearly as much as I wanted to though," he admitted.

Shock scuttled through her, mingled with an entirely different reaction that seemed to settle and burn low in her body. And it shamed her to admit even to herself just how much she wanted to feel him touch her breast again.

"Look, Sophie," he said, his voice sounding as tight as the invisible band around her chest. "Maybe I didn't go about that just right, but—"

Oh, she thought he'd done it splendidly. "But what?" she managed to ask.

"But I'm not sorry."

Thank heaven. She didn't want him to be sorry. She wanted him to touch her again. Despite the risks, despite the danger, she wanted to feel his hands on her again. And she knew she couldn't allow it. But just because there wouldn't be any more kisses in her future didn't mean that right here, she had to pretend to be unmoved by what they'd just shared. "Neither am I."

"Well, then," he said, taking a step closer and reaching for her again.

"But," she said, holding up one hand to stop him in his tracks. "That's not to say I'm a woman of loose morals."

" 'Course not," he agreed, still reaching for her.

"However," she said, already thinking far ahead, "it would probably be best if you didn't do that again."

CHAPTER TEN

Well, she'd surprised him again. The way she'd reacted, responded to him, he'd half expected Sophie to start dreaming of—and *demanding*—orange blossoms. In his experience, a "good" woman who'd been kissed like that would even now be planning a wedding.

Naturally, Sophie would be contrary.

Although, truth be told, the women he usually found himself kissing weren't the kind to be dreaming of courtship and marriage. They were more interested in the solid clink of coins and how to seduce their next customer. So for all he knew Sophie wasn't acting strangely at all. But there was something in her eyes that told him different.

"It was just a kiss," she said softly, unconvincingly.

"That wasn't an ordinary kiss and you know it." Damn it, whatever reason she had for pulling back, he wouldn't let her get away with brushing off a kiss that had rocked him to his socks.

Ridge took a good long look at her, from the flash in her eyes to her lips, red and full from his kiss. The blood in his veins was still boiling. He wanted her. Bad. But even more, he wanted to know why a woman like Sophie wasn't slapping his face and demanding a proposal.

"I think it's best," she was saying, "if we both forget this ever happened."

All right, that was more effective than a slap.

"Why's that?"

"I beg your pardon?"

"Why, Sophie?" he asked, his voice a low hush in the dimly lit room. "Why would a woman like you want to forget about this? Why aren't you trying to trap you a *husband*?"

She blinked. "A husband?"

"Yeah."

"Sheriff Hawkins," she said, straightening up and lifting her chin. "I am not in the market for a husband and if I were, he wouldn't be you."

Ridge felt insulted, damn it. He'd never had any intention of proposing, but knowing she wouldn't have had him anyway stuck in his craw. It wasn't that she didn't like him. He knew enough about kissing that he could damn well tell if a female was enjoying herself or not. So what exactly was going on in that head of hers? Something was wrong here, he told himself. And damned if he wouldn't find out what.

Sophie looked into those pale blue eyes of his and told herself that if circumstances were different, she might very well have reacted as he so clearly had expected her to. Just a year ago . . . heavens, only a month ago, if a man had kissed her as Ridge just had, she would have expected him to come calling at least. But that was out of the question now. She couldn't build a life with a man on a lie—and she certainly couldn't tell *this* man the truth.

No, she'd long since realized that she would never have a family of her own. Five years ago, there'd been a young man. Bernard Hastings, she remembered, the son of the local butcher. Bernard had had small eyes and thick-fingered hands, but he'd been kind and quiet and hadn't listened to the gossip about the Dolan family. That alone had been enough to earn Sophie's affection. When people told him that the Dolan women were touched in the head—that they saw things only God had a right to know—he'd told them all that they were talking nonsense.

And Sophie began to believe that perhaps she might find a bit of happiness after all.

For several weeks that spring, they'd gone on walks together and sat on the porch swing and once, just as the sun was turning the evening sky violet, he'd kissed her cheek. And then Sophie had had a vision. And she'd warned him to not take a particular road home that evening. She'd seen it so clearly. A flash flood, his horse losing its footing, and Bernard going down into the swirling water.

He'd laughed her suggestion away and told her that he didn't believe in "gifts" or visions and he'd ridden off, dismissing her warning. By the next morning, he'd survived the flash flood, packed his bags, and taken the first train to Boston. Without so much as a good-bye note.

He hadn't even been grateful, she recalled. Just scared enough to want to put hundreds of miles between them.

And that was the last time any man had looked at her with more than dread. Until Ridge Hawkins. The one man she couldn't have. A part of her sang with regret, but the more logical part of her mind and soul reminded her that she hadn't come West in search of a man anyway. If she was destined to live her life alone, then so be it. She'd made her peace years ago with the fact that she was going to live and die a virgin.

She simply had never minded that fact quite as much as she did at this moment. Looking into his eyes, she paused briefly to think about what might have been, then resolutely set those notions aside. Taking a deep breath, she braced herself and lied. "It was a lovely kiss, Sheriff, but that's all it was."

"It was a helluva kiss, Sophie," he said, reaching out to run the tips of his fingers along her jawline. "Though it's clear to me it's been so long since you've been kissed, you've gotten a bit rusty at it."

She shivered at his touch and tried to ignore the sting of his words. "I do beg your pardon for disappointing you in any way," she said, sarcasm coloring her tone.

"Didn't say I was disappointed," he corrected her with a wink, "just said you needed some practice."

Which she couldn't risk. Oh, she wanted to kiss him again. More than she wanted her next breath. She wanted to feel that rush of sensation sweeping over her. But as long as she was a wanted criminal and he was a law-abiding sheriff, she couldn't risk it.

"Well," she said briskly, trying to ignore the fresh rush of warmth flooding her. "That's really not your concern." Then before he could respond, she turned around and bent down to snatch up her skirt. But the nails were still holding it in place, so she grabbed the hammer and yanked the nails free. Then she stood up again, still clutching the hammer in a tight fist.

He shook his head and took the hammer from her by easing her fingers back, one by one. His gaze held hers as he set the tool aside. Still holding her hand, he dragged the tip of one finger across her palm and Sophie sucked in air like a drowning woman.

"You know somethin', Sophie?" he said softly. "More and more, I'm seein' just how much you *are* my concern."

Oh, God.

No. She didn't want him thinking about her. Couldn't afford to have him pay even closer attention to her. What if he suddenly became curious? What if he decided on a whim to check into *Mrs.* Sophie Ryan's background, only to discover there *was* no Mrs. Sophie Ryan? Then what? Once he'd caught her in a lie, would he ever believe her attempts at explanations? This just got worse and worse, she thought and pulled her hand free of his grasp. Then, clutching her skirt to her chest, she turned for the door. While she still could.

"Where do you think you're going?" he called after her.

"Home."

"You can't walk through town half naked."

Blast. She glanced down at her petticoat, then said, "I told you before. I am not your concern, Sheriff."

"You are if you leave here like that." He crossed the room toward her.

Outside, the last of the sun's rays had faded and darkness dropped over Tanglewood like a black blanket. It never ceased to amaze Sophie that day slipped into night so quickly around here. Once the sun dropped behind the mountains, it was as if God blew out the single candle lighting the world. But even at night, she was bound to run into one or two people on the street. And she would hardly be able to maintain any dignity as a schoolteacher if she was seen in her undergarments.

Grumbling to herself, she fumbled her way into her skirt just as he came up beside her. Not bothering with the row of buttons, she simply clutched the waistband together in one fist. The quicker she got back to her room, the better . . . *safer* she'd feel.

"Damn it, Sophie, what's going on?" he asked and his voice sounded as soft as the velvety blackness surrounding them.

He took her arm in a firm grip and pulled her close.

As if the last few minutes had never happened, Sophie felt that swirl of exciting sensations ripen inside her again. But she struggled against it. The blasted man was muddling her mind and stirring her body into something she hardly recognized. And she didn't want to like it. And couldn't help it.

"Nothing's going on," she said and wished it were true.

"There's somethin' here, Sophie," he said, cupping her cheek and turning her face toward him. "And I'm not just talkin' about what's between us."

"Ridge . . ." Thank heaven *he* couldn't read minds.

"Whatever it is, I might be able to help."

"No," she said, then tried to correct herself. "There's nothing. Really."

He inhaled sharply, blew the air out in a rush and pulled her closer. Then he kissed her again and she was lost. His lips moved on hers with a gentle sureness, as if he were only waiting for her response. And blast it if her body wasn't doing just that, with or without her mind's cooperation.

She felt herself swaying, surrendering, and delving deep inside herself, she finally managed to find just enough courage to end this before it went any further.

Pulling away from him abruptly, she turned and bolted out the door, into the night.

"Damn it, Sophie," he called after her.

But she didn't listen. She kept walking, forcing her steps to match the hurried pace of her heart.

"You're here early."

Tall half turned in his chair to smile up at the woman standing beside him holding a coffeepot. Mercy James, a tiny thing with dark brown hair and tired green eyes gave him a smile and reached for one of the cups stacked in the center of the table.

"Coffee?" she asked and filled his cup without waiting for an answer.

"Yes, ma'am, and one of your pa's steaks when you get a minute." It was the same thing every night, he thought, looking around the nearly empty restaurant. Saturday nights, the place was packed with cowboys and ranchers, but weekdays, most of the local folks stayed at home for supper. So he generally had the little restaurant to himself but for the occasional straggler.

"No steaks tonight, but I made a nice beef stew," Mercy said.

"Right now, I'm hungry enough to eat the pot you cooked it in," he admitted, stifling a yawn behind one hand.

"Been working down at the school again?" she asked, setting the coffeepot down and easing into a chair opposite him.

"Yes, ma'am," he said with a shake of his head. "And let me tell you, that schoolteacher knows how to make a man work. I'm so tired, I'm afraid to order soup. Might drop my head in it and drown."

"She's a wonder all right," Mercy agreed. "She even got Pa to donate food for the paintin' party she's planning for this weekend."

"Your pa? Donated?" Ethan James was the most tightfisted man in the county. It was said he could squeeze a two-dollar gold piece hard enough to make it three.

Mercy ducked her head then looked up at him from beneath a fringe of hair that dusted across her forehead and ended at her eyebrows. "You gonna be there on Saturday? Painting, I mean?"

"I reckon," he said, wanting to take a nap at the thought of it.

"I'll be there too," she said, then stood up and shrugged as she reached for the coffeepot again. "Serving the food and all."

"Uh-huh," Tall muttered, his gaze drifting past her to the window that fronted the street.

Mercy sighed and wondered what she had to do to catch this man's eye. She'd waited on him nearly every night for months. She always saved him a piece of pie for dessert. And she always made sure his coffee cup stayed full and hot. What more could she do, short of hitting him over the head with her favorite skillet?

"Would you lookit that?" he muttered and pushed up from his chair to walk closer to the window.

"What?" She moved to his side and stood as close to him as she dared. The top of her head came to just about the middle of his chest and Mercy figured that was as close to touching his heart as she was liable to get.

"It's Sophie," he said.

She looked and, sure enough, saw the new schoolteacher fairly flying down the boardwalk, hand fisted

in her middle. And not ten steps behind her came
Ridge Hawkins. As he passed a lighted window, a
slash of lamplight fell on his features and Mercy was
glad it wasn't *her* he was after.

"Now what d'ya suppose that's about?" Tall murmured.

"What else do ya see?" Travis asked, fascinated by the
girl and all the things she knew.

"Lots of stuff," she said proudly and ate another of
the cookies Travis had swiped from his mother's
kitchen.

The scent of ham and potatoes frying wafted
through the open windows and drifted across the yard
to the spot by the fence where the two children sat in
the light of a rising moon.

Travis bit into another cookie himself and thought
about what it must be like to see things ahead of time
and wasn't at all sure he'd like it. After all, knowing
that Jed Foster's old hound dog was going to get run
over by a freight wagon hadn't helped him save it.
Still, thanks to Jenna, he'd found the pocket knife he'd
lost a few months back and he knew that someday he
was gonna grow up and be a doctor. Heck, maybe if
she'd been in town a couple years ago, he might have
been able to save his pa from getting thrown from that
horse.

"Don't worry, Travis," Jenna said and reached over
to pat his hand. "You're gonna get a new daddy soon."

"I am?"

"Uh-huh. Just like me."

"Who's mine gonna be?"

"Reverend Kendrick," she said around another
mouthful of cookie.

"The preacher?" Appalled, Travis suddenly had visions of being toted to church several times a day. "And who're you gonna get?"

"The sheriff."

Travis laughed and shook his head, relieved. "You're wrong, Jenna. Ridge ain't gonna marry your ma. And if you're wrong about him, you could be wrong about the preacher too."

At least, he surely hoped so.

The front door flew open and Sophie rushed in. Hair falling down around her shoulders, her skirt bunched at her waist, color flooding her cheeks, and her breath rushing in and out of her lungs as though she'd been running a foot race.

Hattie jumped up from the settee and dropped the ball of yarn she'd been winding around the reverend's outstretched hands. "Land's sake, girl, whatever happened to you?"

Sophie jumped, looked guiltily from Hattie to the preacher and back again before stammering out a reply. "Uh, nothing. I was uh . . . well, then I . . . and before I knew it . . ." Her voice trailed off into silence.

The Reverend Kendrick set the yarn aside, stood up and moved to align himself at Hattie's side. His kind eyes almost undid her, but Sophie was not about to let these people know what a fool she'd made of herself.

"I'll just go upstairs and—"

"Sophie," Ridge called out, entering the room as if the devil himself were just a step or two behind him. He stopped short when faced with the interested gazes of an audience he hadn't been expecting.

"Just what's goin' on around here?" Hattie wondered aloud and tapped the toe of her shoe against one of her rag rugs.

"Nothing," Sophie said quickly, shooting a meaningful glance at Ridge. "Absolutely nothing."

But clearly, Hattie wasn't convinced. The woman stepped forward, gave Sophie a long look up and down, then shifted a suspicious glare at the sheriff. "Ridge Hawkins," she said tightly, "if you—"

"He didn't do anything," Sophie interrupted her quickly and laid one hand on the woman's arm. Waiting for Hattie's gaze to focus on her, she said, "I fell. At the school. Tore my dress and Ridge . . ."—she forced the next word out—"*helped* me."

All right, it wasn't a very good lie, but it was the best she could do at a moment's notice. And anything was better than the truth. That he'd kissed her and touched her and ignited in her more sensations than she'd known existed before she'd had to push him away. She swallowed hard on that last thought and then shoved it into the darkest corner of her mind. There would be plenty of time later to remember another lost chance at love. For now, she simply wanted to get through the rest of this evening without anyone else knowing what had happened.

"He did, eh?" Hattie asked, and her expression left no doubt in anyone's mind that she knew she wasn't getting the whole story.

Sophie risked a glance at Ridge and saw confusion and frustration etched into his features as he stared at her. Well, better that he be confused than know the truth.

Lifting her chin and keeping her voice level, she tossed her hair back from her face and looked him square in the eye. "Thank you again, Sheriff. For your help."

A muscle in his jaw twitched and she watched as a steely calm seemed to drop over him. He nodded stiffly and said, "Glad I could help, Sophie."

Anxious to escape the remainders of this situation, she turned for the stairs, only partly aware that Hattie was right behind her.

Ridge's gaze followed her up the stairs, and when she disappeared down the landing, he turned his head to meet the calm, interested stare of his friend, the reverend.

"She fell, did she?"

"That's what she said," Ridge told him and yanked off his hat to shove one hand through his hair.

"What do you say?"

"Elias," he started, "don't push me on this."

"That's a good woman, Ridge. She doesn't deserve to be treated as less."

"Don't you think I know that?" he muttered, despite being aware that just a while ago, he hadn't been thinking along those lines.

"A part of you knows it," Elias said softly, "it's the other part I'm concerned about."

Ridge shot him a look and knew his friend was seeing way too clearly. Uncomfortable with the scrutiny, he jammed his hat back onto his head, said, "I'll be staying at the jailhouse from now on. Tell Hattie I'll be by to collect my things tomorrow."

As he turned to leave, Elias's voice stopped him. "You think the jailhouse is far enough away from her?"

"Nope," he muttered and stepped out into the night.

* * *

Once inside her room, Sophie inhaled slowly, deeply, and relaxed for the first time since rushing out of the schoolhouse. Picking up a match, she struck it, then lit the wick in the oil lamp sitting on the table beside her bed. As the flickering light danced around the empty room, she realized she wasn't as alone as she'd thought. Hattie had followed her into the room and was even now closing the door behind her.

"Now," the other woman said, "you want to tell me what *really* happened?"

No, she surely didn't. So she avoided that question by asking one of her own. "Where's Jenna?"

Hattie waved one hand at her and moved to plop down onto the edge of the bed. "Don't you worry about that little darlin'. She's out back with Travis."

Nodding, Sophie took a moment to be glad that at least Jenna was making friends here. She on the other hand seemed to be making nothing more than a mess of things.

"Sophie, honey," Hattie was saying, "I don't want you thinking I'm a busybody . . . but us womenfolks have got to stick together. Which is why I'm going to ask you one question."

"What's that?" she asked and surreptitiously did up the buttons on her skirt's waistband.

"Do I need to load my shotgun and plan a wedding?"

Sophie shot her a quick look and didn't miss the suspicion in the other woman's gaze. "Of course not!" she said, though even she had to admit her voice lacked conviction. So she went on, hoping to sound more believable. "I'm a respectable widow, Hattie."

"Not sayin' otherwise," the woman said with a kind

smile. "All I am sayin' is, that men being what they are, well . . ."

It was the sympathetic concern shining in Hattie's eyes that did her in. The woman wasn't judging her. She wasn't gathering stones to pitch at her. She was simply offering her support. Something Sophie hadn't experienced in far too long.

Giving in to the misery welling inside her, she took a seat beside Hattie and folded her hands in her lap.

"He kissed me," she said, and even as the words left her, she relived the experience, remembering every sigh, every touch, every breath. "Twice."

"Ah . . ." the woman beside her murmured and gave her joined hands a pat. "I figured as much."

"You did?"

"Mmm. You have the look of a woman who's been kissed by a man who knows what he's doin'."

An apt description if she'd ever heard one. Sophie sighed and flopped backward onto the mattress. Staring up at the ceiling, she said, "He certainly does."

"I thought so," Hattie said wistfully. "If I was ten years younger"—she paused to pat her expansive middle—"and a good bit lighter, I might have set my cap for him myself."

Pushing herself up onto one elbow, Sophie looked at the other woman and said, "I haven't set my cap for Ridge Hawkins, Hattie. I'm not looking for a husband."

To her surprise, her new friend laughed, slapped her knee and laughed harder. After several seconds, when she'd caught her breath again, Hattie wiped tears of enjoyment out of her eyes and said, "Honey, it's when you're not lookin' that you usually find 'em."

That was certainly true, she thought. After all, she'd

come to Tanglewood to hide. Not to find romance. And yet, she found herself drawn to a man that could only mean trouble.

"Why," Hattie went on, "I never would've imagined marryin' a preacher. But Elias," she said softly, dreamily, "he's quite the kisser, for a man of God."

"Are you and Elias—" She left the question unfinished.

"Haven't decided yet," Hattie said and tugged her shirtwaist down, emphasizing the opulent swell of her bosom. Then winking, she added, "You'll be the first to know though, I promise."

With that, she left the room and closed the door quietly after her. And Sophie was alone with far too many thoughts.

Next morning, Ridge's back hurt, his legs were cramped from lying all night on the too-short cot in the now-empty jail cell and Ridge had a whole new sympathy for Joe Markham, who'd spent five nights in the damn cell. But now Joe was back home with Maggie and it was Ridge suffering on that damned cot.

And dreaming about Sophie all night hadn't done a damn thing to help the situation any either.

Grumbling about just punishments and what Elias would no doubt call "penance," he poured himself a cup of last night's coffee from the pot on the stove and walked to his desk. Stretching the kinks out of his back, he sank into his chair, sipped at the still hot, muddy brew and shuddered as it slid down his throat.

"Jesus, that's awful," he said on a groan as he reached for the latest stack of papers he'd yet to go through. He sure as hell didn't feel like working, but it was better than doing nothing—which would only give him more time to think about what had happened with Sophie last night.

She'd hurried away from him so fast, her heels had practically set fire to the boardwalk. And blast it, he wanted to know why. Hell, there were plenty of women who'd consider him a fairly good catch. But Sophie wasn't even trying.

Setting the coffee cup down, he untied the string holding the new stack of wanted posters together and started the process of sorting through them.

Three separate piles formed on his desk as he quickly went about the familiar business. One stack for the serious threats; murderers, bank robbers, and the like. Another for the small-time criminals that every town saw sooner or later; cardsharps, road agents, and pickpockets. And the last pile was reserved for the unusual; missing persons, kidnappers. Ridge picked up that last poster and felt his heart do a hard slam against his rib cage. Holding his breath, he stared hard at the artist's rendering of a too-familiar face.

After a long minute, his gaze dropped to the crisp black lettering beneath the portrait and the breath he'd been holding left him in a rush.

**"Sophie Dolan, wanted for kidnapping.
$500 dollar reward. Contact Pinkerton Agency."**

CHAPTER ELEVEN

Something cold and hard dropped into the pit of his stomach. The fog in his head lifted as if wiped away by an invisible hand. He heard each beat of his heart, felt each breath as it labored from his lungs. His grip on the poster tightened as he stared down into the artist's rendering of Sophie's eyes.

Kidnapping?

How did a woman kidnap her own child? But even as that question rose up in his mind, he countered it with another. How did he know Jenna *was* her child? He only had Sophie's word for it, after all.

Well, he'd guessed she was hiding something, hadn't he? Although he had to admit, he hadn't been expecting this.

"Damn it."

Shoving back and away from his desk, he jumped to his feet and, carrying the poster with him, stalked back and forth across the room. His boot heels crashed against the floor and set off a like pounding in his head.

She'd surprised him, he thought, and that hadn't happened in too many years to count. He'd always considered himself a good judge of character. Hell, living the way he'd lived most of his life, he'd had to be. If you couldn't trust the man beside you in a gunfight, you'd end up mighty dead mighty fast.

So he'd watched and he'd learned. He'd taught himself to read a person—man or woman—and to see beyond the face they showed to folks. And he'd been damn good at it. Or so he'd thought.

Until now.

"Son of a bitch," he muttered thickly and stopped beside the front window. Slapping one hand against the window frame, he leaned in and stared out the dirty glass at the town of Tanglewood as it came to life.

Ridge blindly watched his friends and neighbors going about their business. Morton Simpson stood out on his boardwalk, sweeping a night's worth of dirt from in front of his store. Mercy James was washing down the restaurant windows and paused to smile at Davey Sams as he headed inside for breakfast. And a couple of kids raced down the middle of the street, chasing their dog.

He'd come to this place a few years ago and had sworn to protect this town and uphold the law. Lord knew, he'd found the law late in his life. Ridge had ridden more than his share of owlhoot trails, alongside men whose faces were most often found on the kind of wanted poster he still held fisted in one hand. But damn it, he wasn't the same man anymore.

Not since the night four years before when a U.S. Marshal had taken a chance on him. The scene out on the street faded into oblivion as Ridge remembered that night and the man who'd changed his life.

He could almost feel the cold mountain air stinging his cheeks, and if he tried he was pretty sure he'd be able to smell the sweet, warm scent of burning wood.

His horse had been on its last legs when Ridge rode up to the campfire. A lone man sat back from the flames and watched him approach. And any thoughts

Ridge might have had about stealing the fella's horse disappeared quick enough when the old man produced a Sharps rifle and pointed it at him.

"Hey, now," Ridge said and lifted both hands high. No fast moves, he told himself even as he looked for and couldn't find a way out of this predicament. "Ain't no call to go bein' so testy."

"Mister," the man said softly, "you step down easy off that poor horse and keep your hands where I can see 'em."

"I'm not huntin' trouble," Ridge told him as he did just as he was told. He was in no hurry to find out what size hole a fifty-caliber bullet would leave in his body.

"Looks to me like you've already found some, son." The older man waved the barrel of his long gun and indicated that Ridge should take a seat on the far side of the fire.

So he did, needing the warmth even more than he feared that black hole of a barrel pointed at him. His fingers were stiff with cold and it felt as though his butt carried the permanent imprint of that damned saddle.

Crouching beside the fire, Ridge carefully kept his gaze slightly averted as the flames crackled and danced in the wind sliding down off the peaks. A man who stared into the light of a fire would find himself temporarily blinded when he tried to see into the darkness. But he watched sparks lift, wink brightly for an instant, then disappear into the inky blackness.

"Ran into a few bandits some miles back," he lied, since it didn't seem like a good idea to mention the posse he'd spent most of the day losing. "Had to do some fast moving. My horse is about done in, I'm afraid."

"Bandits," the old man said with a slow nod, neither accepting nor dismissing the story. Then he offered, "There's coffee. And beans."

His stomach rumbled and Ridge realized that he hadn't had a bite to eat in nearly two days. Not much time for resting up and such when you were always a step or two ahead of the law. And that bank Jim and Texas Jack had robbed had been sitting right smack-dab in the middle of a town whose citizens apparently didn't know the meaning of the word "quit." Hell, Ridge hadn't planned on being in on a robbery. Rustling a couple of cows here and there, all right. But banks? Nope, he wanted no part of that. Yet that posse of God-fearing Christians were probably still out there on the flats somewhere and Ridge hoped to hell the other boys had gotten away. There was just nothin' meaner than an ordinary citizen who'd been pushed too far.

" 'Preciate it," he said and helped himself. The beans had been seasoned with sage and damned if they didn't smell better than a Kansas City steak. When his hands were full of plate and cup, he heard the trigger on that Sharps snick into a cocked position and the hairs on the back of his neck stood straight up.

Ridge looked up into cold gray eyes that were fixed on him like a snake watching a rabbit. "Mister, I don't mean you any harm."

A dry chuckle issued from the man's throat, sounding like the crunch of dead leaves. "Not while I'm holding this, you don't."

Ridge sighed and tried to remember a time when he wasn't running from or to something. But he couldn't. There'd been too many times like this one, he thought. Staring down into the barrel of a gun and hoping to hell he'd get out of the situation one more time.

"I know who you are, boy."

That got his attention. "Mister, I don't know what you're talkin' about."

The man pulled the edge of his coat back to display a shining silver star pinned to his shirt and Ridge cursed himself for having the worst luck in the world. What were the chances that he'd stumble onto a campfire only to find out his host was a lawman?

"You're Ridge Hawkins," the man said and a flutter of shock whipped through him. Briefly, he considered whether he stood a chance of escaping. But his horse was near dead and he was so damn tired himself that he just plain didn't have the gumption to try it.

So while the old man talked, Ridge figured he might as well eat. If he was going to die sometime soon, he'd rather not do it on an empty stomach. And even if he didn't get shot sometime in the next few minutes, it would be a long, hungry ride to whatever jail the man had in mind for him. Scooping a forkful of beans into his mouth, he barely chewed them before swallowing and taking another.

"You rode some with Billy Bonney, isn't that right?"

He swallowed hard and took a sip of coffee. Getting himself caught was one thing. Turning his friends over was something else again. Finally, he admitted only, "I've seen him a time or two."

"Uh-huh," the old man said with a slow smile. "You saw him down in Santa Fe a few months back, isn't that right?"

Ridge didn't say a word. Hell, he didn't have to.

The old man knew just what he was talking about and he knew it.

"You was in a cantina with the Kid when he pulled a gun on a marshal."

"Yeah?"

"And you talked Billy out of shooting that man, didn't you, son?"

He sure as hell had. Billy'd been on a tear and if Ridge hadn't stopped him he might have shot up the whole bar. "Seemed like the thing to do."

"Some in your place wouldn't have bothered," the old man said, his gaze still fixed on Ridge.

"I don't hold with murder," Ridge said bluntly and set his plate down. Refilling his coffee cup, he shrugged and said, "Defending myself is one thing. Killing a man for the hell of it is another."

The old man smiled and nodded to himself as if pleased with Ridge's answer. Then he lowered his weapon. "Boy, you've been running with the wrong bunch, but it ain't too late for you. Yet. I done some checking on you and the most you've got standing against you is a couple of robberies and some missing cattle. But son, you keep riding with them that kill for sport and sooner or later you'll be doing a fast dance at the end of a short rope."

Talk of hangings was never a pleasant thing. Especially not since he'd been giving the very real possibility of his death some serious thought lately.

"Gunfighting's all I know," he said and eased back against a fallen log.

"Then learn something else," the sheriff told him flatly. "That man you saved in Santa Fe was a friend of mine. You did him a favor and we've been wantin' to return it."

"Yeah?" he asked, suspicious. "How you gonna do that?"

"You keep clear of trouble from here on out and maybe we can get you a pardon."

And with those words, everything had changed.

The old man had been as good as his word, Ridge thought as he let go of the memories and focused once more on the town he'd made his home. With his record wiped clean, he'd been free to start over. And not many men got a chance like that handed to them.

For years now, Ridge had clung to the letter of the law, holding it as tight as Elias held his Bible. And not once in all that time had he been tempted to set what he knew to be right aside. Until today.

He shifted his gaze to the paper in his hand. The law's the law, he told himself. And according to the law, he had to arrest Mrs. Sophie Ryan—or Dolan—or whoever the hell she was, and then contact the Pinkertons.

So why wasn't he already on his way down to the boardinghouse? Because he wanted some answers first, that's why.

If she wasn't who she said she was, then who exactly was she? Remembering the night before and that long, sweet kiss and her eager, but clumsy response, he wondered if that had been an act too. "Hell," he muttered thickly, staring down at her portrait, "for all I know she's a whore, putting on a show."

But even as those words left him, he knew it wasn't so. No whore he'd ever known would have been able to play a stiffly starched lady as well as Sophie did. But instead of answering any of his questions, that admission only deepened the mystery. Why would a *lady* become a kidnapper? And who the hell wanted her badly enough to issue a wanted poster? And just whose child was Jenna?

That cold, hard knot in his gut tightened even further and Ridge calmly, deliberately, folded the piece of paper into a small, neat square. Then he stuffed it into his pants pocket. Couldn't risk leaving it in the desk where Tall might stumble across it.

Until he had some answers, he'd keep this piece of news to himself.

Sophie gathered up her skirts and carefully waded into the icy waters of the creek. The flat, rounded stones on the bottom were slippery and she waved her free arm wildly in an attempt at retaining her balance.

"Hattie was right," she said softly as a breeze rippled along the surface of the water and shook the leaves of the short, squat trees lining the bank.

The older woman had advised her to take some time to herself. To put a bit of distance between herself and Ridge. So instead of supervising the work on the schoolhouse, she'd taken the children for a picnic. And she didn't doubt that the men working today were pleased at her absence.

But with the warm sun beating down on her and the cold water rushing against her bare calves, Sophie had to admit she'd needed this. Time to breathe. Time to let go of worry for just a little while. To remember one of the reasons she'd come to this tiny Nevada town.

Sophie'd been so busy trying to get the school up and running so she could prove her worth to the town that she'd nearly forgotten all about Jenna. And wasn't wanting to give her little sister a normal, happy life the most important reason of all for being here?

"You ain't like our last teacher none," Travis said suddenly and Sophie shot him a quick look.

"You aren't like our last teacher," she corrected with a smile.

The boy grinned, tossed his hair back out of his eyes and shrugged. "Well, I reckon some things is the same. But Mr. Avery, he never woulda come down to the creek with us, would he, Luke?"

The other boy shook his head.

"He was all the time tellin' us to read books and such."

"Reading's important," Sophie told him in defense of the absent teacher. "But so are other things."

"Mama, look!" Jenna squealed, "A baby bird!"

Travis and Luke hurried to the girl's side, but it took Sophie a few extra minutes. Hurrying barefoot on slippery rocks wasn't an easy task.

"Don't touch it," she called as she saw the boys squat down on the creekbank.

Travis snorted and shook his head. "It can't hurt us any."

"I'm more concerned with *you* hurting *it*," she said.

"We wouldn't do nothin'. It's just a baby."

"I know you wouldn't intentionally hurt it," Sophie told him as she finally came alongside the trio of children. "But if you touch it, its mother will smell you on her baby and be frightened away."

Luke nodded. "My pa says the same thing. Says wild animals can smell people a mile off and they stay clear of us if they can."

"Quite true," Sophie said, giving the boy a smile.

He grinned back as though he'd received a grade of 100 on a spelling test.

"It's hurt, Mama," Jenna said softly as she watched

the tiny bird wobble and flop on the ground.

"I don't think so, honey," Sophie said, bending down for a closer look. In the sparse grass, the poor little thing chirped weakly and fluttered its too-small wings futilely. "I think it's just trying to fly and it's too little to accomplish it."

"There's the nest," Travis hooted, pointing up at a branch some six feet off the ground.

Sophie looked to where he pointed and with some difficulty finally saw the tiny circle of twigs nestled into a small fork in the limb of the tree. Shifting her gaze to the boy beside her, she said, "Excellent, Travis. You have quite an eye for detail."

"It ain't nothin'," he said with a shrug, but his pleased grin belied his words.

In the dappled shade of the tree, the three children looked up at Sophie and she recognized the identical expressions each of them wore. They were waiting for the adult to fix the situation. They fully expected that she would find a way to handle this problem and, she told herself firmly, she wouldn't disappoint them.

"We have to get it back into its nest," she murmured thoughtfully.

"How we gonna do that if we can't touch it?" Travis asked.

"An excellent question," she said softly, her gaze sliding from the children to the surrounding area. She noted the rushing creek, the tufts of grass sprouting from the lip of the water, and the low-hanging branches dipping down nearly to the creek's edge, creating a lovely, shaded canopy.

Leaves rustled in a soft wind that lifted a few stray curls from the back of her neck. And as she listened to the soft, papery sounds of the leaves moving against each other, Sophie had an idea.

Stepping out of the cold water, she climbed up onto the bank, walked a few feet and grabbed one of the lower-hanging tree branches.

"What'cha doin'?" Luke asked.

"Well," Sophie muttered as she quickly stripped a few wide leaves from the limb, "I suppose I'm trying to make a leaf glove."

"Huh?" Travis said.

"Which of you is the better climber?" she asked abruptly, moving back to stand near the kids.

"Me," both boys said at once.

Smiling, she shook her head and said, "Truth now. This is important."

"Soph—Mama," Jenna interrupted, pulling at her skirt. "We hafta hurry, the mama bird's comin'."

Luke laughed at the girl's worried tone. "How in the heck do you know that?"

But Travis wasn't laughing. He looked at Jenna, then back to Sophie. "Luke's a better climber, but I'm taller. I can reach higher and longer."

"Hmm." She looked from Travis to Jenna and back again. A small curl of worry unwound inside her. She had the distinct feeling that the boy believed Jenna knew about the mother bird. And later, she'd find time to worry about the fact that a little boy seemed to know their secret.

But for now: "Very well," she said, making a sort of small, delicate shovel with the leaves in her hand. Bending down, she scooped the tiny bird up and cupped it tenderly in the palms of her hands. Carefully, she held the little animal out to Luke, and once he had it, she turned to Travis.

"Come with me," she said and laid one hand on his shoulder. Steering him toward the tree, she talked as she walked. "This is what we're going to do: I'll bend down and you'll get up on my shoulders."

"Your shoulders?" he echoed. "Why don't I just climb the tree?"

"The mother's coming. We don't have time."

He looked directly into her eyes and nodded solemnly.

Nodding, she continued. "Now, when you're in position, Luke will hand the bird to me and I will hand it up to you. Understood?"

"Yes'm," he said.

Luke nodded.

"Mama, hurry," Jenna said and turned her gaze skyward.

"Travis," Sophie said and went down on one knee. The boy clambered up and took a seat on her shoulders. She wrapped her arms around his legs and slowly, carefully, stood up. She staggered slightly and Travis slid to one side, grabbing hold of her hair as he shifted. Pins came loose and she was nearly blinded by a curtain of red curls before she righted herself and the boy again.

"All right?" she asked.

"All set," he answered.

Moving closer to the tree, she asked, "Can you reach the nest?"

"Yes, ma'am," he said.

"Luke," she called and the boy moved to stand directly in front of her. "Careful now," she warned as she let go of Travis's legs long enough to take the leaves and bird from the boy. "Travis, move slowly now or we'll topple over," she said, then lifted the makeshift nest high enough for the other boy to take it.

"Yes'm," he assured her and gently reached for the baby bird.

"Hurry, Travis," Jenna whispered.

"Closer, Miss Sophie," the boy said and she dutifully inched nearer to the tree.

"Easy now . . ." Travis's voice was no more than a whisper.

Sophie blew hair out of her eyes and winced at the steady pressure of a husky seven-year-old's weight on her shoulders. And just when she thought her knees might give out, she heard the boy say, "Finished. You can set me down now."

Keeping one hand on the tree trunk for balance, she slowly lowered herself to one knee and almost whimpered in pleasure when Travis slid off to stand beside her.

"She's comin'," Jenna said and hopped from foot to foot in excitement.

"Come on then," Sophie told them all and herded them to a safe distance from the tree. At the creekbank, they sat down and watched as the mother bird landed on the tree limb and hopped toward her waiting baby who cheeped and chirped excitedly.

Anxious seconds ticked past as they watched, hoping. Then the mother bird jumped into the nest to feed her baby and the three children grinned up at Sophie.

"We did it," Travis said quietly.

"Yes, we did," Sophie answered, letting her gaze drift across each of their faces.

They were all so busy congratulating themselves that not a one of them noticed a solitary man step out of the shadows from where he'd been watching and walk toward them.

"What's all this?" a deep, familiar voice asked and Sophie whipped around to look at Ridge Hawkins as he strolled toward them.

Her mouth went dry as her gaze swept over him. The black shirt he wore seemed to cling to his broad shoulders and the easy stride he affected didn't fool her in the slightest. There wasn't a casual bone in that man's body. His square jaw was tight and his chiseled features looked today as if they'd been hacked out of marble. She met his gaze briefly, then looked away again. Perhaps it was cowardly, but she preferred to think of it as prudent.

After all, there was no point in dwelling on what had happened between them the night before. She'd already told him she intended to pretend it had never happened. And she fervently hoped she'd be able to do just that. Soon.

Despite how much she would prefer differently, there would be no more stolen kisses. There would be nothing between them at all. That was simply how it had to be.

"Been swimming?" he asked and she looked up to find him staring at her bare legs.

"Certainly not." Instantly, she dropped her skirt and curled her toes into the dirt in embarrassment. Then the wind blew her hair in front of her face and she sighed inwardly. Wouldn't you just know she would look frightful the first time she ran into him?

Still, she reminded herself, it hardly mattered what he thought of her, did it?

"We saved a bird," Luke told him proudly.

"Did you now?" he asked, his gaze never leaving Sophie's face.

"It was the teacher's idea," Travis said. "She figured a way to do it so's the mama wouldn't get scared off."

"She's real clever all right," Ridge said quietly.

Sophie shifted slightly under his steady regard and wondered just what exactly he'd meant by that.

"Heckfire," Luke said, "that ol' Mr. Avery never woulda done all that to save some bird."

"Mama's smart," Jenna said, "isn't she, Daddy?"

Luke snorted a laugh.

Travis watched Ridge thoughtfully.

Sophie groaned and rolled her eyes. For heaven's sake. She'd finally convinced the child to call her "mama." Why couldn't she manage to keep her from calling the sheriff *"Daddy"*?

Grabbing Jenna's hand, she passed within an inch of the man and marched toward the bank, calling, "Come along children. I think we'll go eat our lunch. And afterward, you can write a paper for me all about what happened today."

"Oh, shucks," Luke muttered and kicked his bare foot against a tree root.

"There ain't no school yet," Travis whined.

She paused briefly to bend down and scoop up her and Jenna's shoes and stockings, then holding her chin high, Sophie kept walking. "School isn't always to be found in a building. It's wherever you're learning something."

And if that was so, Ridge thought, he was in school right now.

He'd stood back and watched her with the kids.

Seen how easy she was with them. Seen how they responded to her and told himself that a kidnapper wouldn't waste her time playing with children.

He'd looked his fill of her long, bare legs as she waded in the creek and felt the swift, hard punch of desire rock him on his heels. He wasn't sure if it was his body telling him she was innocent or his mind. But he had to find out the truth and he damn well knew it.

Standing alone in the shadows of the trees, Ridge watched her walk away, back straight as an arrow, head lifted, long, loose hair blowing in the wind, and her bare feet picking carefully around the rocks strewn across the ground. Something inside him twisted painfully and he realized that what he'd learned was simple.

He didn't want that poster to be true.

He wanted Sophie Ryan to be exactly who she claimed she was.

But mostly, he wanted *her*.

CHAPTER TWELVE

And as that last thought took root in his mind, Ridge saw Jenna stop dead at the rise of the creek. The little girl slowly turned and looked right at him. Their gazes locked, and even from a distance, he saw the blond sprite smile. Then, not for the first time, Ridge felt that odd little push at the edges of his mind.

It was as if something . . . or *someone* . . . was trying to slip inside his thoughts. He almost laughed to himself at the notion, but before he could, that nudge came again and he had to admit to what sounded like nonsense. Nonsense or not, though, Ridge reacted instinctively to what he saw as an attack. In the next instant, he closed his eyes and deliberately tried to blank his mind by envisioning a thick fog bank. He concentrated on the deep, gray, swirling mists, imagining his thoughts clouded, shrouded in the secrecy most people took for granted.

And that probing nudge faded into the mists.

Ridge opened his eyes again to see Jenna's pouting frown. A chill swept along his spine that had nothing at all to do with the cold wind rippling across the surface of the creek.

Then the moment was gone and Sophie was tugging the girl in her wake again. In a parting gesture, though, Jenna lifted her free hand and wiggled her fingers at him in a tiny wave.

He waved back even as he told himself that something mighty damn strange was going on here. And damned if he wouldn't find out just what.

Sophie and Jenna stopped by the schoolhouse just long enough to see that everything was as it should be. After spending the morning with the children, Sophie was more anxious than ever to get started teaching.

Surprising really, she thought, since back home, she'd never have considered being a teacher. And yet, because of circumstances beyond her control, she'd discovered that not only did she enjoy it, but she actually seemed to have a talent for it.

Remembering the time she'd spent in Hattie's kitchen with Luke, Travis, and Jenna, she smiled to herself. After the boys had written the stories she'd asked for, Sophie had read to all of them from a book she'd loved as a child. It was a collection of mystical stories about dragons and knights and fair ladies, and the two tales she'd read them had inspired Travis and Luke to run out and try to convince Toby to forge a couple of swords for them.

Smiling now, she hoped the blacksmith would stand firm against the wily pair.

"She'll be ready for the painting come Saturday, ma'am," one of the men assured her.

"Excuse me?" Sophie said, dragging her attention back to the matters at hand.

"The schoolhouse," he said. "She'll be ready for paint right on time."

"Oh," she said, "excellent."

"Sound to the ground, ma'am," another man piped up, slapping a palm to one of the brand-new plank walls.

"It certainly looks sturdy," Sophie agreed and stepped farther inside, letting her gaze sweep across the schoolroom that would be her world.

Sawdust littered the freshly laid floor and the smell of newly milled lumber was overwhelming. Sophie loved it. It was the aroma of new starts and second chances. A soft smile curved her lips as she turned in a slow circle. She noted the shining window glass, the rows of low tables and benches where her students would sit, the as-yet untouched blackboard, and directly in front of it, the table and chair that would serve as her desk.

Her desk.

Her school.

Her place in the world.

"Here now, little bit," a man said and Sophie turned in time to see Jenna pick up a hammer.

"I wanna help," the little girl said, holding the tool in both small hands.

"Jenna, honey," Sophie said as she hurriedly crossed the room, "we should go and let the men get back to work."

She thought she saw one of the men heave a sigh of relief, but she couldn't be sure and so refused to take offense at it. Why they should get so upset over a few simple pieces of advice, Sophie didn't know. But after all, she'd read quite a few books about building and architecture. One would think they'd be grateful for her expertise.

"Now," the older man beside Jenna was saying, "if you don't mind, ma'am, we'll let the child hit a nail or two. Let her have a hand in building her new house."

Jenna gave him a brilliant smile and the man's whiskery cheeks split into an easy grin.

"If you're sure it's no trouble," Sophie said.

"No trouble," he assured her and wrapped one large, work-gnarled hand around Jenna's on the hammer. Then gently, he eased her arm back and helped her pound a nail home.

It only took a moment and yet the expression on the little girl's face was one of triumph. As Sophie watched, Jenna turned and hugged the man who'd helped her, wrapping her little arms around his neck and hanging on tight.

He gave her a gentle pat, then set her back from him.

Jenna reached out, laid one palm on his cheek, tilted her head to one side, and said solemnly, "You falled off a horse today, huh?"

The man blinked, startled. "I sure did, honeypie. But how'd you know that?"

Jenna shook her head and whispered, "Don't ride him again 'cause you'll fall again and hit your head and be really, *really* hurt."

"Jenna," Sophie blurted and stepped forward to take her sister's hand firmly in her own. "You shouldn't be making up stories like that, sweetheart."

"But Mama—"

"Shh," Sophie said and gave the man an apologetic smile. "I am sorry, but she's just a little girl."

"Uh-huh," the older man said and pushed himself to his feet.

All around them, the other men worked, oblivious to their conversation. Sophie was vaguely aware of the slam of hammers, the harsh rasp of a saw blade as it bit into wood, and the soft, slightly off-key whistling from one of the men. But it all sounded as though it came from a great distance and she struggled to hear anything over the sound of her own pounding heart.

Hard to believe that only a moment ago, she'd been happy, looking at the beginning of their new life with hope for a normal, happy life. Now, she was staring into the wary eyes of a man whose expression she'd seen so many times before. On so many different faces.

A sinking sensation welled inside her and Sophie fought against giving in to it.

The older man scrubbed one hand across his whisker-stubbled jaws, then shaking his head slightly, he bent over, looked Jenna directly in the eye and asked, "How about if I ride a different horse? That all right?"

"Uh-huh," she said with a smile. "The bad horsey has something wrong with his foot so it hurts and he doesn't want anybody sitting on him."

"That right?"

"Yep," she said with a nod so sharp it sent her soft blond hair swinging into her eyes.

"That's enough, I think," Sophie said and gave Jenna's hand a soft pat before starting past the man who was now looking especially thoughtful.

"Little bit?" he called and Jenna stopped and turned to look back at him. "Thanks," he said, then lifted his gaze to Sophie's. "I 'preciate it."

She didn't see fear in his eyes, Sophie realized with a start. Instead, there was gratitude and a certain . . . admiration. That sinking sensation she'd experienced a moment before lifted a bit, and when she left the schoolhouse, it was with a lighter heart than she'd had in years.

* * *

"So what's botherin' you?" Toby asked.

"Hell if I know," Ridge muttered and rested his folded arms along the top rail of the fence surrounding the paddock. His gaze followed the horses drifting around the enclosure as his mind wandered. Naturally, his thoughts sailed straight back to Sophie.

Durn woman was taking up far too much of his time lately. And it was only going to get worse, he thought darkly, remembering the wanted poster even now nestled in the back pocket of his jeans. Damn it, what was she up to? The woman he'd just seen with those kids was no kidnapper.

So what in the hell was going on?

"I think you know more'n you're sayin'," Toby said.

"I wish I did," Ridge told him and turned his head to watch as his friend lifted a horse's leg and began the process of scraping out and trimming its hoof. In Toby's huge hand, the farrier's tool looked almost tiny, but he wielded it with the same easy grace as he did his sledgehammer.

Turning around, Ridge braced his back against the fence, crossed his arms over his chest, and rested one booted foot behind him on the lower rail. "Damn it, Toby, there's something going on here."

"If you're lookin' for advice," Toby said, shooting him a quick glance, "I'll need to know more than I do now."

He thought about it for a long moment, then shook his head. It wasn't that he didn't trust Toby. Hell, he trusted the man more than he ever had anyone else. But he wasn't ready to talk about that wanted poster yet and he damn sure wasn't going to say something stupid like, "I think little Jenna's wanderin' around town readin' minds."

Ridge needed to know more. He needed to ask questions around town. Talk to people who'd seen Jenna and Sophie together. Find out what the folks around here thought of them.

Then he had to send a wire. A very carefully worded wire to an old friend.

"What do you think of Sophie?" he asked quietly.

Toby paused a beat or two, glanced at him then said, "Nice woman. Good eyes. *Honest* eyes."

"Beautiful too," Ridge muttered, but that didn't help him any.

Toby chuckled. "Hadn't noticed."

Scowling to himself, Ridge asked, "The girl. Her daughter. She seem happy to you?"

"Smiles a lot," Toby allowed.

"She and Sophie seem . . . *right* together?"

Setting the horse's leg down gently, Toby ran one big hand across its back in a tender caress, then walked over to stand beside his friend. "You got somethin' on your mind, Ridge. Spit it out."

"Wish I could," he said. "But I can't. Yet."

The other man nodded in understanding.

Several long minutes passed in companionable silence. Then Toby propped his elbows on the top rail of the fence and looked at Ridge from the corner of his eye.

"Something interestin'," he said quietly enough to grab Ridge's attention immediately.

"What's that?" Ridge asked, pathetically eager to have something—*anything*—else to think about.

The blacksmith waved one hand at the animal still

standing patiently at the doorway to the smithy. "That horse I'm workin' on?"

"Yeah?" Ridge flicked a quick glance at the roan gelding ground-hitched in the dappled sunlight.

"Belongs to Seth Gorman," Toby was saying. "Seems Seth got thrown earlier today."

"He all right?" Seth was the foreman out at the Double T ranch and a good man with a horse. If he got thrown, there had to be a reason. Some said that the old man could throw a rope on the devil himself and ride him straight back down to hell.

"He is," Toby said, "but he told me to check the horse's feet. Said somethin' was wrong."

"Toby," Ridge blurted, impatient now, "you tell a story like you got all the time in the world."

His friend grinned and turned to look at him. "And you got no patience at all."

"Keep that in mind, will you?"

But his friend was clearly in no hurry. While he waited, Ridge watched a dust devil spin into life in the center of the paddock. It kicked up dirt and pebbles as it swept across the yard before petering out. A whole lot of tempest in a little bitty space of time. Just like Sophie in Tanglewood, he told himself ruefully.

"Now," Toby said as he stuck one hand into his pocket and pulled it back out again. "I checked that horse out good and proper and I found this." He held out his hand and there in his wide palm lay a two-inch-long roofing nail. "He'd picked it up, prob'ly over by the schoolhouse, and every time he took a step, it dug into his foot. Prob'ly when Seth climbed up on him, it was more than he could stand."

"What's so interestin' about that?" Ridge asked, almost disappointed. "Hell, lots of horses pick up stones and such in their hooves."

"Yeah, they do," Toby said, rubbing that nail between his thumb and forefinger. "And that ain't what's so interestin'."

"Then what?" Patience long gone, Ridge stared at his friend.

"The child, Jenna? She's the one told Seth there was somethin' wrong with his horse." He looked up. "Told him don't ride it else he'd get hurt bad."

Ridge stiffened and everything inside him went cold and still. Instantly, he recalled again the look on Jenna's face when he'd built that imaginary wall of fog in his mind. There was more going on here than even he'd thought. "How in the hell did she know that? She's just a kid," he muttered, more to himself than to Toby.

"And that ain't all," the blacksmith said.

"There's *more*?"

"Yep. 'Pears the child told Davey Sams where to find his missing rifle stock. Then she let Amy Phillips know that she was a grandma and this two days before Amy got the letter from her boy in San Francisco . . ."

"Good God," Ridge muttered, remembering again that gentle push at his mind. With this information and the memory of Jenna's little pout when he'd blocked her out, he knew that it had been the girl trying to step inside his thoughts. He knew it as well as he knew his own name, but he couldn't prove it. And wasn't altogether sure he'd want to.

"And."

"*And?*"

"She told Henry Fields that his bitch was havin' trouble birthin' those puppies he's been waitin' on."

Henry was a huntin' fool and bound and determined to breed the best hunting dogs in Nevada. Everyone in town knew the store Henry set by his dog Molly. Hell, the man had done everything short of passing out cigars when the dog was bred with some fancy purebred out of Reno.

"What happened?"

"Henry dragged the doc out to his place and they got there in time to save the puppies and Molly." Nodding to himself, Toby added, "Henry was so damn happy, he about busted his buttons."

All of this had been happening and he hadn't heard a damn word about it? "Why didn't I hear about any of this?"

"Guess you been busy, Ridge."

Busy. Yeah, busy making a damn fool of himself over a woman whose face was now folded up and stuck into his pants pocket.

"Why's nobody telling me this stuff? I'm the sheriff here! Didn't somebody think I might want to know what's goin' on in my own damn town?"

"Maybe folks thought you might get upset," Toby said, a small smile tugging at one corner of his mouth.

"Upset? Hell yes, I'm upset! There's a kid wanderin' around town readin' minds and tellin' fortunes, for God's sake!"

"She's a child."

"That makes it all right?"

Toby shrugged massive shoulders.

"If that don't beat everything right down to the ground . . ." Ridge yanked off his hat and slapped it against his thigh. "You're tryin' to tell me this child can see things the rest of us can't?"

"The Indians would call her blessed," the big man beside him said softly.

Shooting his friend a quick look, he noted the far-off expression on his face and knew Toby was remembering the years he'd spent living with the Crow Indians. The man never talked about it much, but Ridge knew Toby'd escaped slavery sometime before the war and had made his way west. Somehow, he'd come to be adopted into a tribe and had lived with them until just a few years ago.

But why he'd left the Indians, he'd never said and Ridge wouldn't ask. A man's past was his own business and not even a friend was welcome everywhere in a man's mind and heart.

"Blessed, huh?" he said, following Toby's stare into the distance.

"Uh-huh. Called it 'touched by the spirits.' " He smiled a bit wearily. "Reckon we'd just say God."

Ridge reckoned some folks might not think it was God giving the child visions or what-have-you. They might just start thinking Jenna'd been touched by something evil. Which could lead into some serious trouble. Damn it all, somebody should have told him.

"And what did Seth think?" he asked.

The blacksmith smiled again. "Said it was right handy having a seer close to home."

"A *seer*?"

"What would you call it?"

"Damn disturbing."

Toby chuckled and shook his head. "That's 'cause you like things to be simple, Ridge. Black and white. Dark and light. Right and wrong."

Yeah he did, Ridge thought, and flicked his fingernail against a rough splinter of wood jutting up from the rail fence.

"Makes life easier," he muttered.

"No it don't," his friend said. " 'Cause even if you don't want to see it, the gray's there. And ignorin' it don't make it go away."

"Grays don't matter a damn when it comes to the law," Ridge snapped and again felt the weight of that wanted poster. If he believed what he was telling Toby—and he did—then he should be arresting Sophie right this minute. His head told him it was the right thing to do. The trouble was, his heart didn't agree.

Toby's features stiffened. "The law's where gray matters most."

"What's that supposed to mean?"

"There's reasons for most everything folks do, Ridge. And that's the gray part. You got to look at the reasons."

That notion went against everything Ridge had lived by for the last several years. Always before, his choices had been easy ones. There was the law and then there was no law.

Did reasons matter when a law was broken? Sometimes, he admitted silently. If one man killed another, but it was done while defending himself, that didn't make the man a murderer.

Sophie's face swam up to the surface of his mind. He saw her eyes, her smile. He felt her kiss and heard the soft sigh of her breath in the darkness and his body stirred. There was no lying to himself. It wasn't because of the law that he wanted to know Sophie's secrets. It was because she'd awakened something inside him that he hadn't even been sure existed.

His heart.

"I seen this kind of thing before," Toby whispered.

"When?" Ridge said, grateful to be pulled away from such dangerous thoughts.

"My sister had the 'sight.' "

"Didn't know you had a sister."

"She died. A long time ago."

Simple words and a world of pain behind them.

"I'm sorry, Toby."

He shook his head and swallowed whatever pain remained. "No need." He looked at Ridge through steady, older-than-the-hills eyes. "That time's passed. But this child," he said softly, "this child is special. She knows things and don't know yet to be quiet about it. Her heart's in her words, Ridge. And that heart has to be protected."

Yes, it did, he told himself. But the question was, who did she need protecting *from*?

"Thank you, honey," Hattie said and handed Jenna a cookie.

"Welcome," the girl said, then took a bite before she skipped out the back door to join Travis in the yard.

"Thank you?" Sophie asked as she came into the kitchen just a heartbeat later.

Hattie spun around, slapped one hand to her abundant bosom, then chuckled as she said, "Lord have mercy, girl, you took about ten years off my life, slippin' in so quiet that way."

"I'm sorry," she said and set her bag down onto the kitchen table.

Sunlight drifted in through the parted curtains and the soft blue material waved in the breeze drifting in beneath the partially opened windows. A three-layer cake sat in the middle of the table awaiting its final layer of frosting and a pot on the stove bubbled with the scent of beef and onions. Twin loaves of freshly baked bread sat cooling on the counter and Sophie's stomach rumbled loudly in anticipation.

"You've been busy," she commented.

"I do tend to cook when I get nervous," Hattie explained.

"Nervous? About what?"

The older woman lifted one hand to smooth her hair unnecessarily, then blushed like a schoolgirl. Her hands fluttered at her waist, smoothing her apron over and over again as she looked guiltily around the room before taking a step closer to Sophie.

"Elias . . . the reverend?" she said.

"Is he all right?"

"Oh." She waved one hand. "Right as rain. And better." A small smile curved her lips briefly before she said in an excited hush, "He's asked me to marry him and—"

"Hattie!" Sophie interrupted, giving the other woman a quick, hard hug. "Congratulations!"

"Thanks, honey," the woman said, giving her a good, solid pat on the back. "Though, to tell you the truth I'd about given up hope the man would ever speak up. I ain't getting any younger, ya know."

Sophie looked at her friend and saw only the shining blue eyes and the easy smile. Hattie was the kind of woman who would never really be old. She would slide into old age gracefully, living life as fully as she did now.

Hard to believe that a month ago, Sophie hadn't even known this woman—this town—existed. And now Hattie and the rest of Tanglewood were such a part of her life, she couldn't imagine being without them.

"But," she asked, "what were you thanking Jenna for?"

A flush crept up and colored Hattie's cheeks. "Well, Elias gave me the prettiest little ol' necklace. And I couldn't find it anywhere. I about tore this house apart lookin' for it, but kept comin' up empty."

"Yes . . ." Wary now, Sophie waited and noted the near guilty expression in her friend's eyes.

"Now darlin'," Hattie said, tilting her head to one side, "I know you don't say nothin' about it, but I've noticed some things, well, about Jenna and—"

"What things?" Sophie asked and felt long, naked fingers of fear scratch at the back of her throat.

"Now, now," Hattie said and all but shoved Sophie down into the nearest chair. "Me and Travis, well, we spend a lot of time with the girl and it'd be plain hard not to notice that she . . . *knows* things."

"You're wrong," Sophie blurted and tried to stand up.

But Hattie kept one big hand pressing down firmly onto her shoulder. "Don't get yourself in a snit, child. There's nothin' to fret over."

Yes there was, Sophie thought wildly. She couldn't let these people know about Jenna. She couldn't confirm what Hattie obviously thought. Because once she did, it would all start over again. The same thing that had happened in Albany. People would whisper about them. They'd point. And stare. And they'd find ways, little ways, to exclude her and Jenna. To make them feel like the outsiders they always were.

Not to mention the threat of word somehow reaching out across the country to Charles.

"You've made a mistake, Hattie," she said hurriedly, her words tripping over themselves. "Jenna makes up stories. Just like any other little girl. She's only playing when she says these things."

Hattie gave her a soft smile and held out her right hand. Turning it palm up, she uncurled her fingers to display the small gold cross on its delicate chain lying in the center of her palm. "Jenna found this for me," she said and waited until Sophie had shifted her gaze from the necklace back up to her before continuing. "The clasp broke and I'd tucked it away in an empty flour tin in the pantry for safekeeping while I was doing the baking. And I plumb forgot about it."

"A lucky guess," Sophie muttered.

"More than luck," Hattie told her softly.

"No," she said stubbornly, shaking her head for emphasis.

"Darlin'," the other woman said, "Jenna couldn't possibly have known where I put this thing. But when I mentioned I'd lost it, she went right to it like a huntin' dog on a full moon."

"Hattie . . ."

"Don't fret, child," Hattie told her and pulled out another chair to sit beside her. "This is a wonderful thing she can do."

"Wonderful?" Sophie repeated with a harsh, bitter laugh. "Is it wonderful to be four years old and have adults look at you like you're a cross between heaven and hell?"

"Nobody'd do that." Hattie sounded appalled at the very notion, which Sophie supposed was one consolation. But only one.

Sophie gave her a sad smile. "*Everybody* does that."

"Now, honey," her friend said, leaning back in a too-small chair that groaned in protest at the movement. "What I think is—"

Sophie didn't hear the rest of that sentence.

A blinding, staggering flash of pain exploded behind her eyes. She gasped, clapped both hands to her head and squeezed her eyes shut. Instantly, a vision rose up from the shadows of her mind and blossomed.

Jenna.

In the schoolhouse.

Screaming.

CHAPTER THIRTEEN

Sophie raced through the back door. Her feet barely touched the steps as she flew down off the porch and hit the ground at a dead run. She threw a wild look around the yard as she ran in a last, desperate hope that her vision was wrong. That Jenna was safe here, with Travis.

But there was no sign of her.

In a heartbeat, she saw it all. The clumps of grass, the windswept earth, the emptiness.

Behind her, Hattie shouted, "What is it? Where are you going?"

But there was no time to answer. No time to waste at all.

Gathering her skirt up in both fists, she hiked the hem high above her knees so it wouldn't slow her down, then pushed every thought but one out of her mind. She had to get to Jenna.

The uneven ground rattled her teeth with every jouncing step, but she paid no attention. Every breath, every silently muttered prayer, was for Jenna's safety.

She took the shortest route possible.

An empty wooden crate lay across her path and Sophie never slowed down. She jumped it like a gazelle, landing hard and still running. Her hair fell from its tight knot to stream behind her in her wake like a living flame, waving and swirling in the wind she created. Her chest tight, she struggled for air and cursed the blasted corset that had her lungs in a stranglehold.

The sun at her back, she kept her gaze fixed on the schoolhouse in the distance. Not so far now, she told herself. Almost there. Jenna. Her eyes teared from the wind and the sun and the fear.

Someone shouted to her, but she didn't take her gaze from her goal. So close. Surely she'd be in time. Why would she get a vision if it wasn't so that she could save Jenna?

A dog bounded out at her from beneath the gunsmith's shop and gave chase, its tail wagging furiously as it joined in the game. Darting in front of her suddenly, the animal destroyed her rhythm and Sophie staggered, caught herself, then fell, sprawling face and hands down onto the pebble-strewn ground.

The dog, sensing there was more fun to be had, jumped onto her back and tugged gently at her hair.

"Down," she shouted, after spitting out a mouthful of dirt. Then half turning, she pushed him off and struggled to her feet again. Sharp, stinging needles of pain stabbed at her palms and her chin ached from where she'd scraped it. The dog jumped up and down around her in a weird sort of dance, but Sophie ignored him and ran again, stumbling now, but still determined.

Then she heard it.

The scream that had ripped through her mind and heart and sent her running through town like a crazy woman.

Ridge heard it, too, and was already moving by the time Toby muttered, "What in hell was that?"

"The school," he whispered to himself and raced

toward it. From the corner of his eye, he noticed Sophie, bedraggled, panic-stricken, stumbling toward the little building from the back way.

But he didn't wait for her. His long-legged strides carried him on and he barely heard Toby and others coming along behind him. Jumping up the front steps, he threw the door open, glanced around with a practiced eye, and then ran through the schoolroom into the back. To the living area that had been built for Sophie and Jenna.

Storming through the partially opened door, he stepped into the tiny parlor and stopped dead.

Jenna, face white, mouth open, stared into the far corner.

Sophie burst through the back door, wild-eyed, like some ancient warrior woman he'd once heard tell of.

Ridge ignored her. His gaze flicked to the corner and even as his heartbeat quickened, his instincts roared into life, leaving him cool and calm. His right hand swept to the pistol on his hip and without thinking, without conscious thought at all, he drew that gun, pointed, aimed, and fired all in one smooth motion.

And the coiled rattler died before it could strike.

The explosion of sound still echoed in the small room as Sophie fell to her knees, grabbed Jenna, and pulled her close. The little girl threw her arms around the woman's neck, held on tight and cried for all she was worth.

Ridge watched the tender scene and could almost feel the girl's sobs and shudders. Sophie's hands moved up and down the child's back as if she were trying to reassure herself of Jenna's safety. Tears slid down Sophie's dusty cheeks, leaving dirty tracks that seemed to lead straight to Ridge's heart.

Damn it, he thought, this was no kidnapper and victim. That child loved Sophie and it was clear to anyone with eyes how this woman felt about the girl in her arms. So where did that leave him? With more questions and fewer answers.

Sophie held the warm, solid little body close and counted each of Jenna's shaky breaths as a blessing. Tremors coursed through her and she wasn't sure if she was supporting Jenna or if it was the other way around. Everything had happened so quickly. Her vision, her race to the school, crashing into the room only to find Ridge already there.

Thank God he'd been here. Her gaze lifted then to meet the hard, even stare of the man across the room from her.

"She all right?" he asked.

"Yes," she said, "thanks to you."

He nodded, then the room filled with other voices, other people.

"What's going on here?" Hattie demanded, panting for breath after her run.

"Ever'thing all right?" Toby's deep voice asked.

There were others, Sophie knew. She sensed them. Absently heard them. But they were nothing more than a low buzz of sound. She felt as if she were floating, drifting farther and farther away from the schoolhouse, Jenna, and the man whose pale blue eyes haunted her waking and sleeping.

She swayed and said, "How odd," as pillars of darkness appeared at the edges of her vision.

"Sophie?"

She squinted at him and saw his lips form her name, but she couldn't hear him. Strange, she thought. Very strange. And then she pitched forward into the spreading blackness.

"C'mon now, Sophie," Ridge said and slapped her cheeks gently. "Wake up. Come on."

Her long, curly red hair lay spread out on the flat pillow and her face looked as pale as the sheet beneath her. He eased down beside her on the edge of the cot and studied her features. As pale as she was, he could count the splattering of freckles across her nose.

"Sophie?" She moaned and turned her face away from him but he wouldn't let her escape him. Damn it, he guessed he couldn't blame her for fainting clean away, but did she have to *stay* unconscious?

Grumbling to himself, he reached out and poured a small splash of whiskey into a drinking glass. Then, lifting her head off the pillow, he held the glass to her lips and eased a bit of the liquor into her.

She sputtered, came up gasping, and twisted away from him.

"What *is* that?" she murmured groggily.

"Whiskey."

"I don't drink, thank you very much."

As pleased as he was to hear her talking again, a part of him recognized that the first words out of her mouth were an argument. Damn woman, he thought with a half-smile.

"Maybe not usually," he said and helped her up as she pushed herself to a sitting position on the cot. "But you fainted. I think you're still in shock. So you'll drink this and be quiet about it."

She reached up and pushed her hair out of her eyes long enough to glare at him. She was still too pale, but at least her eyes were open. "You're a very bossy man."

"So I've heard," he said, holding the glass out to her. "Now drink up."

She took the glass from him, her fingers brushing across his, and Ridge tried to ignore the swift, almost electrical charge that just touching her caused. Staring down into the amber liquid, she grimaced tightly. "It smells terrible. And tastes worse."

"It's an acquired taste," he admitted.

"Why would you want to acquire a taste for—"

"Sophie," he said, "you're stalling. Drink it."

"I'm not stalling, as you put it," she said, "I simply asked a question."

His gaze narrowed into slits.

"Fine," she snapped and lifted the glass, pouring the whole drink down her throat in one gulp.

Ridge's eyes widened.

Instantly, *her* eyes welled with tears, and she clutched at her throat with one hand and gasped her way into a choking cough. "Oh, sweet heaven!" she finally managed to say.

"You get used to it," he told her and poured another good-sized shot of whiskey into the glass before handing it back to her.

"No more," she said and tried to hand it back, but he refused it.

"One more." He nodded at her. "You're not as pale as death anymore. Let's see if we can't get some color in your cheeks before we talk."

She went completely still. Except that her grip on the glass tightened until her knuckles shone white against her already milky skin. "Talk? Talk about what?" Then, as if it had just occurred to her, she glanced around the tiny cell, taking in the high, narrow window lined with iron bars and the slashes of sunlight painted across the floor. She sucked in a slow, deep breath and asked, "Why am I in jail? Where's Jenna?"

"Jenna's with Hattie," he said. "I asked her to take care of her for a while so you and I could talk about a few things. And you're not *in* jail. You're *at* the jail. There's a difference." He waved one hand at the open doorway. "You're not locked in."

Sophie shot him another long look from the corner of her eye and scooted to the edge of the cot. "Good. In that case, I'll just be going over to the boarding-house to check on—"

"Jenna's fine," he interrupted her. "In fact," he said, "you're in worse shape than she is." He took one of her hands and studied the palm, scraped and dirty. He sighed and ran the tip of his finger along the scratches, feeling her tremor as his own.

"I fell," she said, shrugging it off. "I was running and there was a dog and—"

"You were running," he repeated and watched her turn wary eyes on him. "Why?"

"Jenna," she said quickly, shoving her hair back from her face again. She seemed irritated by the fall of thick, luxurious curls and it was all Ridge could do to keep from spearing his fingers through the mass and finding out for himself if her hair was as soft as it looked.

"She was in trouble," Sophie said quietly. "I had to get to her."

"How'd you know?" Ridge asked in a whisper.

"What?" She blinked up at him.

"I said, how'd you know she was in trouble?" He took a step closer to her. "You were running for her long before she screamed. How'd you know?"

Sophie stared at him and let her mind race as she
fought desperately to come up with something that
would appease him and convince him. Something
short of the truth, of course.

"I, uh . . ." She shifted her gaze to the amber liquid
swirling in her glass. Why couldn't she think?

"There's something going on here, Sophie, and I
want to know what it is."

But she couldn't tell him, could she? Everything
depended on her keeping her identity—and Jenna's—
a secret. If he found out who she was and why she'd
left Albany, wouldn't he be duty-bound to turn her in?
To arrest her or something?

Her gaze shifted again, sweeping over the interior
of the tiny, whitewashed jail cell. One small, narrow
cot and slices of daylight piercing through the iron
bars and little else. This could be her life. All it would
take was Charles Vinson catching up with her and she
would be in prison and Jenna would be—in a completely different sort of prison. At the mercy of a man
who wanted her only for what she could do for him.

No. How could she possibly risk all of that by trusting a man who represented the very law she was trying
to hide from?

Decision made, she nodded, and without thinking,
lifted the glass and downed the liquor in one long
drink. Liquid fire snaked down her throat, stealing her
breath and watering her eyes, but she didn't cough
this time. The heat suffused her instantly, easing
away the last of the chills hiding in the dark corners
of her heart.

Now she knew why people called hard liquor "liquid courage." At the moment, she felt strong enough

to stand against an army of sheriffs. She only hoped the feeling lasted.

Handing him her empty glass, she tossed her head to one side, swinging the long, loose fall of her hair behind her shoulders. "I don't know what you mean, Sheriff," she said, taking one small step toward the open door and safety. "As far as I know, nothing is 'going on.' "

"You're a poor liar, Sophie," he said.

"I beg your pardon?"

"You damn well should," he told her, "but I doubt you really are."

Her head swam and she slapped one hand against the cold, stone wall for balance. Once she was steady again, she looked at him and tried to brave it out. "I really don't feel like talking at the moment."

"Too bad," he said, catching her upper arm in a tight fist.

She looked down at his hand, then lifted her gaze to glare at him. "Would you mind unhanding me?"

"Don't pull that 'grand lady talking to the peasant' routine on me, Red," he said.

"I don't know what you're talking about," she said and noticed that her tongue felt too thick.

"Oh, you know, all right."

"You're hurting me," she said, though he really wasn't. But as she'd hoped, he released her instantly and she moved to walk past him. Which would have worked fine if she could have convinced her feet to move. How very odd.

"You're drunk."

"Im-possissible." She frowned to herself. That hadn't sounded correct. She ran her tongue around the inside of her mouth hoping to thin it down a little.

"Damn it, Sophie," he muttered, pushing her back down onto the cot. "Did you have anything to eat today?"

"Oh my, yes," she said, waving one hand and then staring at her fingertips as though she'd never seen them before. "I had some lovely coast and toffee this morning."

"Toast and coffee?" he muttered.

"Yes, with your lovely deputy Mr. Tall and that sweet Mercy woman who likes him so much." She leaned toward him and asked, "Why is my tongue so big?"

"What?" Mercy James liked Tall? He shook his head. That wasn't important now.

"Hmm?" She blinked up at him, giving him a smile that in other circumstances he might have been happy to see.

"Your tongue is big because that whiskey hit your empty stomach then ran up and slammed into your brain."

She scowled at him and lifted her fists like some second-rate boxer. "Who hit me?"

"Nobody," he said, disgusted with himself. He couldn't get answers from a woman who was too drunk to know her own name. Good God.

"Oh, thank goodness," she said, letting her hands drop to her lap. "If someone hit me, then I would have to hit them back, and," she added, leaning toward him, "I feel very odd right now."

"Is that right?" he asked, and though he was frustrated, he felt a smile tugging at one corner of his mouth. She looked so damned serious. So damned . . . appealing.

A long lock of red hair hung down in front of her

right eye and she plucked at it with her fingertips but couldn't quite seem to catch it. He moved it for her.

"Thank you." Then she stood up, wobbled a bit and laughed uncertainly. "I feel strange. Sort of airy." She scowled. "Not a word, is it? A rhyme? Oh, airy, fairy, scary . . ."

"You're scary all right," Ridge muttered as he watched her turn in a slow circle, her arms outstretched and her head tilted back so she could watch the ceiling spin past.

She staggered, then stopped and frowned at him while she clapped one hand to her forehead. "Are you scared of me too?" she asked, then without waiting for him to answer, went on. "See, I don't know why. I'm not scary. I'm Sophie."

"Too," she'd said. And he told himself that if he picked and chose throughout her blathering, maybe he could get a few answers after all. "Who's scared of you, Sophie?"

"Oh," she said with a wave of her hand, *"everybody."* She tried to snap her fingers and when they wouldn't cooperate, she shrugged good-naturedly and gave it up. "You will too be. Be too. Just like everybody else."

"Except your husband?"

"Who?" She blinked at him again, then drew her head back to focus on him. "You know," she said thoughtfully, "you theem . . . seem like a nice man."

"Thanks," he said wryly, accepting now that he wouldn't be finding out a damn thing from her today.

"And," she added, lifting her index finger as if about to make a point to a judge in court. "You're a good kisser."

His body leaped to attention. Damned if a look

from her didn't get him up and runnin' like the starting shot at a race.

Her eyes went wide. "Oops. Shouldn't thay sat— *say that*." She hiccupped and covered her mouth. "Pardon me."

Drunk as a skunk on two piddly little glasses of liquor. And she probably didn't have one idea what she was doing to him. "Why not?"

"See?" she asked. "Nice."

He didn't feel nice at the moment. He felt all wound up with nowhere to go. His insides were coiled like a spring and even the blood in his veins seemed to be on a high boil. No sir, "nice" had nothin' to do with what he was feeling right now.

And there wasn't a damn thing he could do about it. Keeping that thought in mind, he tried to force his brain away from wishing for things he couldn't have and asked instead, "Sophie, can you tell me who you think is scared of you?"

"Oh no," she said and leaned in, putting her finger to her lips as if hushing a child. "I can't tell you, thilly." She frowned and carefully corrected herself. *"Silly."*

"Who can you tell, Sophie darlin'?" he asked, his voice a low murmur of sound as he stared into her wounded green eyes. There was more going on here than a wanted poster. There was old hurt in her eyes. Old pain, and he needed to know what it was. Needed to ease it if he could.

And that thought brought him up short. Damn, he was getting in deep, here. Deeper than he'd ever thought possible. This woman should very well be locked up in his jail right now, and instead, she was digging her way further into a heart he'd thought long dead. He told himself to not be foolish. Reminded himself that he was the law here. With a responsibility both to the town he'd sworn to protect and to the badge he wore with pride.

Then her eyes welled up and he was lost.

"Nobody," she whispered and covered her mouth with one hand. Straightening up, she turned her back on him and stared up at the barred window as if her life depended on it. "Can't tell," she said, more to herself than to him. "Never tell."

Ridge moved to stand behind her, and giving in to the urge to touch her, to comfort her, he wrapped his arms around her middle and pulled her against him, her back to his front. She rested her head on his chest and kept her gaze locked on the slanting bars of light dazzling the otherwise darkened cell.

Every breath she drew, every beat of her heart, seemed to echo inside him. Her body felt warm and supple against his, and if she hadn't been a little tipply, he might have given in to one or two other urges. The urges that had been riding him day and night almost from the moment they met.

"What's scarin' you, Sophie?" he asked, and his breath ruffled her hair. "What're you runnin' from?"

She tipped her head back to look at him and smiled. "Should run from you," she said.

"But you're not."

She shook her head slightly. "Not yet."

His arms tightened around her middle as he instinctively sought to keep her close.

"Never," he said.

But she'd turned back to stare at the sunlight slanting through the bars again and he heard her murmur, "Never's a long time."

CHAPTER FOURTEEN

His arms around her waist felt so good. So strong. Sophie closed her eyes and took just a moment to enjoy the sensation of being held. Her brain pleasantly warm and fuzzy, she sighed and nestled back against Ridge's hard-muscled chest. She didn't want to think about the future. Didn't want to remember that she couldn't be involved with a sheriff. That she was running from a man who would stop at nothing to catch her. That the man holding her right now was the very man who could end her freedom.

"Sophie, darlin'," he whispered and she smiled, relishing the timbre of his voice so deep and intimate, so close to her ear. Her insides melted. That was the only explanation for the watery consistency of her knees and her swirling stomach. "How'd you know Jenna was in trouble? How'd you know to come a-runnin'?"

Her eyes opened and she frowned to herself as she tried to concentrate on his question and not the sound of his voice. But it was too hard. The whiskey, she thought, and wondered why she'd never taken a drink before this. It was lovely, really. This mind-numbing sensation and the added bonus of feeling laughter bubbling inside her.

"Sophie . . ."

She smiled. "You have a vice noice." A chuckle

erupted from her throat as she very carefully corrected, *"Nice voice."*

He sighed. "Damn it, Sophie."

"Ramn it, Didge," she said and turned abruptly in his arms. She felt the room teeter precariously for one brief, exciting moment before righting itself. "Oh my."

"You're drunk."

"You're handsome."

He frowned at her and shook his head. "Come on, I'll take you back to the boardinghouse."

"Nope," she said, reaching up to grab two handfuls of his shirtfront and holding on. Then, tilting her head back, she looked up at him and was almost undone by the quiet concern in his eyes, not to mention the flash of heat simmering at the center of those icy-blue pools. Giving in to the sudden, urgent need rising up within her, she murmured, "Kiss me," and pursed her lips.

"Sweet—" His voice broke off and he sighed again before saying, "Darlin', as temptin' a package as you make right now—and believe me when I say it's damn temptin'—there's rules to these things."

"Piffle," she said and laughed at the funny sound the word made. "Don't wan' rules. Wanna kiss." And before he could argue her out of it, she went up on her toes, tilted her head to one side, and planted her lips against his. For several seconds, he held strong against her, but finally, he surrendered to his own needs and parted her lips with his tongue.

Sophie groaned and leaned in to him, giving herself over to the magic she felt in his arms. His hold on her tightened until she could hardly draw a breath. And she didn't mind in the slightest. His hands shifted, moving up and down her back with a ferocious desperation that fed the fires swamping her.

Again and again, his tongue invaded her warmth, caressing, demanding, urging her on, to give more, take more. Mindless moments flew past and all she knew, all she wanted to know, was Ridge's touch. Heat flashed through her, boiling in her veins, throbbing deep and low within her. Her knees wobbled, her head swam, and Sophie's world spun out of control.

She tore her mouth from his and dragged in a long, uneven breath while tightening her hold on his shirt. Swaying slightly, she narrowed her gaze, looked up at him and licked her lips. Sighing, she asked, "How many eyes do you have?"

A brief, hard snort of laughter shot from his throat, then Ridge rested his forehead against hers. "Come on, Sophie. I'll take ya home."

"Home," she repeated, and in the recesses of her mind, she heard a tune playing and a moment later, she was singing it. " 'Be it e-ver so hum-ble, there's no-oo place like home.' "

Ridge sighed and said, "Yeah."

Sophie awoke to a headache between her eyes and finally understood the penance paid for drinking. But it didn't seem fair that she should be the one to pay since it hadn't been her idea to drink at all.

Sitting up in bed, she thought back to the day before and tried to remember everything that had happened. But most of it—after finding Jenna safe—was a blur. She did know she'd been alone with Ridge for quite some time and he'd given her some whiskey for her shock, but that was pretty much all she could really put her finger on.

What had she said? she wondered. What had she told him? What had she *done*? Panic quickened inside her briefly, then just as quickly subsided. She must not have told him much or she wouldn't have been waking up in her own bed. She would have greeted the morning from the narrow confines of that cot. Only this time, she thought, that iron door would have been closed, locking her in.

Oh, the very notion gave her cold chills. Dropping her head into her hands, she lifted it again immediately and stared at the clean white bandages wrapped around her palms. Good heavens, she didn't even remember having her hands cared for.

A knock at the door interrupted her thoughts, for which she was grateful. "Come in."

Hattie opened the door and peeked her head in. "Good, you're up."

"I'm awake," Sophie corrected quietly. "Up is something else again."

Shaking her head, the woman stepped into the room, set the tray she carried on the foot of the bed, then marched directly to the window. There she threw the curtains back with a quick swipe of her hands and opened the window to let the late morning breeze in.

Sophie grimaced slightly at the brightness as it played against the backs of her eyes. But even in her sorry state, she appreciated the soft coolness of the draft sliding into the room.

"What time is it?" she asked.

"Oh, about noon, I suppose," Hattie told her and came back to pick up the tray.

"Noon!" Embarrassed to be so late abed, Sophie instantly tried to swing her legs off the mattress. And regretted the quick movement a heartbeat later. Her head throbbed as though it were a bass drum played by a ham-fisted, untalented circus strongman.

"Now, now," the other woman told her firmly, "you just stay put. You try to stand up too fast and your head just might roll right off your shoulders."

She had a point, Sophie thought with a silent groan as little men with big hammers attacked what was left of her brain.

Plumping the stack of pillows behind her, Hattie then eased Sophie back against them, and situated the tray across her lap. "I brought you some good, strong coffee and some dry toast. Always best to go easy on your stomach after a night of drinkin'."

A night of drinking? The woman made it sound as though Sophie had staggered from tavern to tavern along the waterfront, looking for a good time. However, since she couldn't remember a thing she'd done . . .

"You're lookin' some better today, girl. Your mouth ain't all puffy and red anymore." Hattie winked. "You best tell Ridge to shave before you two get to kissin'."

"Kissing?" Sophie searched her fairly spotty memory and thought she did remember a long, intimate kiss. Oh, good Lord. What else had she done that she couldn't—or *wouldn't*—remember?

"Oh, sweet heavens," Sophie muttered and cupped her face in her palms again. "What you must think of me," she moaned, gingerly shaking her head.

"What I *think*, missy," Hattie said, pouring a cup full of coffee from a flowered, ceramic pot, "is that you had you quite a scare yesterday and then the whiskey Ridge gave you—strictly for medicinal purposes, mind you—went straight to your head." She handed her the coffee, then stood back and smiled benevolently.

"True," Sophie murmured, taking the cup between her palms and wincing slightly as the heat of the drink branded her scraped flesh.

"Now don't you worry 'bout your hands," Hattie told her quickly. "They're just a mite scratched up, is all."

"Thank you for taking care of me," she said. "I do appreciate it."

"Ridge did the bandaging, honey. When he brought you home last night, you was all taken care of and singing."

"Singing?" she repeated, horrified at the idea.

"Yes, indeedy," Hattie said with a grin. "Quite a little ditty, as I recall."

"Oh, please . . ." Sophie murmured, hoping this was all a hideous dream.

Hattie's smile widened even further as she tipped her head back, tapped her index finger to her chin, and mused, "Let's see now, it was somethin' about a man named Finnegan and the wake his friends gave him."

" *'Finnegan's Wake'?"* Sophie moaned silently at the humiliation of it all. Not only was she quite possibly the world's worst singer, but she'd chosen to sing an old Irish drinking song that had been one of her stepfather's favorites.

"I'll have to leave town after all," she whispered.

Hattie laughed. "Not until you teach me that song, you're not. Had quite a little bouncy lilt to it. You was even doing a dance that had some mighty fancy steps."

This just kept getting worse as the seconds ticked past.

"I did a jig?" she asked, cringing.

"That's what you called it," Hattie told her. "Lots

of jumping and your feet just flyin' like they'd minds of their own."

"Oh, for heaven's sake." She hadn't done a jig since before her stepfather had died and that was more than four years ago now.

Chuckling, Hattie shook her head. "Don't be so bothered by it, honey. We sure weren't."

"We?"

"Me and Elias and Ridge, o'course, though he wouldn't dance no matter how many times you asked him."

She'd asked Ridge to dance with her. She'd done a jig, sung a song, and in general made a complete jackass of herself. Well, at least now she knew why she couldn't remember what she'd done the night before. Her mind had—*thankfully*—blacked it out.

"There's no excuse for my behavior," she finally said, pausing a moment to inhale the delicious scent of the coffee until she felt the fog in her mind begin to lift. Which she wasn't entirely sure was a good idea.

"Don't need an excuse, child," Hattie told her as she scurried about the room, dusting this, straightening that, all with a brisk, no-nonsense manner. "Everybody's had a snootful at one time or another, I expect."

"Not where I come from," Sophie said softly, trying to imagine some of her more straitlaced neighbors with a "snootful." But no matter how she tried, she couldn't quite carry it off. And what those neighbors would have had to say if they'd seen her dancing and singing drunkenly in the streets didn't bear thinking of.

"Piffle."

"I beg your pardon?"

Hattie came back to the bed and tugged at the quilt

atop the mattress until every last wrinkle had surrendered. "You ain't from there anymore, are you?"

"What?" Sophie said after a swallow of hot, wonderful black coffee. Its strength seemed to seep into her bones and she felt as though, with a little luck, she might not slide off the face of the earth.

"I said, you're not from there anymore. You're from here." Hattie planted both hands at her hips, cocked her head to one side, and looked down at her meaningfully. "This is home now, isn't it? Here in Tanglewood? You're one of us. So what do you care what some beady-eyed, long-nosed so-and-sos back East might say?"

You're one of us.

Tears stung the backs of Sophie's eyes at the simple words that meant so much. She'd been accepted. She was a part of this town every bit as much as it had become a part of her. And apparently, not even an evening of dancing and singing in the streets was enough to change that. She and Jenna belonged.

At least, she thought, until people started whispering. Until the rumors began flying. Until Tanglewood became too much like Albany. After all, as Hattie had said, everyone got a "snootful" once in a while, but not everyone could see into the future. And those who couldn't were generally afraid of those who could.

Regret pooled within her as Sophie realized that she must prepare herself for the inevitable. Hattie and the few others who had guessed about Jenna's "gift" didn't seem concerned, true. But that had been the case back home as well.

There'd been a handful of people who either hadn't cared or hadn't believed the rumors about the women in the Dolan family. But unfortunately, it was the others—those people ready to believe the worst about anything—who were the loudest.

"Am I right?" Hattie asked.

"Hmm?" Brought back from her thoughts, Sophie forced a smile on the woman who had become her first real friend.

A small line of worry etched itself into the space between Hattie's blond eyebrows. "You *are* one of us now, aren't ya? I mean, you're not plannin' on leavin' or anything, are ya?"

Not unless Ridge showed up with a pair of handcuffs. But there was no point in courting trouble. Not when it would find her soon enough on its own. Meanwhile, she would try to enjoy the sensation of belonging. The feeling of being wanted. Needed. For however long it lasted. "You're absolutely right, Hattie," she said and watched the other woman's smile blossom. "I belong here, now. Tanglewood is home."

The other woman smiled in satisfaction.

And only silently did Sophie add, For now.

"A *kidnapper*? Here? In Tanglewood?"

Ridge hissed out a breath and gave a quick look around and behind him. Thankfully, the three-times-weekly train had just pulled out of the station, leaving the tiny depot as empty as a fool's wallet. A blast from the departing train whistle rattled the office window-panes and the slow chug of iron wheels on steel tracks vibrated across the floor. Ridge glanced outside, but years' worth of grime encrusted the windows, so that the world beyond the glass looked like little more than a shadowy blur of movement.

"We've never had a kidnapper before. Imagine that, someone out there stealing children." He clucked his tongue like an old biddy. "What is the world coming to?"

Scowling, Ridge shifted his gaze back to the man opposite him. If there'd been any other way to do this, he would have found it. But he was trapped between the devil and the deep blue sea and he needed help. Fast.

Slapping his palms flat onto the countertop, he said, "Now damn it, Clarence, this is official business."

"No need to get your back up, Sheriff," the little man on the other side of the counter said with a sniff. His thick spectacles magnified tiny black eyes and his nose twitched in readiness for one of his constant sneezes. His short, thin fingers unnecessarily smoothed the telegraph message with quick, nervous strokes until Ridge wanted to jump out of his own skin. The rabbity little man always made him a little skittish.

Clarence ran the train depot, the freight office, and the telegrapher's office, mainly because no one else wanted the jobs. He wore a white shirt with sleeve garters and a green visor positioned low enough over his spectacles that he had to tip his head back to look up.

"All I asked was if we should be worried about a criminal on the loose."

"You just worry about loose tongues, Clarence."

The little man pursed his lips and tapped his fingertips against the counter. "I took an oath, y'know."

"Just so you remember, 'cause I'm tellin' you," Ridge continued, his voice low and meaningful, "that if I hear so much as a whisper of a mention about what's in that wire, I'll slap you into a cell faster'n you can sneeze."

"Ahhhhh—choooo!"

Ridge frowned. "Bless you."

"Thank you."

"Now you send that wire fast, Clarence. Then you bring me the answer yourself."

The man swallowed hard and looked as if he might argue the point, then thought better of it. "Right away."

Ridge stood there a moment or two longer, watching the little fella turn, take a seat behind the desk, and rest his fingertips on the telegraph key. As the delicate clicks sounded out, Ridge thought about the words on that wire and hoped he'd been specific enough without giving too much away.

Wanted poster from Pinkertons stop Female kidnapper stop Need any information you have on who issued poster stop Ridge end

Through the magic of the telegraph wires, his old friend U.S. Marshal Sam Bennet, all the way in New Mexico Territory, would be receiving that cable within the next hour or two. Then hopefully Ridge would get some answers from the one man he could trust. The man who'd made him a lawman.

Irritation rode him hard and Ridge left the depot office a moment or two later, unable to stand still. He stepped out from under the overhang and into the street. He'd have to keep a sharp eye on Clarence. Not that the man was much of a gossip. But Ridge couldn't afford to take a chance this time. He didn't want talk of hunting down a kidnapper to get back to Sophie. At least, not until he'd had a chance to figure out what to do.

A couple of kids ran by, kicking up dust as they went. A heavy farm wagon creaked along the street, its wheels etching the ruts in the road a little deeper.

Afternoon sunlight warmed Ridge's back but did little to ease the chill inside as he tried to figure out what his next move should be.

And the fact that he was so damned confused was what really had the burr under his saddle, so to speak. His back teeth ground together and he kicked at a rock in his path. Damn it all to hell and back, this should be easy. He had a wanted poster. He had Sophie. She should be in jail. Simple.

But nothing about Sophie Ryan was simple as he well knew. Hard to believe that it was only a couple short weeks ago that she'd stepped off that train and thrown his life into complete discombobulation.

Hat brim pulled low over his eyes, he kept walking down that familiar street and silently wondered why it all felt so different today. But he knew the answer to that question well enough. It was because of her and the mystery that surrounded her. Sophie Ryan. Or Dolan or whatever the hell her name was.

That woman had somehow wormed her way under his skin until he couldn't even remember a time when he didn't have her to spar with. When he couldn't hear the click of her heels against the wooden walkway. When he didn't dream about holding her, touching her, tasting her.

"Hey, boss!"

Grumbling, he half turned to look at Tall, ducking his head to leave the restaurant. The deputy loped lazily across the street, dodging in and out of the way of horses and wagons. Stopping in front of Ridge, he grinned and said, "I been lookin' for you."

"That's why you're a lawman, Tall," Ridge said, forcing a smile. "You found me." When the other man only looked confused, he asked, "What did you need me for?"

"Oh, it ain't me, boss," he said. "Miss Sophie? She's wantin' to talk to ya. Said you should come over to the schoolhouse."

"She did, huh?" Ridge glanced off in the direction of the school and asked, "She say what about?"

"No, sir, she didn't," Tall answered then grinned. "She just said you should come."

He'd been *summoned*. Like a peasant called to the Lady of the Manor. If she wanted to see him then she could damn well come to him herself. Who the hell did she think she was, sending his deputy out on errands? A slow burn churned in his gut and Ridge let it rip. Better he be mad than all torn up with want and need that couldn't be satisfied.

Abruptly, he turned around and started for the livery stable.

"Boss?" Tall called after him. "Ain't you goin' to see Miss Sophie?"

He stopped and a horse and rider were forced to go around him. The cowboy muttered something insulting, but he paid no attention. Glancing back over his shoulder, he said, "No, I'm not. You tell Sophie that I'm a shade too busy to come runnin' just 'cause she crooked her finger."

Tall just nodded, though his expression said plainly that he'd rather not deliver that message.

Still grumbling, Ridge stomped off toward Toby's. What he needed was some distance. Some time away from Sophie so that he could think clearly. But even as he thought it, he knew it was no use. Because thoughts of Sophie were always with him now. He was never free of her image, her voice, her scent.

And those same dreams would be haunting him even if he had to lock her up. Only then, he'd be tormented with visions of sparkling green eyes trapped behind cold, steel bars.

He hardly looked at Toby as he went straight back to the farthest stall where he kept his own horse. Throwing the blanket and saddle on the big animal's back, Ridge cursed whatever laughing gods had sent this woman to him.

And as he stepped into the stirrup and swung aboard the horse, he dared those same gods to take her from him now.

CHAPTER FIFTEEN

She walked slowly through the newly finished school-house, letting her fingertips trail across the sanded tabletops. Her footsteps echoed in the room and she realized it was the first time she'd been alone in the building since this had all begun. But the men had completed the work yesterday and now all that remained to do was paint the structure.

And with the painting party scheduled for tomorrow, she could hold her first official class by Monday morning.

Hopefully, the throbbing ache behind her eyes would have disappeared by then. Sighing softly, she reached up and rubbed the spot between her eyes, but finding no relief, she gave it up. Just punishment, she told herself, and there was more to come.

Facing Ridge Hawkins after what had happened last night was not something she was looking forward to. But she had to do it. And not just to apologize for her drunken behavior. But to find out just what exactly she might have said to him. Sophie's stomach rolled as a wave of nervousness passed over her.

She laced her fingers together at her waist and continued pacing. Her mind raced from one thought to the next, each more horrifying than the one before. If she'd told him everything, he might even now be on his way to the schoolhouse determined to arrest her.

What if he brought a posse? Oh, good God, perhaps he'd march her down Main Street with her hands tied behind her back. Children would throw stones at her. Decent women would turn away and men would shout crude remarks.

Was tarring and feathering still fairly common-place?

And once in jail, then what? Would he send her back to Charles? Or would she go directly to prison? And what would happen to Jenna?

Oh Lord, Jenna.

Maybe he'd already picked the girl up from Hat-tie's. Maybe the poor little thing was right now sitting in a jail cell, crying her heart out while Ridge Hawkins stood over her mouthing platitudes about the law being the law.

Nervousness abated and in its place came the soft, certain stirrings of anger. More comfortable with that emotion, Sophie encouraged it, giving in to the embers of righteous indignation quickening in her belly. How dare he frighten a child? How dare he set himself up as judge and jury? How dare he decide that she, So-phie, wasn't fit to be a teacher. Or Jenna's mother.

That he'd done none of these things didn't seem to matter at the moment. Her imagination had already shown her the lengths to which he'd go to protect his law. His town.

"Well," she muttered darkly, staring at the stark, empty surface of the chalkboard. "If Ridge Hawkins thinks I will slink quietly away, he's delusional."

"What's that mean, exactly?"

She spun around to face the man who'd entered the schoolhouse without her even noticing. Heaving a re-lieved breath, she said, "Deputy. You startled me."

"Sorry, ma'am," he said, then frowned. "But that word, 'delu—' "

" 'Delusional.' "

"That's the one. What's that mean?"

She could hardly give him the definition of the word, since she'd used it to describe the man's employer. So instead she said, "Another time, Deputy." Then she looked past him at the empty doorway and the yard beyond. "Where is the sheriff?"

Tall ducked his head and reached up to run one finger around the inside of his collar like a man trying to stretch out a noose for a little extra breathing room. "He ain't comin', ma'am."

"He *ain't*?" she repeated.

"No, ma'am," Tall said, "he uh . . ."

"He what?" Sophie demanded and took a step toward the man.

He backed up. "Well, ma'am, Ridge said he was too busy to come a-runnin' just 'cause you said so."

Instantly, the small fire burning within erupted, sending sparks of flame to every inch of her body. Here she stood, ready to apologize, to humble herself in front of that man, and he refused to come? Sophie took several small, even breaths, but rather than cooling her off, the extra air just seemed to fan those flames into a near inferno. "And may I ask what he is so busy doing?"

Tall winced. He knew an angry woman when he saw one and damned if he didn't experience a sharp stab of pity for Ridge. Poor man. When this female caught up to him, it would be like a mountain lion cuttin' loose on a housecat. Just wasn't fair, he thought. Men were raised to treat a woman kind and gentle, but when that woman turned on you, there was just plain nothing you could do to fight back.

Except maybe to get out of her way. Which is just what he planned to do. Ridge was on his own.

"I saw him go on over to Toby's. I figure he took his horse out for a ride on the mountain."

Her red eyebrows shot straight up on her forehead and Tall knew instantly he'd said the wrong thing.

"He went for a *ride*? That's his important business?"

"Yes, ma'am?" He gave her a tentative answer. Hell, when she said it like that, it didn't sound so good.

"We'll just see about that, won't we?" she whispered, more to herself than to him, and Tall was grateful. She sailed past him like he wasn't even there and when she hit the front porch he swore her feet never touched the ground. Hefting the hem of her skirt up clear of the dirt, she marched like a soldier on parade straight for Toby's place.

You could almost *see* steam coming out of her ears.

Tall shook his head, thought about his friend up there on that mountain, and wondered if maybe he should ride out and warn him. But in the next instant, he set that notion aside. No, sir. The only safe place in this mess was out of range. Tall would back his boss in a gunfight with no hesitation. But like every other man when it came to women problems . . . from here on, Ridge was on his own.

"Now, Miss Sophie," Toby said, shaking his head, "this ain't a good idea."

"Thank you for your concern, Toby," she said and smiled, despite the fury nearly blinding her. "But I shall do quite nicely."

The big man grumbled to himself, wiped one hand across his mouth and asked, "You ever ride with a Western saddle before?"

She looked up at the saddled beast beside her and thought for just an instant she caught a mocking gleam in the animal's eye, but dismissed that notion quickly. The horse was merely a conveyance, she told herself. A wagon without wheels. A carriage with teeth. She frowned to herself, then shifted her gaze back to Toby. "Actually, no."

He opened his mouth to protest.

"But," she cut him off before he could. "I've read several books on equestrian arts and I'm quite sure the horse and I will get along splendidly."

"Wish I had a sidesaddle," Toby muttered.

"It wouldn't matter," she said, laying one hand on his forearm. "I've never ridden with one of those either."

He groaned. "Miss Sophie, I can't let you do this."

"Toby, you can't stop me."

"I don't have to rent you this horse," he said sternly.

"True," she said and wished he would stop arguing. She was going onto that mountain to find Ridge Hawkins if she had to crawl all the way. "However, if you don't, I shall simply borrow a horse from someone in town."

Defeated, the big man's shoulders slumped. Catching her eye, he said, "You're a mite hardheaded, aren't you, ma'am?"

Magnanimous in victory, Sophie smiled. "Yes, I suppose I am." Then turning to look at her horse again, she asked, "Are you sure you don't have a smaller one?"

He grumbled again, but she didn't quite catch what

he said. "Moonlight here is real gentle. She shouldn't give you any problems. But if she does, you just let go of the reins and she'll trot on home."

She frowned up at him. In all the books she'd read, she distinctly remembered that they'd made quite a point of the rider keeping a firm grip on the reins at all times. "Really?"

"Nothin' she likes better than her own stall. You just hang on to the saddle pommel and she'll bring ya home."

Sophie nodded abruptly, pushed her straw hat back into place, and said, "Thank you. That's very good to know. But could you tell me what exactly *is* the pommel?"

His brown eyes rolled as he slapped one huge hand onto the leather hump jutting up at the front of the saddle.

"Of course," she said. "Now, if you'll excuse me . . ." She stuck the toe of her shoe into the stirrup, held on to the *pommel,* and hopped up and down in an attempt to swing her right leg up and over the broad back of the beast. To no avail. Strange, it looked much easier when other people did it.

Toby tried not to watch.

Her hat slid down over her left eye and she looked at him from the corner of her right. "If you would be kind enough . . ."

"I'm gonna regret this, I just know it," the man said softly as he grabbed hold of Sophie's waist, lifted her as easily as though she were a child and plopped her down onto the saddle.

"Oh my," she said, her fingers curling around the very handy pommel. "This is very high up, isn't it?"

"Miss Sophie—"

"It's all right, Toby," she assured him, smiling down into his worried brown eyes. After all, it wasn't Toby she wanted to shout at. It was his friend. "If you could just hand me the reins now."

She took a leather strip in each hand and, holding them up and away from her body, nodded a thank-you at the watching man and said clearly, "All right now, Moonlight, I believe the term is 'giddy-up.' "

"You should hold 'em together in one hand, ma'am," Toby said softly, wishing to hell he was anywhere but here.

"Of course." She took them in her right hand, still holding them high in the air. "Come, Moonlight," she said. "Let's be off."

"You stick to the trail now, Miss Sophie," Toby said, pointing off toward the mountain. "It's real clear, you can't miss it."

"I will," she told him. "Thank you for your help."

"And you remember what I said about the horse bringin' you home."

"Of course," she said, sighing just a bit. "But how do I make her *leave* home?"

Toby muttered a heartfelt prayer to the Indian gods and gave Moonlight a gentle swat on her backside. The horse lurched forward and Sophie teetered precariously for a long moment, before catching her balance.

"Thank you," she called as the old mare trotted off toward the mountain.

Toby watched her go for a long minute. He figured the way Sophie was bouncin' around in that saddle, she had about an hour before her behind was so sore, she'd give up this notion and come on back before she got into trouble. Then again, she was so damned stubborn, she probably wouldn't quit at all until she'd found Ridge.

And Toby wondered if it might not be safer for him to leave town before Ridge came down off that mountain.

A quiet ride through the high country was generally enough to fix whatever ailed Ridge. The soft plop of his horse's hooves on the forest floor, the sigh of the wind through the treetops, a stream chuckling across the stones in its bed . . . all of it was as close to a religion as Ridge had ever been.

It was like riding through God's church. No walls. No people. Just the trees and the earth and the sky. And normally, he'd have felt refreshed. Renewed.

But not today.

Just one more thing to blame on Sophie Ryan, he thought, disgusted with the turmoil still boiling and churning inside him. Maybe he should have gone to see her, he told himself. Maybe it would have been best to just face her down, tell her about the damned wanted poster and demand an explanation.

But even if she'd given him one, how could he have believed her? Wouldn't a woman wanted for kidnapping lie her fool head off to keep from getting caught? And now that she *was* caught, what was he going to do about it? Could he really turn his back on everything he believed in? Had made his life into?

Damn it.

No peace. No peace anywhere. In the clear, still air, he heard the low hum of activity from the lumber mill farther up the mountain. A brace of birds shot up from a clump of bushes as his horse walked past and the skitter of small feet sounded above him in the trees.

Hell. Even the squirrels were keeping shy of him today.

"Well, this was a waste of time, boy," he said quietly and leaned forward to run the flat of his hand along his horse's neck. The big animal shook its head, sending its black mane flying.

Then reaching up to yank off his hat, he shoved one hand through his hair before jamming that hat back on and gathering the reins in one clenched fist. He should have known that getting Sophie out of his mind would require more than a ride through the forest.

In fact, he had the distinct feeling that thoughts of her would plague him long after his death.

Turning his horse, he headed farther up the narrow path that passed as a trail, aiming for Foster's meadow. A cool, pine-scented breeze drifted past him, tugging at his shirt collar and stirring the fallen needles at his feet.

His horse moved quietly enough that a whisper of sound reached him above the soft thud of his own animal's footsteps. He pulled up short on the reins, turned in the saddle to face back down the trail and listened for a long minute.

Sophie bounced in the saddle and tried to understand why *anyone* would choose such a means of travel deliberately. Moonlight seemed a good-natured animal, but her back was broad enough that the muscles in Sophie's legs were screaming from having to straddle her. And she was absolutely certain that her behind had been broken half an hour ago.

"Where is the wretched man?" she muttered as she rode deeper into the treeline. Dappled shadows stretched out to meet her, wrapping her in blessed coolness. The mare's hooves sounded muffled against the pine-needle-littered ground, making an eerie sound that felt almost like a heartbeat in the still forest.

Her own heart quickened slightly as she realized just how alone she was at the moment. If she couldn't find Ridge . . . if she got lost . . . no. She was perfectly safe, she thought, remembering Toby's words. All she had to do was drop the reins and Moonlight would go home, taking Sophie with her.

Still, she looked around at the shadowy darkness surrounding her, noticing that the sun barely reached the forest floor through the thick stand of trees. Ridge could be five feet from her in these woods and she wouldn't know it unless he spoke up. And, she told herself with a frown, he probably wouldn't. So, it would be up to her to find him and she would if she had to comb every foot of this forest.

"Come along, Moonlight," she said and rocked in the saddle trying to convince the mare to pick up her pace a bit. When she did, though, Sophie had to muffle a groan as her backside slapped the saddle. As the narrow track curved to the right, her gaze landed on a man on horseback in the shadows and she gasped, startled.

"Damn it, Sophie," Ridge nearly growled. "Can't you give a man a moment's peace?"

Her heart dropped from her throat back to her chest and she drew in a long, steadying breath.

"I beg your pardon," she said, wincing slightly as Moonlight hurried to meet the other horse. "But if you had bothered to come and talk to me as I asked, this trek through the forest primeval wouldn't have been necessary."

"What in the hell are you doing up here?" he demanded.

She winced. "Please don't shout," she said quietly.

"Hangover, huh?"

"You don't have to sound so pleased at the thought," she said.

"Look, Sophie," he said, shifting his gaze to the meadow just beyond the treeline. "This isn't a good idea, you being here."

"Perhaps not," she said, "but we have to talk and—"

"You want to talk?" he asked suddenly, cupping both hands on the pommel of his saddle and leaning in toward her. "Fine. We'll *talk*. How about we start with, how did you know that Jenna was in trouble yesterday?"

"What?"

"You heard me," he said. "You busted into the schoolhouse out of breath and half out of your mind just a second or two after she screamed. That means you started runnin' a long time before anyone knew something was wrong."

Sophie swallowed hard and told herself she should have expected this. But somehow, she hadn't. "Instinct," she blurted. "It was a . . . feeling."

"A feeling."

"That's right."

He shook his head. "There's more to it, Sophie, and you damn well know it. You're keeping something back. Why?"

She'd always heard that the best way to defend yourself was to attack your attacker. "Aren't there things in your life you'd rather not talk about?"

"This isn't about me."

"I saw you shoot that snake," Sophie said, reliving the moment again. "You drew your pistol, fired, and had it back in its holster almost in the same motion."

"So?" He drew his head back and stared at her like she was crazy.

"So, I've read books about gunfighters and—"

"Books again!" He lifted one hand high into the air and let it fall again.

"That's right, books," she said. "Books have taught me everything I know about life."

"That explains a lot."

"There's no reason to be nasty."

"Sophie, go home."

"So when we're talking about you, you don't want to talk."

"I don't have questions about me," he told her.

"I do." Sophie watched him as she asked, "You were a gunfighter, weren't you?"

"And if I answer that one, do you answer my questions?"

That stopped her cold. Slamming her mouth shut, Sophie stared at him, wishing things were different. Wishing she could tell him everything. It would feel so good to be able to talk to someone. To *him*. To feel as though she weren't all alone. But she couldn't risk it. There was simply too much at stake.

Her expression must have told him everything he needed to know because he said, "Sophie, you found your way here, you can find your way home." Tugging on the reins, he pulled his horse's head around and headed off.

"You're just going to ride away?" she called after him and urged Moonlight on as the mare chased after his horse.

"Red, we're through talkin'."

"This is about last night, isn't it?" she asked, almost afraid of what he might say.

Ridge shook his head, pulled his horse to a stop again and waited for her to catch up. When she had, he looked into that forest-green gaze and knew that every time he saw her eyes he would remember this moment. This time in the woods, when the trees reflected the color of her eyes and made them seem deeper, more mysterious than ever.

Damn it, he wanted her more than his next breath. And because that need was strangling him, his voice sounded harsher than he'd planned when he said, "Forget about last night. I'm tryin' to."

"I don't see why *you're* so angry," she muttered and shifted uncomfortably in the saddle.

"You sure don't or you wouldn't be here," he said tightly. He had too many questions. Too many feelings. And didn't know what to do about any of 'em.

"It's not as if *you* made a fool of yourself, singing and dancing in the street," she said, as if he hadn't spoken.

He laughed shortly, despite the situation, remembering her enthusiastic, if off-key voice. Then other, stronger memories intruded and his laughter faded away. Staring directly into her eyes, he felt his defenses weakening. Damn it, it didn't matter who she was or what she'd done. He needed her like he'd never needed anyone else in his life. His gaze moved over her face, and he memorized every line, every curve, until he knew that fifty years from today, he could recall this one image of her and relive the moment completely.

Everything inside him tightened almost unbearably as he said simply, "Go home, Sophie."

She licked her lips, shook her head slowly, and said, "No."

Later he wasn't exactly sure how it happened, but suddenly, he was reaching out, she was leaning in toward him, and he scooped her off her saddle and dragged her across his lap.

"Ridge," she said, looking up at him, "I think we should talk about—"

"No more talkin', Sophie," he muttered, his right hand moving to cup her face. "You should have let me be, darlin'," he said softly. "Because once we start, there'll be no stoppin'. You know that, don't you?"

She swallowed hard, blinked once, then nodded. "I know. I think I knew that when I followed you."

His thumb traced gently across her cheekbone and she turned into his touch, letting her eyes slide shut.

Bending his head, he claimed her mouth in a kiss he'd been thinking about since last night. And with the first brush of her lips on his, he knew he was *lost*.

Chapter Sixteen

Sophie closed her eyes and gave herself up to the wonder of his touch, his mouth. Swirls of sensation pooled within her and rippled out to the tips of her fingers, her toes. She felt as though every inch of her body had suddenly leaped into life. Her skin where he touched her burned with a deep inner fire.

This is why she'd followed him up onto the mountain. Whatever other excuse she'd given herself paled beside this one reality. She'd needed to be held by him again. Needed to feel the flames only he could stoke. The fears and doubts that plagued her constantly faded into the background. The risk of becoming too close to this man was now overwhelmed by the want claiming her.

For once in her life, Sophie needed to know what it was to be *wanted, needed.* And if this moment never came again . . . if this was the only time with him she would ever have, then she would make it be enough.

Wrapping her arms around his neck, she arched into him, lifting herself off his lap, to press her chest against his. To feel their heartbeats pounding in time together.

His hands moved up and down her back, scooping high into her hair, releasing it from its knot and scattering hairpins like pine needles on the earth below. Her hat fell off and lay forgotten as the big horse moved forward restively on the trail. And still Ridge kissed her, his lips and tongue working her into a frenzy of need that sizzled through her bloodstream like a fireworks display on the Fourth of July.

Her breathing labored, she struggled for air even as she admitted that if she'd had to make a choice between breathing and feeling his mouth on hers, she would have chosen the latter. Nothing, nothing could be as important to her as tasting him on her lips.

And then he lifted his head, breaking that contact and she wanted to weep for the loss of him. Opening her eyes, she looked up into his gaze and read the same hunger she felt shimmering in her own.

"Decide, Sophie," he whispered brokenly, his voice catching on the words as his gaze moved over her face, her throat, her breasts.

Her nipples tightened in anticipation and a low curl of something wickedly exciting unwound in the heart of her.

"Decide?" she repeated, touching his cheek, his hair.

"We stop now and I take you home," he said through gritted teeth, "or we go on and nothing is ever the same between us."

Her heartbeat fluttered wildly and her mouth went dry. She didn't want to think. She wanted only to feel. To experience everything she'd always dreamed of. But a small, niggling voice in the back of her mind demanded caution. Demanded that she recognize what he was saying.

He was right, she knew it. If they went on, it would change everything. More than even he was aware of. It was a risk, giving her body, her *self,* to the one man who could ruin the rest of her life. But it was a risk she knew she had to take. She couldn't leave now. She couldn't walk away from what he was offering. So she made the only choice she could.

"We go on," she told him after a long moment.

He nodded slowly, and deliberately shifted his right hand to cover her breast. Even through the fabric of her dress, Sophie felt the heat of his hand brand her skin and instinctively she moved into his touch.

"We go on," he said softly, his thumb tracing gently across her nipple.

She shivered in reaction, riding the crest of the unexpectedly wild series of tremors racing through her. Then she held tightly to him as he cradled her body with his left arm and gathered the reins in his right hand.

"Hang on to me," he said and nudged the horse into a trot. "There's a place up ahead just a bit."

She nodded against him, burrowing in closer to his strength, his warmth. His heartbeat thudded beneath her ear and she felt its rhythm, breathed with it. It didn't matter where he was taking her. Sophie's body felt liquid, fluid, and she knew if he let go of her now, she'd simply slump to the ground, her muscles too weak to hold her upright.

Then she remembered something. "My horse—"

"She's already started back down the trail."

Sophie looked over his shoulder and saw Moonlight ambling back down the mountain just as Toby had said she would. That problem taken care of, she settled back down into the crook of his arm and tried to close her thoughts to anything beyond this moment.

Overhead, the canopy of tree limbs thinned as Ridge guided his horse along the trail and out of the shadows. Dappled light gave way to a soft, buttery, sunlit glow that crowned a meadow filled with fragile stalks of tall blue flowers and shorter plants with splashes of deep red blooms.

Sophie sat up straighter on his lap, looked around the tree-edged clearing and sighed at the beauty of it. Her gaze swept across the flowers waving gently in the soft breeze, then shifted to take in the stand of pines that stood sentry around this small, but perfect garden. "It's beautiful," she whispered, glancing up at Ridge.

He nodded. "Foster's meadow. Named for the fella who once built a cabin here. See?" He lifted one hand and pointed to the far right corner of the meadow.

She hadn't noticed it before, but now that he'd pointed it out, Sophie saw the remnants of a chimney jutting up drunkenly from the sea of flowers. And before she could comment on it, Ridge urged his horse into a trot, aiming right for it.

Most of the cabin had long since disappeared, fading back into the ground from which it had sprung. Blue and red blossoms crowded the remaining planks until all that was left of the cabin was the crumbling chimney and a few weathered floorboards.

Ridge swung down from the horse, then held his arms out to her. Sophie placed her hands on his shoulders, and as he lifted her down, he let her body slide along the length of his. Her breasts ached and somewhere low inside her a throbbing need pulsed, demanding to be acknowledged.

Standing there, amid the flowers, he bent his head to claim a kiss and Sophie went up on her toes to meet him. A soft wind caressed them, lifting the scent of the flowers and spinning it about them until Sophie's head swam with the thick sweetness.

She opened her mouth to his gentle prodding and gasped anew when his tongue swept into her warmth, stealing her breath, vanquishing the last of her doubts. His arms came around her like twin bands of steel, pressing her close, molding her body to his as though, if he tried hard enough, he might make them one.

The sun poured against her closed eyes, dazzling her mind with flashes of brightness. She clutched at his shoulders, digging her fingers into the soft, worn cloth of his shirt. She wanted more. Needed more. And as if he heard her silent plea, he broke the kiss, set her back from him, and half turned to his horse.

She staggered slightly and reached out one hand to him. He gave it a squeeze, then quickly untied the blanket roll he kept behind his saddle. Tucking it under his left arm, he grabbed her hand and said softly, "Come with me."

He stepped into the center of the fallen cabin, swept the area with a careful but quick gaze, then released her long enough to open the blanket roll and spread it onto the ground.

Sophie's throat closed and she wasn't entirely sure if it was caused by fear or excitement. And at the moment, she didn't really care. She'd waited her whole life for this—had actually given up hope that she would ever know a man's touch—and now that the time was here, she didn't want to miss a minute of it.

"I need you, Sophie," he murmured, stepping closer. "I didn't want to, but I do."

She sucked in a gulp of air and held it in on the off chance she'd be unable to draw another. "I know," she whispered, as if she were in church. "I feel the same way."

He lifted his hands to the buttons at the neck of her dress and as his knuckles brushed against her throat she felt her heart hammer wildly in her chest. One button, then two, slid free and his fingers continued on down the long line of pearl buttons that swept from her throat to the hem of her pale green dress.

Her gaze locked with his as the cool wind dusted across her bare chest. Goose bumps ran up and down her spine and she tossed her windblown hair back from her face with a quick shake of her head. Her stomach churning, she felt his fingers slip into the valley between her breasts. She gasped aloud, briefly closing her eyes in anticipation of more to come.

"You're beautiful, Sophie," he whispered, and let his fingertips trail across the tops of her breasts.

She swallowed hard, swayed a bit, then locked her knees in an effort to stay upright. She watched him look at her and for the first time in her life Sophie *felt* beautiful. His hands moved quicker now, his deft fingers undoing the buttons until he'd freed enough that the dress slid down off her shoulders and over her hips to lay pooled at her feet. He looked at the corset, clucked his tongue, then turned her around. In seconds, he'd loosened the ties binding her, allowing her to draw her first easy breath, and then he was tossing the corset aside and turning her back in his arms to face him.

Now all that stood between them were the clothes he was wearing and her chemise and petticoat. "Is it my turn?" she asked and, before he could answer, reached up with trembling hands and opened the first button of his shirt. The backs of her fingers brushed across his throat and she felt the pulse beat there quicken. She smiled to herself as she realized that he was as affected by her touch as she was by his. A thrill of power swept through her, and setting the last of her shyness aside, she quickly unbuttoned his shirt, eager now to touch him, to feel the soft strength of his skin. She laid her palms flat against his chest and she heard a dark, low groan slide from the back of his throat.

Catching her hands with his, he held her still and she felt his heart thundering wildly beneath her palms.

"Jesus," he muttered, his gaze moving over her with a hunger that she'd never thought to see directed at her. "What you do to me. One touch," he said, "and I'm like some kid out on his first Saturday night."

"Is that good?" she asked.

"Hell yes, it's good," he said, reaching for her, "and it's about to get better."

He pulled at the pink ribbon holding her shimmy tightly closed until the fabric lay open, her breasts exposed to his gaze. Gently, he cupped her breasts in his palms and Sophie sucked in air like a drowning woman. She clutched at his shoulders, her short, trim nails digging into his skin. "Oh, my goodness," she whispered as his thumbs teased the tight, erect buds of her nipples. She groaned aloud, surprising herself at the husky need rippling from deep within her.

Then he stunned her by bending his head and taking first one hard, pink nipple into his mouth and then the other. Over and over again, he nipped at her tender flesh with teeth and tongue. She fought to stay upright, clutching at his shoulders and swaying against him. Tendrils of pure, undiluted pleasure snaked through her with abandon and she let her head fall back on her neck as she concentrated solely on the magic of what he was doing to her.

"Don't stop," she said softly and heard the plea in her voice. "Don't ever stop."

He chuckled against her, his breath puffing across her skin like a caress. "Don't plan to, ma'am."

Then he suckled her and Sophie's knees gave out. She collapsed in his arms and he instantly caught her and laid her down on the blanket he'd prepared for them.

"You stopped," she accused as she struggled for air.

"Not for long," he assured her and quickly stripped out of his clothes.

Sophie stared up at him, boldly curious, and wasn't disappointed. His body was just as she'd imagined it. Hard, strong, with muscles carved into his broad chest by a God who'd taken the time to do it right. Her gaze strayed lower and a small spark of doubt flared up inside her as she wondered for just a moment how on earth their two bodies could possibly fit together. Then she gave up the worry, leaving it in his hands, so to speak.

He lay down beside her on the blanket and pulled her into his arms. She pressed herself close to him, brushing her breasts against his chest, loving the feel of his skin touching hers.

Ridge couldn't touch her enough. He swept his palms along her body, learning her curves, her valleys, her secrets. He pushed himself up onto one elbow and looked down at her as he touched her, loving the flash of eagerness that lit her eyes. He brushed his thumb across one of her hardened pink nipples and smiled to himself when her body jumped.

"Pleased with yourself, are you?" she asked, one red eyebrow lifting into a high arch.

"Damn right," he said, repeating the touch, just to

watch her eyes darken again. Bending his head, he kissed the corner of her mouth and whispered, "I think I finally found a way to keep you quiet, Red."

Her lips twitched as she returned his teasing. "Quiet? In the books I've read, the heroines are usually shouting the hero's name. Are you saying you can't make me shout?"

"Is that a challenge?" he asked, letting the tips of his fingers circle her nipple until she was twisting beneath him.

"Mmmmm," she said, "yes, I believe it was."

"You're on," Ridge told her and bent his head to let his tongue trace a path around the tip of her nipple.

"Oh my," she said on a sigh and arched her back, offering herself to him.

And he took her. He lavished attention on the fair, milky-white skin he'd dreamed of for too long. He found the few golden freckles dusting her body and kissed each one of them until Sophie was twisting and moving beneath him. Every touch stoked the fire within. Every caress fed the flames. Every breath pushed him nearer the edge.

"You're mine, Red," he whispered against her throat. "No matter what, you belong with me."

She caught his face in her hands, looked at him for a heartbeat of time, then brought his mouth to hers. She kissed him, long and slow and deep, driving his need into a fever pitch that threatened to consume him. And when he couldn't breathe, she broke the kiss to move her mouth along his neck. The tip of her tongue drew a damp, warm line that arrowed straight into his heart. And Ridge knew he was done for. He felt the hunger in her blossom and grow and knew this was the woman he wanted for the rest of his life. He didn't care what lay in her past. He only cared about her future. *Their* future.

Sophie felt him sweep her petticoat down and off, freeing her legs to the sun's warmth and the gentle kiss of the wind. The scent of the wildflowers surrounded them, drowning them in a rich perfume that staggered the senses. Ridge took her mouth, staking a claim on her mind and heart, his tongue mating with hers in a silent dance of advance and retreat.

Her hands slid up and down his naked back, and she relished the feel of his skin beneath her palms. The hard strength of him, the cool softness of his flesh.

Then he tore his mouth from hers and laid down a trail of damp, warm kisses along the line of her throat, across her chest, to the tips of her nipples again. Once more, he suckled her breasts, each in turn. With the earth beneath her, steadying her, she gave herself up to the sensations clamoring within. She arched into him, silently offering him more, silently demanding he take it.

And he did. His lips and teeth tormented her while his right hand swept down, along her rib cage, over the curve of her hip and back up, to trail across her abdomen with light, tender strokes. Sophie stared up into the cloud-tossed sky and stared at heaven while Ridge showed her a different heaven, here on earth.

Suckling her, he dipped his hand down, past the soft curls at the apex of her thighs, to the dewy warmth of her center. When he touched her, her body jumped in his arms at the shock of the gentle invasion, but he didn't give her a chance to withdraw, instead he pushed her on, further, higher than she would have thought possible.

He touched her intimately, his fingertips stroking,

soothing, teasing. Sophie sighed and moved against his hand, lifting her hips, twisting into his touch. She felt something inside her tighten, like a spring wound too tight. His mouth worked her breasts and she held his head to her, tried to keep him there even as he left her to trail his lips and tongue down the length of her body until at last he shifted, moving to kneel between her thighs. His hands stroked up and down the inside of her legs, gently, softly, the merest of touches, designed to drive her wild, to push her to the edge of insanity. Her fingers curled into the blanket beneath her, holding on tightly, fisting the rough material as though her grip on it would determine if she lived or died.

She lifted her head and watched him scoop his hands beneath her bottom. Felt him lift her high off the blanket until her legs hung free on either side of him and her body lay open to his gaze. Warmth stole through her, a rushing heat that filled her cheeks and swamped her soul. Caught in the grip of his strong hands, she moaned softly as his fingers kneaded the soft flesh of her behind, then he lifted her higher still and as she watched him he lowered his mouth and took her.

"Ridge!" Her shout broke the stillness of the air and he lifted his head long enough to grin wickedly at her.

He'd won their bet. She nodded, breathless, and said, "If you keep doing that, I'll shout your name until I'm hoarse."

"Deal," he whispered.

His wonderful mouth did things to her she'd never dreamed of. His tongue traced wild, delicate patterns over sensitive flesh until she writhed and twisted in his grasp, eagerly chasing the delight she felt lying just out of her reach. His strong hands supported her as he tasted and explored her secrets. Sophie looked at him—forced herself to *watch* him—and felt the excitement inside her quicken to a blistering pace.

And the spring within her tightened further. She felt it. Harder, tighter, stronger. Always growing, expanding, tightening. She hurtled toward something she'd never known and fought to reach it. Her hips rocked in his hands. Her hands fisted, opened, and fisted again in the blanket beneath her. Tossing her head from side to side on the hard earth, she struggled forward, reaching, striving, and suddenly she felt that spring snap and, with one last gasp of stunned surprise, called out his name and dissolved.

And while her body still rocked with gratification, Ridge laid her back down and gently pushed his body into her tight, damp heat with one swift, sure thrust.

Ridge stopped dead, stunned. Seconds ticked past and he held himself perfectly still as he waited for the tension in her face to drain away.

Then she moved beneath him, setting off a delicious friction between their bodies. She dusted her fingertips along his chest and instantly a greater need asserted itself. Ridge rocked his hips against hers and she moaned softly, lifting her legs to encircle them around his hips, pulling him closer, deeper.

And his thoughts ended. He'd think later. Try to figure this all out, later. Right now, all he wanted . . . *needed* . . . was to join with her. Be a part of her. Be taken so deeply within her that he'd never be alone again.

Bending his head, he kissed her as he advanced and retreated, leading her in an age-old dance that felt as new as a fresh morning. He gave himself up to the wildness he'd felt since the moment he'd touched her. The control he'd maintained while he had pleasured her disappeared in the rush to find the peace he knew was waiting for him.

In a few fast, sure strokes, his body erupted, and as he gave her all that he was, he claimed a kiss to seal the unspoken bargain they'd just made.

"Looks good," Tall said as he took the tray from Marie's hands.

"Fresh apple pie, venison stew, and hot coffee," she said, wishing he'd look at her with the same kind of appetite he reserved for her cooking. Then sighing, she told herself that one of these days, she'd have to take things into her own hands if she expected to ever leave the maidenly life behind. Some lawman he was, she thought, with a shake of her head. Couldn't see what was right in front of his face.

"Thanks for bringin' it over," he said as he carried the tray with him to Ridge's desk. "With the sheriff gone, I didn't figure I ought to get too far away from the office."

"I don't mind," she said, following him across the room. Then perching on the edge of the desk, she asked, "You gonna be at the painting party over at the school tomorrow?"

"Sure," he said around a mouthful of stew. "Ain't everybody?"

"Uh-huh," she said, adding, "Pa's bringing his fiddle."

"That'll be fine," Tall told her. "Your pa plays a mean tune."

"Maybe you'll dance with me?"

He looked up at her and blinked. "Well, I, uh—"

"Is the sheriff here?" a voice from the doorway asked.

Tall stood up.

Marie silently cursed the little telegrapher for his poor timing.

"No, he ain't, Clarence," Tall said. "But I am."

The little man shook his head and pushed his thick spectacles higher up on the bridge of his nose. "He told me to bring this wire soon's I got it in."

"Well, give it here then," Tall said, holding one hand out for it.

"Nope. He said I should give it straight to him."

The deputy glanced at Marie, then frowned at the man in the doorway. "I'm in charge when Ridge ain't in town, so you should just give it over, Clarence, and stop tryin' to . . ." He searched for a legal-sounding phrase and found it. "Obstruct the law."

"I ain't obstructin' nothin'," the little man said and scurried across the floor to slap the wire into Tall's outstretched hand. Then he left, muttering something about a man trying to do his job and getting nothing but a headache for his trouble.

Tall smiled at Marie and said, "I have to read this. Official business."

She nodded and settled down to wait. She wasn't going to leave until she at least got him to promise to dance with her.

A moment or two later, though, Tall was racing across the floor and grabbing his hat off the peg by the front door. "I got to go, Marie. I'll see you later." He ducked his head and ran out, sprinting toward the train station.

Left alone in the office, she stood up and kicked

the sheriff's desk. Then disgusted and limping, she headed back to work.

"Oh Lordy," Sophie murmured and her breath brushed Ridge's shoulder.

His body still cradled deeply within hers, Ridge felt the magic of the last few moments slowly fade away. Cold, hard realization settled in his chest like an icy stone as he levered himself up onto one elbow and looked down at her.

Her green eyes mirrored his own sense of uneasiness and he knew without a doubt that whatever was coming wasn't something he wanted to hear. But damn it, he *needed* to hear it. Both as a man—and as a sheriff.

She reached up to smooth his hair back from his forehead and he steeled himself against the gentleness of her touch and the warmth still pooled within him. As much as he wanted to just enjoy what he'd found with her, there were too many unanswered questions. Rolling to one side of her, he pulled her close, still needing to feel her against him, despite the misgivings roiling within.

"What's goin' on, Sophie?" he asked.

She laughed shortly. "I should think that's fairly obvious."

He shook his head and cupped her face in his palm. "You know what I'm talkin' about," he said.

"No," she said, shaking her head.

Was she just trying to brazen it out? Or was she innocent enough to think he wouldn't notice? "Sophie, up until a minute ago, you were a virgin."

Color filled her cheeks instantly as she denied it. "Don't be ridiculous," she said.

"I'm not," he said. "Wish I was." Just as he wished so many things. That she wasn't lying to him. That he didn't know she was wanted by the law. That there was a way out of this mess—for both of them.

"Can't you just leave this alone?" she asked. "Can't we just have this moment? This one moment?"

"Don't you think I want that too?" he asked, rubbing the pad of his thumb beneath her eye. Hell, he wanted many more moments. But neither of them could have that until he knew the truth.

"Then stop, Ridge," she said, grabbing his hand and holding it. "Stop now. While we still can."

"And live with secrets?" he asked, shaking his head. "No. I want more than that, Sophie. I want it all. Present, future, *and* the past. And none of that can happen until you stop lying to me."

She pushed herself into a sitting position, batting his hand aside as she grabbed at her chemise. Holding it up in front of her, she looked at him through wide, wounded green eyes. All Ridge wanted to do was grab her, hold her tight, and tell her everything would be all right. But he couldn't. Not until he knew what he was up against. Not until she told him what she was hiding. Not until she trusted him enough to give him more than her body.

She pushed her hair behind her back and the simple movement distracted him, sending a warning pulse through his body that told him if he wasn't careful, he'd forget all about answers and just look to bury himself inside her again. Swallowing hard, he said softly, "No more lies, Sophie. Not now. Not anymore."

She threw her chemise on, covering the breasts he ached to caress again, then slipped into her petticoat, tying the strings at her waist. Looking at him, she shook her head, sending that lion's mane of red curls flying about her face.

"I can't," she said simply.

"Can't or won't?"

"Does it matter?"

"Hell yes, it matters," he shouted. "Everything about you matters to me. Don't you see that?"

She stood up, pulling the edges of her chemise together and holding on for all she was worth. Turning to face the wind, she closed her eyes as the breeze rushed past her, and for one long moment, Ridge just looked at her, knowing he would remember this image of her for the rest of his life. With the blue mountain lupine at her feet and the red wave of her hair flying out behind her and the soft white cotton of her petticoat fluttering in the wind, she looked as far from his life as an angel dropped to earth.

But, he told himself as he stood up and grabbed her arm, turning her to face him, she *was* in his life and he didn't want to lose her now. And God help them both, he would unless he could get her to talk to him. Give him something to work with. Something to *do*. "Sophie, tell me. Tell me what you're hiding."

"I can't."

Still shutting him out. Even after what they'd just shared. Her refusal to trust him hit him harder than he might have expected. Holding on to her upper arms, he pulled her close and she tipped her head back to look up at him. "Then I'll tell you what I already know," he said. "I know you were a virgin up until about ten minutes ago."

She sucked in a breath.

"And Sophie darlin', as far as I know, there's only been one virgin birth and you ain't it."

"Ridge . . ."

"So you're not Jenna's mother."

She shook her head.

In spite of already knowing he was right, a sinking sensation hit him hard. "Who is she to you?"

"My sister," she said and a single tear escaped the corner of her eye to roll along her cheek.

Sister? Why would she have had to kidnap her own sister? Misery clouded her eyes and his heart twisted in his chest, but he fought against the rush of protectiveness he felt toward her. He had to know it all. "You kidnapped her."

She fell back a step. "Kidnapped? Why would you say I kidnapped her?"

He shoved one hand through his hair and kept his hold on her with the other. "I got a wanted poster on you. There's a five-hundred-dollar reward out for Sophie *Dolan*."

"Oh God . . ."

"Sophie . . ."

She yanked free of his grasp and shoved at his chest. He didn't budge. He wouldn't let her go. Not now. Not when he was so close to finding out the truth behind that poster. The truth that would either set them free or separate them forever.

"I didn't kidnap her," she said, pushing her hair back from her face with a nervous gesture. "I rescued her. From a man who would have made her life miserable."

"Damn it, Sophie." It was true, then. She was the kidnapper the poster accused her of being. Changing the wording of the act didn't change the act itself.

"I'm not sorry," she snapped, her green eyes blazing. "So arrest me, Sheriff—or so help me, the minute I get back to town, I'll grab Jenna and run again."

CHAPTER SEVENTEEN

Panic reared up inside him. Instantly, he imagined his life without her. He saw the coming years stretching out in front of him like some vast desert—empty of anything and everything that might have made life worth living. Ridge had spent years living on the outside—and damn it, he was tired of it. He wanted in. He wanted a life. And love. And by God, he wanted it all with Sophie. Hearing her talk of throwing away what he'd only just found made him want to howl in frustration.

"You're not goin' anywhere." Grabbing hold of her, he yanked her close, loomed over her and stared down into her wide, green eyes. "Understand that, Sophie. No more lies. No more runnin'."

She looked up at him and shook her head. "You don't understand . . ."

"Then tell me."

"You know all you need to know," she snapped, pulling free and looking around for her dress. Spotting it in a clump of lupine, she grabbed it up and stepped into it. She pulled it on, shoved her arms into the sleeves, then started buttoning, though her fingers were shaking so badly she made a fine mess of it. She'd only done up half of them when she gave it up with a hiss of disgust. "I'm a criminal, you're a sheriff, and never the twain shall meet, I believe the phrase is."

"Don't you climb up on that high horse with me now, Red."

"I *do* beg your pardon, *Sheriff*," she practically snarled.

He grabbed up his pants, tugged them on, then stomped into his boots. Damn woman. Thought she could keep quiet *now*? Thought she could turn into that prissy Easterner again and make him back up and sit down? Well, she had another think comin'. He'd ridden the outlaw trails. He'd been in gunfights. He damn sure wasn't about to turn tail and run because his woman turned that barbed-wire tongue of hers loose.

Twisting around to face her, he shoved both hands through his hair, then stabbed the air with his index finger. "You think I'm just gonna step aside and wave you on past?" he asked, swinging one arm wide for emphasis. "You really expect me to say, 'Well, thanks a bunch, Sophie. Haven't enjoyed a roll in the hay so much in a long time!"

"A *roll* in the *hay*?" she repeated, splotches of red dotting her cheeks even as sparks of anger glittered in her eyes. Stepping up close to him, she planted both hands against his chest and shoved him, hard. "That's what this was to you?"

"No," he shouted, then, frustrated beyond belief, lowered his voice and repeated, "*No*. Aren't you listenin'? I'm tryin' to tell you that what just happened was the most amazing thing I've ever had in my life and I'm not gonna let you walk away from it. From us."

"There is no us," she whispered.

A sheen of tears swam in her eyes and an invisible

hand squeezed Ridge's heart until he thought he might howl with the pain of it.

"Tell me, Sophie," he said instead. "Tell me the rest of what you're trying so hard to hide. Trust me."

She slumped against him and his heart broke for her. Damn, it was a hard thing, to see a strong woman look beaten.

"What is it you need to hear?" she asked, resting her forehead against his chest.

"Jenna," he said. "She knows things. Things she shouldn't have any way of knowing."

Sophie was silent. Too silent. Pulling back, he tipped her chin up and he looked at her, not surprised in the least to see that stubborn expression he'd become so used to seeing on her face.

His tone gentled in response to that stubbornness. He knew it was hard for her. Hell, he felt as though he'd been kicked in the stomach. How much worse would it be for her to realize that her masquerade was falling apart? "Toby claims the Indians would say Jenna's been touched by the spirits."

Now she did surprise him by flashing a small, brief smile. "Touched by the spirits," she echoed, her voice soft and wistful. "What a lovely way to put it. And how very different from what I'm accustomed to hearing."

Ridge nodded. "So she does have the 'sight.' "

"Yes," Sophie said and stepped back from him, wrapping her arms around herself and holding on tight.

"Thought so," he said softly, remembering the times Jenna had looked at him and he'd felt that tiny touch inside his mind. Shaking his head, he choked out a laugh and added, "Thought I was going crazy the first time I felt her inside my head."

"What?"

"Jenna," he said, and wondered why she looked so surprised. "She slips into my head. I can feel her there. Even shut her out once. She looked mighty upset about it too."

Sophie lifted one hand to cover her mouth. "I didn't know she'd done that to anyone but me. Oh God."

"What about you?" he asked, reminding her, "The day of the rattler . . . you ran into the schoolhouse just a heartbeat behind Jenna's scream for help. You couldn't have heard her and reached her in time."

She reached up and rubbed the spot between her eyes. "I—"

"You have it too."

"Not like Jenna," she said quickly, and it was as if now that he'd finally gotten her to talk about it, the words couldn't tumble from her fast enough. "The women in my family have been *blessed*"—and she said the word so sarcastically he winced in sympathy— "for generations." Rubbing her hands up and down her arms, she continued. "We see bits and pieces of the future. Never the whole. Just snatches, images. Although my mother's gift was stronger and Jenna seems to have far more power than I ever had."

"This is hard to take in," Ridge admitted, not sure if he was comfortable knowing that Sophie could see more than he could.

"It always is," she snapped, and frustrated with the wind tossing her hair, she grabbed the mass and began to braid it with nervous hands.

"You know," he pointed out, "you've had your whole life to get used to this. I've had about two minutes."

"Doesn't matter," she said with a forced laugh that

sounded like it scraped along her throat. "Do you think you're the first person to look at me as though I'm crazy?"

"I'm not—" he argued, defending himself.

"Of course you are," she said quickly, waving one hand at him. "You're staring at me and wondering right now if I can read your mind—I can't—and you're wondering what I can see about you or the future or—It doesn't really matter, does it?" Shaking her head, she tossed the thick braid behind her back and started pacing. "I've been called names, I've had people cross the street to avoid me. I even had to smile when the man I thought loved me ran away because I'd saved his life with a vision."

One word in that last sentence stopped him cold. "Man? What man?"

"He isn't important," Sophie said. "What is important is that I've spent most of my life trying to smother the visions that jump into my mind. I don't *want* these images. I want to be normal."

"So that's why you became a *kidnapper*?" he asked shortly. "So you could have a normal life?"

"No," she snapped at him. "So Jenna could have a normal life."

"Explain." It was an order. He needed to hear her explanation even if it wouldn't change a damn thing about the situation.

She did, talking quickly, her quick steps matching the rhythm of her words, and as she talked, Ridge listened, silently scrambling for a way out of the mess they found themselves in.

"So," she finished, scrubbing her hands across her face, "somehow Charles convinced my mother to name him Jenna's guardian just before she died."

"And?" he prompted.

"And he told me what he'd planned for her. He wants her to help him in his investments. To build a fortune. He'd keep her locked away in a room, bringing her out only to use her." She shivered and added quietly, "I couldn't let that happen."

"I understand," he said.

Sophie wanted to believe him. More than anything, she wanted to be able to trust Ridge Hawkins. But the simple fact was he represented the very law that would snatch Jenna from her in an instant. It had felt so good to finally talk to someone. To tell him the truth, to tell him who she was and why she was here, in Tanglewood.

But now that she had, what would happen? Oh, she didn't doubt that he felt something for her. But was it enough? Would he choose her and Jenna's safety over the law? Or would his own sense of right and wrong force him to arrest her and send Jenna back to Charles? Just the thought of that made her want to hike up the hem of her dress and start running. Briefly, she considered jumping onto his horse and riding off across the meadow and back down the mountain. Then she could grab Jenna and get out of town. Before he could stop her. Before he could lock her up and ruin Jenna's life.

A short, humorless laugh bubbled inside her chest. To do any of that would require her actually being able to *mount* the big animal. And without Ridge's help, she'd never be able to accomplish it. She lifted one hand to her mouth and absently chewed on her thumbnail as she considered and discarded other options. She could try to take his gun away from him. No, she'd never be able to do it. Besides which, she didn't have the slightest notion how to fire the blasted thing. She could hit him over the head and make a run for it. But she didn't want to hurt him. She could wail and weep and throw herself on his mercy.

Her spine stiffened as that image appeared. Sophie Dolan would *not* beg. Besides, she had the distinct feeling that a man as devoted to the law as Ridge Hawkins was, would be unmoved by a criminal's pleas for mercy.

Running her palms up and down her arms, she tried to recapture the feeling she'd had just a few short minutes ago. Shifting her gaze to the blanket-covered ground, she remembered it all. The soft swipe of his hands against her skin, the warm puff of his breath at her throat, the hard, solid strength of him lying atop her. The incredible sensation of his body sliding into hers. She sucked in a gulp of air and bit down on her bottom lip. For one brief moment, she'd felt as though she weren't alone anymore. Tears stung the backs of her eyes and she furiously blinked them away.

She'd waited all her life for what she'd found here, in this meadow. And now, in the space of a single conversation, it was all over.

There was a wanted poster out on her. She was a criminal. Bounty hunters like the type she'd read of could right now be on her trail. Images of scowling men with bandoliers of ammunition crisscrossed on their chests filled her mind.

"Sophie," he said, laying one hand on her shoulder and turning her around to face him. "We'll find a way out of this."

"How? I'm a criminal. My face is on a wanted poster." Oh God, she heard the pitiful whine in her own voice and couldn't do anything to stop it.

"I know, but—"

She shook her head, and when a single tear escaped the corner of her eye, she brushed it away impatiently with the back of her hand. "There is no way out," she said, wishing things were different. Wishing she could stay here. With him. And be a part of this place and his life.

"Charles will never give up," she said softly.

"Charles isn't here," Ridge told her. Then more firmly this time, he said, "I'm not sayin' this'll be easy. There's plenty for me to work out. But one thing's for sure."

"What?"

"If you run, it'll only make things harder. On both of us."

He must have seen the panic in her eyes, she thought. He must have guessed how badly she wanted to take Jenna and disappear. And she knew he would never allow that. His feelings for her aside, she'd broken the law and Ridge Hawkins wouldn't let a wanted criminal escape him.

Then he drew her close and wrapped his arms around her. Resting his chin on top of her head, he held her tightly to him and Sophie listened to the reassuring rhythm of his heart. "You have to try to trust me, Sophie," he said softly.

The wildflower-scented wind kicked up, and Sophie wrapped her arms around his waist and held on, looking for shelter from the cold.

Tall was antsy.

He marched back and forth from the desk to the front door and back again. Where the hell was Ridge? Stepping to the edge of the boardwalk, he craned his neck and looked past the last of the afternoon's stragglers. Most folks had headed off for home, getting ready for supper.

And just the thought of the word made his stomach rumble. His gaze shifted to the restaurant and through the front window, he spotted Marie, wandering from table to table, lighting the oil lamps. Flickering shadows danced across her face and Tall found himself smiling. She sure was a busy little thing, he thought. And pretty too.

He frowned as the realization skittered through his brain, wondering where it had come from. But before he could think on it some more, he heard Ridge's voice.

Smiling now, Tall turned to see his boss swinging Sophie down from his horse. As Ridge stepped down too, Tall jumped off the boardwalk and crossed to meet them.

"Head on home to Hattie's," Ridge was telling her. "I'll come down after supper and we'll talk this through."

"There's no point," Sophie said, and the afternoon sun gilded her long, loose hair, making it shine as if her head were on fire. "We've already said all there is to say."

"No we haven't," he said, lifting one hand to touch her face. "Not by a long shot."

She closed her eyes and shook her head, looking as though she wanted to weep. But a moment later, she seemed to gather herself and opened her eyes to look at Ridge again. "All right," she said at last, "we'll talk."

Then giving Tall a half-smile, she turned and walked off toward Hattie's.

Ridge flicked his reins across the hitching rail, tore his gaze from Sophie's back, looked at his deputy, then looked at her again. Even in the half-light of twilight, he saw the stiffness of her spine and the lift of her chin. Damn it, he wanted to go with her. He wanted to stay by her side—not just because it tore at him to be farther than an arm's reach away, but because he couldn't be sure she wouldn't grab up Jenna and make a run for it.

Oh, she'd promised not to. But he had reason to know just how stubborn the woman was. It'd be just like her to figure that running would keep Jenna safe and keep him from having to break the law he was sworn to defend.

Gritting his teeth, he glanced at his deputy again and asked, "What is it? You look like you're fit to burst."

"You got a telegram while you was gone," Tall blurted out.

Telegram? Then he remembered and could have kicked himself for leaving town before that wire arrived. But if he hadn't ridden out, then he and Sophie wouldn't have found each other in that meadow and that was worth anything.

"Let me see it," he said tightly.

Tall reached into his back pocket, pulled out a wrinkled slip of paper, and handed it over.

Holding it up to the dying afternoon sunlight, Ridge read, *Man issued poster, Charles Vinson, Albany, New York stop Contact him for more information end*

Charles Vinson. Even the man's name hit Ridge like a fist to the guts. Memories swam in his mind. The image of Sophie's face when she cried. And Charles Vinson had brought her to that. He'd taken a strong, proud woman and reduced her to breaking the law and running across the country looking for a place to hide.

It had been a lot of years since Ridge had wanted to hunt a man down and beat the crap out of him just for the sake of meanness. But the feeling was riding him now and the only thing saving Charles Vinson from the beating of his life was the fact that the man was too damn far away to reach.

Then Tall's voice worked past the fury in Ridge's brain, and as he realized what he'd just heard he jerked the man a look and said, "What? What did you just say?"

Tall shrugged his shoulders, jammed his hands into his pants pockets, and repeated, "I sent a wire off to that Vinson fella. Don't know who it is he's lookin' for, but I figured you'd want him to know that you're on the trail."

His heart stopped. It felt like a stone in his chest. Sweet Jesus. "What made you think I'm on a trail? I never said anything to you."

"No, sir," Tall said, shuffling his feet and ducking his head. "But why else would you be sending off wires lookin' for information?"

" 'Cause I'm the sheriff, that's why. It's my job to look into these things."

"Yeah, but—"

"Damn it, Tall," he snapped, "you shouldn't have done anything without talkin' to me first." Though it wasn't Tall's fault. It was his own. He should have been here. And he hadn't been.

"Sorry, boss," the other man said, wincing slightly. "Thought it was important."

Ridge took a deep breath, looked off toward Hattie's, then back at his deputy. Through gritted teeth, he asked, "What did you say in your telegram? Exactly?"

Clearly uneasy now, the man rubbed the back of his neck and said, "I just told him you was onto somethin' and that you'd be in touch."

Son of a bitch. Now he had to think of something fast. From what she'd told him about Vinson, Ridge had the feeling that the man wouldn't waste much time comin' after her.

The question was, how was Ridge going to protect her when Vinson had the law on his side?

"So who is it, boss?" Tall asked, lowering his voice and looking over his shoulder.

"Who is who?"

"The kidnapper," the deputy whispered in a tone that was just a shade lower than a shout. "Can't hardly believe there's a real live criminal right here in Tanglewood. I mean, we know everybody for miles around," he went on, talking more to himself than to Ridge. "So don't know who it could be."

"Doesn't matter," Ridge said tightly, not about to tell Tall any more than the man already knew. Not until he had some idea on how to get out of this.

The deputy's features twisted into a mask of disappointment. "Hell, boss. You can trust me."

Yeah, he could. The problem was, Ridge wasn't sure he trusted himself to do the right thing. Whatever that was. Pushing past the man, Ridge muttered, "Let it be, Tall. Just let it be."

Then he stomped into the office, leaving his deputy in the dwindling twilight.

ALBANY

Charles leaned back in the plush, oxblood leather chair, crossed his neatly shod feet on the ottoman and picked up his glass of sherry from the gleaming mahogany side table. Holding the crystal up to the firelight, he paused long enough to admire the golden light shimmering deep in the heart of the liquor.

Then he tasted it, held it on his tongue for a long moment and swallowed, making a ceremony of his nightly drink. He allowed himself this one glass of fine liquor every evening because a gentleman must be able to recognize and appreciate the finer things in life. "But," he murmured, smiling to himself, "a wise man is temperate in all things."

A discreet knock on the library door made him frown. He disliked having his evening ritual disturbed and his maid knew it. "Yes?" he asked, irritation clear in his tone.

The door swung open and a middle-aged woman with graying dark hair entered the room. "I'm sorry to interrupt you, sir," she said, "but a boy just delivered this telegram for you. I thought it might be important."

She scuttled toward him, handed over the yellow envelope, then hurried away again, closing the door quietly behind her.

Frowning slightly, Charles set his sherry aside and opened the envelope. Pulling out the sheet of paper tucked inside, he unfolded it and tilted it toward the lamplight on his right.

Need more information on your wanted poster stop

Am on the trail stop Sheriff Hawkins, Tanglewood, Nevada end

"Nevada," he said, a slow smile curving his mouth.

Carefully, despite the flush of excitement sweeping through him, Charles folded the telegram neatly, slipped it back into the envelope, then tucked it into his inside jacket pocket. He reached for his glass of sherry, stood up and crossed the room to the hearth. Staring into the fire as the flames licked at the oak logs, Charles lifted his glass of sherry and downed the smooth liquid in one long gulp. Then he hurled the empty crystal into the hearth and smiled again at the tinkle of broken glass.

CHAPTER EIGHTEEN

"Miss Sophie," Travis said, swinging his fall of brown hair out of his eyes. "Me and Jenna are gonna go help the men, that all right?"

"Yes," she said, giving the boy a smile despite the turmoil bubbling within her. Then smoothing Jenna's hair back, she bent down and kissed her forehead.

The little girl frowned and shook her head. "Don't worry, Mama," she said. "Daddy'll fix it."

"Fix what, sweetie?"

"Your hurt in here," Jenna said, patting Sophie's chest.

Sophie sighed, gave the child a brief, hard hug, then said, "You two go off and help. Just don't get in the way."

"We won't," the boy shouted, already dragging Jenna off behind him toward the school.

Jenna meant well, she knew. But Ridge couldn't fix the hurt she felt. No one could.

Alone, Sophie stared at the scene in front of her.

The tables nearly groaned with the mountain of food piled high on them. Somewhere nearby, nimble fingers played a fiddle and a banjo. Children laughed and ran through the crowd, dodging their parents and laughing at secrets and jokes only they understood.

Sophie's gaze darted from one face to the next as

she watched them all. There was Hattie, flutteringly happy about her romance with the sweet-faced reverend. And Marie, directing longing glances at Tall, who was too busy studying the crowd looking for "criminals" to notice. And Mr. Simpson, the owner of the mercantile, dancing attendance on all five of his young daughters while his wife sat, one hand lying protectively atop her slightly rounded belly.

A pang of regret stabbed at her chest as Sophie realized how much these people had come to mean to her. In Albany, she'd never had this sense of closeness with her neighbors. She'd always been "that Dolan girl," stared at, avoided, feared. Here, she was part of a growing community. An important part.

She shifted her gaze to the schoolhouse, where the men of Tanglewood swarmed over the building like red ants on an anthill. While their women prepared the food, the men wielded paintbrushes, making the new schoolhouse come to life. The soft yellow paint and dark green trim were just as Sophie'd seen it in one of her visions, yet she took no comfort in it.

How could she, when she didn't know if she'd ever hold a single class in that tiny school?

Wandering in and out of the crowd, she forced a smile and tried to join in the fun. This was what she'd been working for since she arrived in Tanglewood. A schoolhouse, a new life for her and Jenna. Yet now that the day was here, she couldn't enjoy it. There was a cloud hanging over her head and she felt as though she were here in town on borrowed time.

No matter what Ridge said, and she told herself he'd said plenty last night, there was no answer to the problem lying between them. She'd seen him these last few weeks. She knew what the law meant to him.

She'd heard everyone in town talking about the man who put the law before everything else.

How could she expect him to put all of that aside for her? And how could she go on living here, constantly looking over her shoulder?

It didn't make the slightest amount of sense, but she almost expected Charles to arrive on today's train. Of course he couldn't. Even if he'd left the moment after he'd received Tall's telegram, he wouldn't be here for another three or four days.

Cold fingers touched her spine and she shivered, despite the sunshine pouring down from a cloud-spattered sky.

Oh God. He knew where she was.

Her gaze flicked to Jenna and it took every ounce of her self-control to keep from grabbing the girl and running for the train. She could be packed in just a few minutes and then by the time Charles arrived in Tanglewood she and Jenna would be long gone.

"Don't even think about it," a deep familiar voice said from right behind her.

She whirled around to look up into Ridge's deep blue eyes. "What?"

"I said don't even think about it."

"I don't know what you're talking about."

He laughed shortly and shook his head. "Hell, Red, you've practically got one foot on the train right now."

Apparently, he didn't need the "sight" to know what she was thinking. She ducked her head, glanced around to make sure there was no one close enough to overhear them, and said, "It'd be best for all concerned if we simply left town today."

"No it wouldn't."

"Ridge—"

"I thought we talked this out last night."

"We did," she said, remembering their chat in Hattie's parlor and the stolen kisses that had punctuated it. God, she couldn't stay and didn't want to leave. "But—"

"No buts," he interrupted and lifted one hand to cup her cheek.

She tried to step back. "Someone might see."

"I don't give a good damn who sees, Red."

A flush of pleasure swept through her despite the situation. She'd waited so long to be wanted. To be needed. Now, finally, she'd found the man who returned her feelings and she couldn't enjoy it because of the sword poised over their heads.

"What're you thinking?"

"That I wish things were different," she blurted.

"Me too . . ."

"It's not that easy," she said, giving him a wry smile.

"Don't lose all that starch on me now, Red," he murmured.

"I beg your pardon?"

He grinned. "There you go."

She frowned at him and tried to turn away, but he held on to her and waited until she was looking at him before continuing. "I never in my life met a more determined, single-minded female than you. I swear, you could push the mountains to the sea if you put your mind to it."

"Ridge . . ."

He shook his head. "No, ma'am. You keep on fightin', Red. And you keep trusting me. 'Cause I swear, there's nobody can beat us when we stand together."

Her throat closed up tight with emotion. He was on

her side, no matter what it cost him—his honor, his job, his life. And a pang echoed inside her as she realized what she had done to a man who believed in nothing more than the law.

Looking up into his deep blue eyes, Sophie felt her heart swell until she thought it might burst from her chest. She loved him. More than she'd ever believed it possible to love anyone. And more than her next breath, she wanted a life with him. She wanted to go to bed lying beside him and wake up in his arms. She wanted children with him. She wanted to grow old with him.

She huffed out a sigh and bit down hard on her bottom lip in an effort to stem the dampness filling her eyes. Blast him anyway.

He held her upper arms and she felt the warmth of his touch right down to her bones. His strength poured into her, and as it did, Sophie reached inside herself and found the starch he'd spoken of. If he was willing to risk everything he had, everything he was, how could she do differently? Stiffening her spine, she lifted her chin, looked him dead in the eye and said, "You're right."

Surprised, he grinned and asked, "I am?"

Her lips twitched. "Yes, you are," she said then warned, "And enjoy hearing me say that now. It probably won't happen often."

"No doubt," he said.

"I do trust you."

He nodded. "Good."

"And I won't run."

"Good. 'Cause I'd come after you."

"And when it's over—"

"Yeah?" One dark eyebrow lifted.

Whatever she might have said was forgotten when she saw his expression shift and his gaze dart to the crowd behind them. "What is it?" she asked.

"Jenna," he said quietly. "I just heard her call."

"I didn't hear anything."

"No," he said, shaking his head and starting past her. "I heard her *inside* my head."

She didn't doubt him for an instant. No one who saw the expression on his face would have.

Sophie hurried after him, but Ridge didn't even notice. His gaze swept the crowd, looking for one little girl. The fact that he could hear Jenna's cries in his mind didn't even bother him now. All that mattered was finding her and making sure she was all right. When he spotted her, the child was running toward him, her eyes brimming with tears. He dropped to one knee and held out his arms.

"Daddy!" She flung herself at him, wrapping her little arms around his neck and holding on for all she was worth. His heartbeat returned to normal as he realized she was safe and unhurt.

Sophie was right beside him, smoothing the child's tangled hair back from her tearstained face, and a few other folks gathered close as the girl's cries were noticed.

"What is it, darlin'?" Ridge asked, peeling her off him and holding her back he could see her face.

"Jenna, sweetie," Sophie said, "what is it?"

"The ponies," Jenna said around a choked-off sob. "The ponies' house is burning down."

"Ponies?" he repeated, shooting a look at Sophie, who shrugged helplessly. Then lifting his gaze to one of the men standing close by, he asked, "You know anyone around here who keeps ponies, Ed?"

"Can't say that I do," the older man muttered.

Then Toby spoke up and his deep voice carried over the whispers scuttling through the air. "They ain't ponies," he said, "but John Farmer's mare had twin colts last week."

Baby horses would seem like ponies to a child, Ridge thought, and turned his gaze back to Jenna. "Is that it, darlin'?" he asked. "Are there two ponies?"

"Uh-huh, and the big white barn where they live is burnin', Daddy," she said in a rush. "You have to save 'em."

"How's she know a barn's on fire?" someone wanted to know.

Another man in the crowd muttered, "Didn't John just paint his barn white last month?"

"What in the sam hill is the child talkin' about?" someone else asked.

"Heck if I know."

"You think there's anything to it?" someone else wondered aloud.

"Look at the girl," another voice piped up. "Looks to me like *she* believes it."

Ridge lifted Jenna in his arms and stood up, staring down into Sophie's worried green gaze. "She's usually right, isn't she?"

"Usually," she said and took the girl as he handed her over.

"All right, then," he said, and shouted, "Tall? Where are you?"

"Right here, boss." The man pushed his way through the crowd, eager to be of service and still trying to make up for sending that wire.

"Is John Farmer here today?"

"No, sir, I ain't seen him."

"You goin' out there, Sheriff?" Mort Simpson asked.

Ridge shot Jenna another look. The girl's tears were real. The touch in his mind had been real. He was ready to bet that fire was real too. And if it was, John Farmer might need help fighting it. "I sure am."

A few of the other men spoke up, and before he knew it, half the town was bundling into wagons and onto horses for the ride out to Farmer's ranch. Sophie and Jenna hopped into Hattie's carriage and he didn't even argue. It would have been pointless.

Besides, until this matter of Charles Vinson was settled, he preferred having them close at hand. Stepping up into his saddle, he pulled on the reins, wheeled his horse around and spurred it into a gallop. The men on horseback soon left the buggies and wagons behind on the three-mile ride to Farmer's place.

John Farmer stopped dead in his tracks as damn near the whole town of Tanglewood rode into his ranch yard.

Ridge pulled his horse to a stop and swung down, holding on to the reins as he let his gaze drift across the peaceful place. He noted the smoke coming from the chimney at the main house, then looked at the outbuildings, the corral, and most especially, the freshly painted white barn . . . none of which were on fire.

Scowling to himself, he rubbed the back of his neck and tried to figure out what was happening. He'd been so sure. *Jenna* had been so sure.

"What's goin' on, Sheriff?" John asked, wiping his forehead on his shirtsleeve.

"Your barn ain't on fire," Tall accused, his gaze

locked on the building as if he expected flames to suddenly sprout from the roof.

"Well, who the hell said it was?" the man snapped.

"You got no call to be so durn cranky, John," a man in the crowd yelled out. "We only come here to put out your danged fire."

"What fire?" John demanded.

"Looks like we come all the way out here for nothin'," someone else said.

"You don't have to sound so disappointed," Ridge told the man sharply.

Sighing, John Farmer looked at the buggies and carriages rolling into the ranch yard, then shifted his gaze back to Ridge. "You want to tell me what you're all doin' out here?"

"We come out to help you fight your fire," Mort Simpson told him hotly. "A body'd think you'd be some grateful."

"What fire?"

"The child said she saw some ponies burnin'."

"What child?" John said, sounding more and more confused.

And Ridge didn't blame him a bit. Hell, he was just as confused and he knew what was going on. He would have been willing to bet that Jenna was right. Now he wasn't sure what to think.

"Is somebody gonna tell me what's happening around here?" John asked, irritation coloring his tone.

But before Ridge could say a word, the double doors to the barn burst open and one of John's hired hands came running out, leading one of the new colts and waving his arms like a crazy man. "Fire!" he shouted, then staggered in surprise when he saw all of the people in the yard.

Tendrils of smoke drifted from the open barn doors, twisting in the cold mountain wind before snaking out toward the crowd like a beckoning finger.

"By damn," Mort muttered, "there *is* a fire!"

"The little girl was right," someone else pointed out unnecessarily.

"Son of a bitch, my barn!" John shouted, already sprinting toward the building. Glancing back over his shoulder at his friends and neighbors, he hollered, "Well, give us a hand!"

Sophie held Jenna on her lap and kept her arms wrapped tight around the girl. She watched Ridge and the other men run into the barn and saw them lead the animals to safety before forming a bucket line from the watering trough to the flames growing inside the building.

"Are the ponies all right?" Jenna asked, putting both hands on Sophie's cheeks and demanding her attention.

"Yes, honey," she said tightly. "Look. Over there. See? They're with their mama."

Jenna looked to where the colts gamboled and jumped in the paddock near their weary mother. Then the child heaved a sigh and sat back with a pleased smile on her face. "Oh, good."

Hattie turned from the front seat, gave the girl a pat and Sophie a knowing glance. "Lucky thing for John that Jenna happened to be around, wouldn't you say?"

"Yes," she said, "I suppose it is."

Her gaze drifted to the water line, where Ridge stood closest to the flames, tossing bucket after bucket of water onto the fire. Smoke billowed out from the inside of the barn, like a New England fog, and the stench of burning hay and charred wood stung her nostrils.

Now everyone would know, she thought, resting her cheek atop Jenna's head. Everyone in Tanglewood would know her and Jenna's secret. Now there would be no question of remaining here. Even if Charles didn't come for them, they wouldn't be able to stay. Everything would be different, now. The whispers, the stares, the name-calling, would all begin soon and it would be Albany all over again.

Only this time, it would hurt so much more.

It was a tired bunch of citizens who made the long ride back to Tanglewood. John Farmer's barn was still standing. A bit worse for wear, but he'd only have to replace a few boards and repaint it. It could have been worse, as they all knew.

One of the new colts had kicked a lantern over into the haystack and it had taken only seconds for the flames to consume one corner of the barn. Without help, John never would have been able to keep the fire from spreading. Jenna's vision had come in damn handy.

Ridge helped Sophie down from Hattie's buggy, then picked up Jenna and set her on his hip. Such a tiny thing to be a heroine, he thought.

The little girl patted his cheek. "You saved the ponies, Daddy."

She looked at him like he was one of Sophie's storybook heroes and Ridge silently admitted just how much it meant to him to hear her call him "daddy." For the first time in his life, he was important to someone. And when she looked up at him with those pale green eyes full of admiration and love, he wanted to be everything she thought he was. He wanted to protect her. To love her. To be the father she wanted him to be.

"It wasn't me, squirt," he said, tapping the end of her nose with a fingertip. "It was *you* who saved the ponies."

She giggled and the sound shot straight to his heart.

Staring up at him, she said, "Can we go see 'em tomorrow? Maybe I could play with 'em and then maybe me and Travis could have one of 'em, too, and we could ride it all the time and—"

"Hold on there, sweetness," Ridge told her with a chuckle, getting tired just listening to her. "Let's wait and see about the ponies, all right?"

Jenna sighed heavily as only a child can and grudgingly said, "All right, Daddy."

"For now," he said, chucking her under the chin, "let's get you and your mama home, huh?"

Jenna nodded, resigned, and he turned to look down at Sophie, walking beside him. She smiled sadly and Ridge wondered what she was thinking. Then her gaze drifted past him to the townspeople slowly walking by them on their way back home, and he knew. She'd told him all about her life back in New York. He knew that she was used to being snubbed and feared, and now she was waiting to have the same thing happen all over again.

His gaze slipped from her to the people he'd known for the last few years and he wished he could reassure her. Tell her that no one here would do to her what had been done in the past. But it didn't matter what he said. The only way she'd believe in anything now was if she saw it for herself. He could only hope the folks of Tanglewood wouldn't let him down.

"Sophie, darlin'," he said softly, taking her arm, "don't worry. Everything'll be fine."

She nodded and tried to give him a smile, but it died before it could complete itself. Though he felt a flash of pride when she lifted her chin and walked beside him like a damn queen down the middle of Main Street. Whatever she thought was going to happen, she was ready to meet it on her own terms. And damned if he didn't love her for her guts.

"G'bye," Jenna called to the people watching them pass.

"Goodbye, little one," Toby called and Ridge shot him a grateful nod.

They kept walking, and as they neared the boardinghouse, he noticed Sophie hurried her steps as if she couldn't wait to get behind closed doors away from the curious glances of the people she'd thought her friends.

Just before they turned into the walk though, Morton Simpson stepped up to them. He looked long and hard at Sophie, and Ridge, beside her, felt her stiffen, almost as if she were expecting a blow.

"That's a fine thing your girl did today, Miss Sophie," he said, then turned a smile on Jenna. "You're a pistol, child," he said, then moved off again, still shaking his head.

Sophie turned her head to look after them, stunned surprise evident on her face.

"Not Albany, huh?" Ridge muttered and she flicked him a quick look. He saw the hope shining in her eyes and his heartbeat staggered with the need to protect her. To keep her from ever feeling lost and alone again.

Davey Sams walked up to them next. "G'night,

Miss Sophie," he said, then grinned at Jenna. "You surely did save them ponies, didn't you, punkin?"

"Uh-huh," Jenna said, pleased to be the center of attention.

Hattie came out of the boardinghouse, a wide grin on her face, and marched right up to them. Snatching Jenna from Ridge, she said, "Turned out to be a fine day, didn't it?"

"Yes," Sophie said hesitantly, "I guess it did."

Ridge grinned at her and dropped one arm around her shoulders as the rest of Tanglewood surrounded them, everyone talking at once.

"Damn handy child to have around, I say," someone said from the back of the crowd.

"If she'd been here last year, maybe I wouldn't have lost my field to that brushfire."

"Don't you just know it," another voice called out.

"My goodness," a woman said breathlessly, "I feel safer knowing she's in town."

Sophie drew strength from the arm Ridge kept tight around her and she felt his pleasure, too, as she turned from one smiling face to another, still amazed by the reactions of those around her. Never in her life had she experienced anything like this. Not only were these people not afraid of her and Jenna, they were actually *happy* to have them around. *Grateful* for Jenna's vision. Tears stung the backs of her eyes and Sophie blinked furiously, to keep them at bay. She didn't want to ruin this moment with tears. She wanted to enjoy it all, burn the memory into her mind so that years from now, wherever she was, she would be able to recall what it felt like the moment she realized she'd finally found a home.

CHAPTER NINETEEN

Two days later, Ridge was a man on the edge.

Time was running out and he was no closer to figuring out what to do. Damn it, he was expecting Charles Vinson to show up any time now. From what Sophie had told him about the man, Ridge guessed he'd set out from New York the minute he'd received Tall's telegram. Which could put him in Tanglewood as early as tomorrow.

Pushing back from his desk hard enough to make the chair legs scrape against the wood floor with a shriek, Ridge propped one booted foot on the corner of his desk and stared blankly at the wall of wanted posters opposite him. He'd never really thought about the faces on those posters before. The men and women behind the faces, rather. Their reasons for doing what they did. For ending up on some sheriff's wall.

Mind you, most of them were no better than they should be, he knew. Hell, you couldn't ride with outlaws for years and not learn that the majority of 'em weren't worth the gunpowder needed to blow 'em to hell. But there were others too. Folks who for one reason or another either stumbled into or got pushed into a life they hadn't wanted.

Like Sophie.

What was it Toby had said? The law wasn't all

black and white. And it was the gray that mattered the
most. He'd never believed that before.

Jumping to his feet, he crossed the room in a few
long strides, the only sound his boot heels clacking
against the wooden planks. Stopping at the front window, he stared out at Tanglewood and thought about
her situation. Hell, she hadn't asked to go on the run.
She hadn't *planned* on changing her name and hiding
out in a backwater part of Nevada. But she'd done
what she had to do. He didn't doubt her for a minute
when she said that Jenna was in danger from Vinson.
It had taken a lot of guts to break the law and up and
move across the country. To take a stand that she had
to have known could land her in jail. But she'd put
that child's safety above all else and, damn it, he
couldn't—*wouldn't*—do less.

And if that meant turning his back on the law and
the life he'd found, then so be it. He wouldn't lose
Sophie. Or Jenna.

The office door flew open and Tall stepped inside,
smacking his forehead on the door sash. "Dadburn it,"
he muttered, rubbing at the spot and sweeping his gaze
around the room until he spotted Ridge.

"Hey, boss," he said, nodding.

"Tall." Ridge turned away and walked back to his
desk. Damn it, if there was one thing he didn't need
at the moment it was another go-round with Tall. The
man had been at him for two days, pestering him for
the name of the "criminal" mentioned in the telegram.

"Y'know, boss," Tall said, clearly aiming to go
straight at it again. "If you'd just tell me who it is
you're worried about, I could maybe help."

"There's nothin' you can do," Ridge snapped as he

sat down and scooted his chair in closer to the desk.
"Like I keep tellin' you."

Still rubbing his forehead, Tall shook his head and
said, "Don't you trust me?" Then without waiting for
an answer, he went right on. "I'm your deputy, boss.
I know I sent that wire when I shouldn't have, but if
you don't tell me what's goin' on, how can I keep
from doin' something stupid again?"

"Tall," he said, leaning back in the chair, "it's not
that I don't trust you . . ." And that was the truth. He
had no reason to doubt the man's integrity or his courage. "It's just that I don't know yet what I'm gonna
do and you shouldn't be involved. It'll be safer for
you this way."

"Now, damn it," Tall said, laying both palms flat
on the desk and leaning in. "If I was worried about
bein' safe, would I be wearin' a badge pinned to my
shirt?"

"Guess not," Ridge allowed. There were far safer
jobs to be had than being a lawman. It was said that
the only thing a badge did was to give a gunman a
target to aim for.

"Then how about tellin' me the truth about what's
goin' on?"

Ridge thought about it, then decided to tell him.
After all, if it came down to him, Sophie, and Jenna
runnin' for the hills, then Tall would be left in charge
here. The man had the right to know. "Fine," he muttered and stood up again. Reaching into his back
pocket, he pulled out the wanted poster he'd kept there
for safekeeping. Unfolding it, he briefly looked down
into Sophie's face, then handed it over.

Tall rubbed one hand nervously across his face as
if now that he'd gotten what he wanted, he wasn't

entirely sure he wanted it after all. But then he took the poster, glanced at it, and lifted his gaze to Ridge. "Sophie? *She's* the kidnapper?"

"She's no kidnapper," Ridge snapped, then rattled off the whole story, telling it as quickly and as thoroughly as he could. When he was finished, Tall crumpled that wanted poster in one fist and slapped himself in the forehead with the flat of his other hand.

"And I turned her in," he said, disgusted.

"You didn't know."

"Damn it, Ridge, I sent a telegram telling that son of a bitch where he could find her."

"It's not your fault," Ridge said tightly.

"Damned if it ain't," Tall muttered, pacing wildly back and forth across the room. "Hell, you shoulda shot me. *I* woulda shot me."

"Thought about it," Ridge said with a half-smile. The man was punishing himself far more than Ridge could have. Guilt was stamped all over his features and his gaze when he looked up again was clouded by shame.

"It ain't too late," Tall muttered, spreading both arms out wide. "Pull your gun, I'll stand still."

"Maybe I would if it'd help," Ridge said, shaking his head. "But it won't."

"What will?" Tall asked, walking toward him.

"I don't know," he said, then slowly looked up into Tall's level gaze. "But one thing I do know. I won't let Sophie go to jail. And I won't let that bastard have Jenna."

" 'Course not," Tall agreed.

"Even if it means the three of us leave here and disappear again." Hell, he'd lived on the dodge most of his life. He could do it again. He knew how to hide better than most men would.

Glancing down at the badge pinned to his shirt, he realized that for the first time in a long time, he was thinking seriously about turning his back on the law.

"You'd leave Tanglewood?"

"If that's the only way."

"Hell, Ridge," the man said and kicked the corner of the desk. "I don't wanna be sheriff. We'll think of somethin' else."

Ridge pushed up from his chair with a tired sigh and walked across the room to the front door. He plucked his hat from a peg on the wall and tugged it on. Then he turned to look at his deputy. "I've been tryin' to do just that for the last few days and haven't come up with anything yet. Why don't you give it a try?"

"I will, boss," Tall told him. He raised his voice to be heard as Ridge walked outside. "You wait and see. This'll work out."

Later, at the restaurant, though, Tall had to admit he hadn't thought of a damn thing either. "And it's all my fault," he muttered into his cup of coffee, barely noticing as Marie sidled up to refill his cup.

"What's your fault?" she asked.

He flinched and told himself it was a wonder Ridge kept him on the job at all. Damn fool. Always shootin' off his mouth or sendin' wires when he should be quiet. Lord help Tanglewood if Ridge up and left, leaving Tall as sheriff.

"Nothin'," he said, and held out his cup.

Marie poured more coffee, then set the pot down onto the table and took a seat opposite the lanky deputy. He seemed about as miserable as a man could get, she told herself, and wondered what it was that had him looking like someone had shot his dog.

"Tell me," she said simply and folded her hands atop the table.

"I can't, Marie," he said, determined to finally keep his peace and not make more of a mess by shooting off his mouth. With a quick glance around the otherwise empty restaurant, he added, "Official business."

She shook her head, reached across the table and covered one of his hands with hers. Surprised, he looked down at their joined hands before lifting his gaze to meet hers again. "Marie . . ."

"Tall Slater," she whispered tightly, "I been serving you coffee and such for nearly two years."

"Yeah, but—"

As she talked, her frustration mounted and she squeezed his hand tightly in reaction. "I'm the one you talk to when you're worried. I'm the one you tell when you're happy. If you don't know that you can trust me by now, then you never will, blast your eyes."

"Now, Marie . . ."

"Now, Marie nothing," she snapped and squeezed his hand tight enough to make him wince. "I *love* you, you big oaf, but I'm not gonna wait forever. I want to have me some babies before I get too old to rock 'em myself. And if you ain't interested, you tell me now and I'll look elsewhere."

Tall just blinked at her, stunned.

"Some lawman you are," she muttered. "You didn't guess my feelings?"

He shook his head, but smiled.

"Well," she snapped, letting go of his hand, "now you know. So, do you tell me what's going on or do I get up and leave you on your lonesome for good?"

When he didn't say anything right away, she shoved back from the table, but he grabbed at her hand and held on as tightly as she had before.

"Don't go, Marie."

"Why not?" she asked, and held her breath, hoping he'd say the right thing for once.

"Because I do trust you," he said softly, looking up at her with those big ol' eyes of his. "And I need your help."

"Is that the only reason?" she prodded.

He swallowed hard and his Adam's apple bobbed up and down once or twice. "No, ma'am," he said finally, "it ain't." He smoothed the pad of his thumb gently across her skin before admitting, "There's a few things I'd like to say to you too." Then he took a deep breath and added, "But before we talk about havin' them babies, we got somethin' else to figure out first."

Marie looked into his eyes and, in their depths, finally saw what she'd waited two long years to see. Inhaling sharply, she let the air slide out of her lungs again as she sat back down. Smiling now, she said, "Then let's get busy, I ain't getting any younger."

"Yes, ma'am," he said, and gave her another squeeze as he started talking.

"He's here," Sophie whispered late the next afternoon as the train whistle sounded out long and lonely in the still air.

"He?" Ridge asked, following her gaze down Main Street toward the train depot beyond.

"Charles," she said and backed up a step.

Ridge caught hold of her and stepped into her line of vision. She shook her head and looked up at him. "Let me go, Ridge. I can get Jenna and—"

"And what?" he demanded through gritted teeth. Panic reared up inside him and he had to fight to draw a breath. He wouldn't lose her. Not to Charles and not to her own desperation. His hands came down hard on her shoulders. Yanking her close against him, he forced her head back and when their gazes locked he asked again, "What can you do? Sneak onto the train when he isn't lookin'? Run somewhere new? With him just a step or two behind you?"

"We've been through this," she reminded him stiffly, and shot a quick look at the street, making sure no one could overhear them.

"Yeah and we decided we wouldn't run."

"You decided."

"Damn it, Sophie—"

"No!" she said and jerked free of his hold. Backing up another step and then another, she kept her gaze locked with his and muttered thickly, "You don't understand. He'll take her. He'll take Jenna and I won't be able to stop him."

"No he won't," Ridge swore, to her and to everything he held holy. "I won't let him." He wasn't sure how he'd stop him yet, but surely *something* would come to him.

"There's nothing you can do. He has the law on his side," she reminded him, taking another step to keep him at arm's length. "And he'll expect to have you on his side as well. I won't let him have her. I *can't*."

"And I can't lose you," he murmured fiercely. "*Or* Jenna." Closing the gap between them quickly, he grabbed hold of her and pulled her close to him. "Trust me, Sophie."

"I do trust you," she said, her gaze moving over his face like a caress. "But—"

"No buts," he warned her, then turned her around. Giving her a little push, he said, "Go to Hattie's. Wait there for me."

She looked back at him over her shoulder and Ridge saw the fear and pain in her eyes. Helplessness rode him hard, and as he headed for his office, he was almost looking forward to meeting Charles Vinson. He needed a target for the fury raging inside him.

Charles left the train station behind and walked into the heart of Tanglewood, Nevada. His upper lip curled at a rising swirl of dust as a horse and wagon trundled past without a care for the pedestrians it passed. Impatiently waving one hand in front of his face, he reminded himself that the privation and discomfort of his trip West would all be worth it soon. All he had to do was find the sheriff who'd sent him the wire.

He supposed he had taken a chance in coming all the way out here without first making sure that Sophie was still in the vicinity. But he hadn't wanted to risk her running off again. And surely she would have heard if he had made inquiries.

His gaze took in the miserable little town and he wondered idly why in heaven anyone would *choose* to live their lives in such squalor. Hard to believe that such outposts still existed, he thought. Back East, people tended to think of the frontier as nothing more than a setting for dime novels. And frankly, Charles preferred it that way. The sooner he collected Jenna and returned east, the better.

When he spotted the grimy window with the word "Sheriff" painted on it, Charles smiled to himself and hurried his steps. He was so close to his goal now he could almost taste success.

He stepped inside and immediately crossed the room to where a lone man sat behind a cluttered desk. "Sheriff Hawkins?" he asked, in his most officious tone.

The man lifted his head to look at him and Charles stared into a cool pair of blue eyes. For one brief moment, he reconsidered his opinion of this backwater town. The sheriff looked to be a shrewd, hard man. But then, Charles thought, so was he.

"That's right," the man said and leaned back in his chair.

"I'm Charles Vinson," he countered, lifting his chin and idly brushing at the dust marring his well-tailored black coat. No harm in showing the lawman that he was now dealing with a man of means. "You sent me a wire? About Sophie Dolan and a missing child?"

Ridge forced a slow smile despite the cold, hard knot in his gut. Even if Sophie hadn't told him all about this fella, Ridge would've taken an instant dislike to him. He had small eyes and soft hands. And to Ridge's way of thinking that meant he saw too little and worked not enough. The man stood as if he expected mud to be flung on him any minute and damned if he didn't sniff as if the very air offended him.

"Jenna's not missing," Ridge told him, taking pleasure in it. "She's right here."

"Excellent," Charles said and rubbed his palms together in anticipation. "I've come a long way to collect her, so if you wouldn't mind fetching her from wherever she is—"

"I don't think so," Ridge said, and stood up, preferring to face his enemy eye to eye.

"I beg your pardon?" Charles went perfectly still

and it was clear he wasn't a man to take being bested lightly.

"I said, Jenna's not going anywhere with you until the circuit judge comes to town."

"That's outrageous."

"Maybe," Ridge mused, running with the idea that had just sprung into his mind. "But that's the way it'll be."

"I am the child's legal guardian," Charles said and reached into his inside pocket to pull out a sheaf of papers. "Read this."

He ignored the papers being waved under his nose. "The judge can do that."

"Now listen to me, Sheriff."

"No, sir, I don't have to do that," Ridge said and enjoyed the look of pure apoplexy on the other man's face. "What I can do is contact the judge and see how soon he can get here."

Charles stared at him for a long moment and Ridge could almost see the steam lifting off the top of the man's head. He looked fit to bust. Apparently, people didn't buck him real often. Well, Ridge was proud to be one of the few.

"Fine," he muttered, tucking his papers back into his coat. "But while you do that, I'd like to see my ward."

"Nope."

"What?"

"See, I only have your word for what you're sayin'," Ridge said, and folded his arms across his chest. Bracing both feet wide apart, he gave the other man a long look and added, "I'm not about to tell you where to find one of our citizens without talkin' to her first."

"This is outrageous."

"So you said."

High spots of color flagged Charles's cheeks and he struggled to hold on to a temper that was clearly on the rise. Good, Ridge thought. A man who lost his temper wasn't thinking clearly. And right about now, he needed every advantage.

"You know," Ridge suggested, "you look like you could use a drink. Why don't you go on down to the saloon and I'll come get you as soon as I know something?"

He wanted to argue. But there was just nothing he could do about it. And Ridge had to give him marks for knowing when to back down.

"All right, I'll do that, *Sheriff*."

"Good," he said, smiling and nodding encouragement.

As Charles left, he stopped in the doorway and said, "I'll be expecting you shortly."

Ridge waited until the man had gone past the front window and his footsteps had faded into the distance before turning and walking through the jail to the back door. There, he stepped outside, and sprinted for Hattie's.

"Are you out of your mind?" Sophie demanded.

"You're not the first to suggest it," Ridge said.

She stuck her right arm through the iron bars of her cell, made a wild grab for him—and missed.

"Now, Red . . ."

"Don't call me that! I can't believe you did this to me!" She grabbed hold of the iron bars and gave them a shake. They rattled, but held. Then kicking them, she whirled around and marched to the opposite side of her cell. Pacing back and forth in its narrow confines, she kept up a muttered stream of conversation, giving in to the rush of emotion charging through her. "I'm in a cell. Behind bars. Pacing. I can't believe you did this to me. After . . . after . . . what we *did*."

He opened his mouth to speak, but she turned her back on him.

"I trusted you," she said, shaking her head in disbelief. She never should have. She'd known better. He was a *sheriff,* for pity's sake. Hadn't everyone in town told her how stern Ridge was about the law? About how he treated the sheriff's office like his own private church? About how his badge was his Bible? She should have listened. Should have known that a man so devoted to the law wouldn't be able to bend it. Even for love.

And sure enough, Charles had only been in town fifteen minutes when Ridge had rushed down to Hattie's, tossed her over his shoulder, and carried her back to the jailhouse where he'd promptly locked her into a cage.

A *cage.* Her gaze shifted to the twilight sky just beyond her tiny window. The first stars twinkled in a lavender haze. This was how she'd see the world from now on, she thought, cringing at the thought of years in prison. How would she stand it? How would she live with the memory of Ridge betraying her? How would she live with the pain of not watching Jenna grow up?

"Sophie, damn it," he said and grabbed one of the bars. "If you'd just listen to me for a minute—"

"Listening to you is what put me in this . . . *trap*!" She whirled around again to sneer at him. "Did Charles pay you the reward he promised? How much was it again? Five hundred dollars?" One red eyebrow lifted. "Betrayal certainly pays better than thirty pieces of silver these days, doesn't it?"

"All right, by damn," he muttered thickly, "that's enough."

Reaching for the key, he jammed it into the lock, turned it and swung the door wide. She made a break for it instantly of course, but he caught her and held her tight despite her kicking feet and the fact that she landed a good kick to his kneecap.

"Ow! Cut it out, Sophie!"

"I will not," she vowed, throwing her hair back behind her head and giving him a glare that should have roasted him on the spot. "I will fight you with my very last breath." Pushing against his chest with all her strength, she said, "I curse you, Ridge Hawkins, and all of your descendants if you should have any! I hope you don't have a moment's peace the rest of your life for what you're doing tonight."

"I probably won't," he agreed and carried her over to the cot. Sitting down, he plopped her onto his lap and held her there.

"You'll regret this, you—you—*bastard*!" She continued to struggle, her pain nearly choking her. He'd made his choice, her mind screamed. He'd chosen his precious law over her and now everything was over. Her freedom . . . Jenna's life . . . Oh God. Her gaze swept the cell frantically, searching for an escape that wasn't there. How could this have happened? How could he have turned against her like this? Had what they shared meant *nothing* to him?

At that thought, she balled her fist and took a swing at him.

"No doubt," he grumbled and muttered an oath

when her small fist connected with his jaw. "Now are you gonna listen to me?"

"No!" The pain in her fist was *nothing* compared to the sharp ache squeezing her heart. "I listened to you once. When you told me not to run. When you told me to trust you." She spat the words at him. "And you see where listening to you got me!"

"Then if we're not gonna talk . . ." He speared his fingers into her hair, tipped her head back, and laid siege to her mouth. She fought him at first, as he'd expected, and he really couldn't blame her. After all, she was in jail. But damn it, she should trust him.

He parted her lips with his tongue and darted into her warmth, feeling the strength and passion he found within her surge through him. This woman was everything to him, he thought as he felt her surrender to the power of what lay between them.

She pressed herself close to him, arching her breasts into his chest and every inch of his body burst into flame. There on that narrow cot in a small cell, he held his world in his arms and as he swallowed her sighs he knew he would do anything he had to, *anything,* to keep her.

"It seems," a voice tinged with amusement said, "I've arrived just in time."

Ridge lifted his head and Sophie blinked blindly like a woman coming up from underwater. She felt short of breath, her head was spinning, and her heartbeat thundered in her chest. It just wasn't fair that she could still respond to a man who was going to ruin her life.

"Evenin', Reverend," Ridge said and Sophie turned her head to see Elias, Hattie, and Jenna standing in the open doorway.

Confusion mixed with embarrassment sputtered through her and she shot Ridge a look, silently asking for an explanation.

"That's what I was trying to tell you," he said with a helpless shrug. "I figured the only way to make you see reason was to lock you up while I told you my plan."

"Which is . . . ?" she asked.

"We're getting married," he said bluntly and for the first time in her life Sophie was absolutely speechless with surprise. For a few seconds, anyway.

She looked up at him and saw the earnestness in his eyes and knew he was dead serious. A pang of regret tingled inside her.

"Because a man can't be forced to testify against his wife?" she asked and wondered if he heard the ache in her voice.

"For God's sake, Sophie," he muttered.

"We're not getting married, Ridge."

"Don't argue with me, Red," he ground out.

"Thank you for offering to do this," she went on, "but I won't get married just to be safe."

Ridge shot a look at the people in the doorway and they backed up a step or two, allowing him and Sophie a touch more privacy. Then turning to face her, he cupped her face in his palms and she felt the hard warmth of him shine brightly all the way to her soul.

"Red, I never thought I'd say this to anybody," he whispered, his gaze moving over her face as if he were trying to memorize her every feature. Finally, though, he shifted his gaze to hers, looked deeply into her eyes and said, "I *love* you."

Sophie's breath caught in her throat. *This* she hadn't expected. Tears stung her eyes until she was forced to blink wildly just to be able to see him clearly. "No," she whispered, shaking her head. "You don't."

One corner of his mouth lifted. "Yeah I do. Didn't mean to." He smoothed her hair back from her face. "You kind of sneaked up on me, but I do, nonetheless. I love the way you yell at me. I love the way you tilt your chin up when you're getting ready for war."

She opened her mouth to argue, but he cut her off.

"I love your courage, your strength. You are the only woman I've ever wanted in my life, Red. Don't say no." His gaze locked with hers and she read the emotion shining in his pale blue eyes as he added softly, "Don't leave me alone."

Sophie's heart filled her throat. She'd desired him, hated him, fought with him, and loved him almost from the first moment she'd seen him. And to have this joy at the darkest moment of her life was the greatest gift she'd ever been given.

"Marry me, Red. And trust me to find a way out of this. Let me be Jenna's daddy for real. Let's make us some more babies to keep her company."

"Do it, Mama," Jenna called and Sophie laughed shortly. "You're s'posed to. I can see it!"

"Well," Sophie said, reaching up to rub the pad of her thumb across his bottom lip. "I suppose that settles it."

"Damn right," Ridge said, grinning. "You already told me she's never wrong."

"There's only one problem," she said.

"Red . . ."

"I cursed you," she reminded him. "And your descendants."

"Well, I figure if you put the curse on," he said, with a half-smile, "you can take it off. You reckon?"

Sophie looked directly into his deep blue eyes, smiled and said softly, "I reckon."

CHAPTER TWENTY

Two days later, the saloon had officially been closed and turned into a makeshift courtroom. The place was packed to the rafters with the citizens of Tanglewood and all the folks who'd come in from the outlying ranches.

Sophie sat beside Ridge at one of the tables up front wondering if it was too late to run. But even as she considered it, she knew she'd never get out of the saloon. If Charles didn't stop her, her new *husband* would. Ridge had hardly left her side in the last two days, and though he kept insisting that she trust him, he hadn't bothered to tell her what he had in mind. And please God, he *did* have a plan.

Folding her hands together tightly, she flicked a glance at Ridge and wished she felt half as confident as he looked. His black broadcloth pants had been brushed and pressed and his boots polished. He wore a black fingertip-length jacket over a starched white shirt and the silver star pinned to his lapel seemed to catch every light in the room until it gleamed with what looked like an inner fire. He leaned back in his chair with a casual ease that Sophie envied until she noticed a muscle in his jaw twitching and she realized he wasn't any calmer than she was.

That knowledge terrified her. He, too, must hear the sound of an imaginary cell door slamming behind her.

Sophie's throat closed up tight. There just didn't seem to be a way out of this mess, and knowing that in a couple of hours' time she could very well be on her way to prison wasn't exactly making it easy to breathe.

Nervous, she let her gaze drift across the familiar faces crowding the saloon. She could feel their curiosity. Feel their stares. *Kidnapper,* they whispered and looked at her with what she could only guess was a mixture of fascination and fear. She squirmed uncomfortably in her seat. The only person missing was Toby, who'd volunteered to look after Jenna while court was in session. Muttered conversations rose and fell as rapidly as the paper fans being wielded by nervous hands.

A trickle of perspiration rolled down Sophie's back and again she shifted uneasily. Despite Jenna's assurances that everything would "be all right," Sophie was worried. Charles wasn't a man to give up. And now that he'd found Jenna, she knew he would do whatever he had to do to keep her.

As if sensing the turmoil spinning inside her, Ridge glanced her way, gave her a half-smile, then reached to pat her hand. "It's gonna be fine, Sophie," he said quietly.

"I hope so," she told him, grabbing hold of his hand and holding on tight. But frankly, she didn't know how it could be.

"Come to order," the judge hollered and smacked his gavel down onto the bartop.

Sophie's gaze swung in his direction. About sixty, Judge Elijah Forrest was small and wiry with sharp gray eyes, grizzled hair, and salt-and-pepper whisker stubble he hadn't bothered to shave that morning. His black suit was dusty, his white shirt less than spotless, and he sat on a tall stool behind a bar in a Western saloon. Yet with all that, he carried a sort of legal dignity with him and the crowd hushed when he spoke.

"Now," he said, thumbing through a sheaf of papers in front of him, "the way I hear it, this fella . . ." He paused and pointed to Charles, sitting alone at a table opposite Sophie and Ridge. "Says he has legal claim to the child, Jenna . . ."

"Hawkins, Your Honor," Ridge supplied easily.

One gray eyebrow lifted into a high arch. "She's your daughter then, Ridge?"

"Yes, sir, she is," he answered.

Sophie felt all the air whoosh out of her lungs. She stared at his profile, stunned. Ridge had *lied* to the judge? She'd no more expected that than she would have the sun suddenly deciding to rise in the west and sink in the east. Dozens of questions chased each other through her mind, but there were no answers to be had. By not even a flicker of an eyelash did Ridge let on that he knew she was surprised by his statement.

Whispers rustled through the crowd like autumn leaves caught in a sudden gust of wind.

"That's a lie," Charles shouted, jumping to his feet. "I have the paperwork to prove it. Just look through it, for heaven's sake!"

The judge picked up the gavel again and slammed its head against the bar. "You sit down, until I call on ya."

Blustering, obviously disgusted, Charles did as he was told.

Dutifully, the judge riffled through the papers again, frowned to himself, then looked up, pinning Ridge with a look. "You say the child's yours."

"Yes, sir," Ridge lied again without hesitation and took Sophie's hand in his. "Mine and my wife's here."

She blinked back a sudden sheen of tears and felt her heart swell in her chest. His strength poured into her, his love flowed deep into her soul and filled her to overflowing, like the banks of a rain-swollen river. She held on to him tightly, wanting to let him know, if only silently, that she knew what he was doing now and that she loved him for it.

Nodding, the judge folded his hands atop the paperwork and asked, "So what we have here is one man's word against another."

"And the legal papers naming me guardian," Charles reminded him, jumping up to protest again.

"Mister," the judge warned quietly, "I already told you to sit down till I call on ya."

"This is ridiculous."

"If I fine you for contempt of court, you're goin' to find it a mite less funny," Elijah told him sternly.

Clearly furious, Charles took his seat.

"Now," Elijah said to Ridge, "you got any other proof of what you're sayin' besides your word? Not that I don't believe ya, boy. But this fella did come loaded for bear with all his paperwork here."

Ridge gave Sophie's hand one last squeeze and stood up. "Your Honor," he said, his voice clear and strong, "I don't need anything besides my word. I'm paid to uphold the law. I do my job. I don't lie. I figure my reputation ought to be worth as much as Mr. Vinson's papers."

His word. Sophie listened to him, heard him lie to the judge and knew she'd never been loved so much in her life. Ridge was giving up everything for her. Everything he was. Everything he believed in. For her sake, he was offering up his honor, his reputation, his pride. For love of her, Ridge Hawkins was turning his life upside down.

Heart full, she stared up at him and knew that no matter what happened, she would always have this moment.

This one moment when a proud, honest man was willing to sacrifice himself for her.

Elijah rubbed one hand across his whiskery cheek as he did some thinking. After a long moment, though, he shook his head and said, "Son, I'd like to say you're right. But legally, if all we've got is one man's word against another, then his papers carry a mite more weight."

A soft moan slid from her throat and Ridge sat down beside her, reaching blindly for her hand again.

"It's not just one man's word," someone in the crowd said suddenly.

Elijah's head snapped up and his gaze narrowed as he searched the crowd. "Who said that?"

"I did." Mort Simpson stood up.

As one, Ridge and Sophie turned to stare at the storekeeper as he turned his hat over and over in nervous hands.

"Step forward," the judge commanded and Mort did just that, walking to stand in front of the bar.

Elijah glared at the man. "You swear to tell the truth so help you God?"

"I do," Mort said after clearing his throat.

Nodding, Elijah looked him dead in the eye and asked, "To the best of your knowledge, is the child Jenna the daughter of Ridge and Sophie Hawkins?"

The storekeeper glanced at the two people sitting

at the table, then turned back to face the judge. "Yes, sir, she surely is."

Ridge slanted a slow, disbelieving grin at Sophie and she blinked away tears to smile back at him. Hope, fragile as a breath, rose up inside her once more and Sophie clung to it desperately.

"This is outrageous!" Charles was on his feet and shouting to be heard over the rumble of sound from the audience.

The judge ignored him and, when Mort finished testifying, asked, "Anybody else got somethin' to say?"

The scrape and scuffle of chairs moving and feet shuffling filled the room and Sophie sucked in a shaky breath as at least a dozen others stood up. They formed a line that snaked from the bar clean out the front door to the boardwalk.

Ridge pulled her close and draped one arm around her shoulders. It was as if the sun was peeking out from behind a threatening bank of black clouds. She wanted to believe. Wanted to hope.

Swiveling her head, she glanced at the judge, who allowed himself a small smile as he studied the growing line of "witnesses." Daring a look at Charles, she watched as the man's features darkened with rage.

"Appears to me," the judge announced over Charles's objections, "that we got us a few more testimonies to listen to."

Ridge held her tight, pressing her to him as, together, they listened to one person after another come forward to testify under oath that Jenna was Ridge's daughter. Men and women she'd known only a few weeks stood before a judge and lied through their teeth to protect her and Jenna.

Her heart swelled to the point of bursting. Her throat tightened and tears stung the backs of her eyes. She clung to Ridge and felt the solid, warm comfort of his support as she listened to their testimony. She'd come to this place a stranger, expecting nothing, hoping to find a refuge.

And, she realized, as she held on to Ridge, she'd found so much more. She'd found *friends*. A home. And she'd found a love deeper and stronger than she'd ever believed possible.

Ridge gave her a squeeze, and she rested her head against his shoulder as Hattie finished her speech.

"I'm tellin' you, Judge," the woman said, dabbing at her streaming eyes with the tip of her hanky. "Ridge liked to walk a hole through my floor the night Jenna was born. All his worryin' and carryin' on, I practically had to order him out of the room at gunpoint. But I swear, you've never seen a happier man than Ridge when he first saw his baby. Why," she added with a shake of her head, "when I handed him his newborn daughter, the man had *tears* in his eyes!"

"Is that right?" the judge asked, sliding Ridge a look. Ridge held Sophie closer and nodded.

"May God strike me dead if I'm lying," Hattie proclaimed.

Sophie didn't know whether to laugh or to leap out of the way of a heaven-sent thunderbolt. But she did neither, instead shooting a glance at Charles, who quietly fumed at his table. He'd already been fined fifty dollars for his constant objections and since then he'd kept his mouth shut. But his silence didn't hide his contempt for the proceedings. His fingers tapped against the tabletop and his gaze was fixed to a spot on the wall behind the judge's head.

When the testimonies had ended Judge Forest cleared his throat. Instantly, he had the attention of everyone in the room.

"Well," he said slowly, rubbing his whiskery jaw with one hand. "I've read all the papers, I've heard all the testimony, and now I reckon it's time for my decision."

Sophie shot Charles another look. He hadn't changed position. Ridge tightened his hold on her. She clung to him as if it meant her life. As, in fact, it did.

"Mister," the judge said, giving Charles a steely-eyed look. "I don't know you from Adam's great-aunt. You show up here claiming the right to steal another man's child and you believe I ought to help you do it."

"She is *not* his child," Charles argued.

"That ain't what I'm hearin'," the judge said, waving the man into silence. "I got a whole town who swears that child belongs to Ridge and his wife. I got the word of a lawman whom I trust. I got the word of a *preacher* who swears he married these two and I got the word of the woman who helped deliver the child."

"Lies," Charles muttered, slanting a vicious glance at Sophie. "All of it. Lies. I don't know how she's done it. Or what she's promised them—"

"Mister," Judge Forest shouted and banged his gavel. "You are startin' to try my patience. You hush up or so help me God you'll be hearin' my decision from the inside of a jail cell." Wagging that wooden gavel at him, he then warned, "You know, we don't take kindly to them that tries to steal children. You best watch your step before you find yourself the guest of honor at a tar-and-feather party."

Sniffing loudly, the judge then turned to face Ridge

and Sophie. "The court finds Jenna Hawkins to be the natural and legal daughter of Ridge and Sophie Hawkins. Charles Vinson has no claim to the child. And if he makes a move on her, he ought to be shot on sight."

A roar erupted from the crowd as the judge slammed that gavel down one more time and shouted, "Case dismissed. Court's closed, bar's open! Give me a drink!"

Slowly, as if he couldn't believe it was over, Ridge stood up and pulled Sophie into his arms for a squeeze hard enough to keep her from drawing a single breath. Tears coursed down her cheeks. Her heartbeat thundered in her ears and as Ridge bent his head to claim a long, deep kiss she felt a rush of gratitude and love sweep through her.

Then their friends were surrounding them, pulling them apart to congratulate them. People crowded close, everyone talking at once. Sophie was pushed from embrace to embrace, spinning from one friend to the next as she laughingly accepted their good wishes and tried desperately to think of a way to thank them all for what they'd done.

A few minutes later, she found herself on the opposite side of the room from Ridge. She watched as he grinned and yanked Hattie into a heartfelt hug that lifted the big woman clean off her feet.

But Sophie's smile froze in place as a sharp, stabbing pain sliced through her mind. She cupped her head in her hands and closed her eyes tight, riding the wave of pain and helplessly watching as a vision blossomed in her mind's eye.

Charles. He had Jenna and the child was screaming. Toby lay stretched out on the ground, motionless, while Charles threw Jenna across a saddle in front of him. Helplessly, Sophie watched Ridge try to stop him and she saw a black swirl of danger surround the man she loved.

Terror closed her throat and clawed at her heart. She opened her eyes and didn't even see the people standing in front of her. Gasping for air, she blinked the mental images aside and, throwing one last glance at Ridge, pushed her way through the crowd toward the door. She couldn't risk his safety. She couldn't ask him to fight one more battle for her. He'd already sacrificed his professional pride and his self-respect. She wouldn't let him lay down his life. This time the fight was hers. She would save Jenna and she would defeat Charles. No matter what.

Outside, she hiked the hem of her skirt up and ran down the center of the deserted street, her gaze fixed on the distant stable, where she knew Charles and Jenna waited.

The babble of excited voices was almost deafening, but even with the outside distraction, he heard Jenna call him. Instantly, his head came up and his gaze swept the sea of faces, searching for Sophie. But she was gone. As was Charles.

Jenna's silent shriek echoed in his mind again and this time Ridge didn't hesitate. Shoving past his friends and neighbors, he crashed through the crowd, ran through the front door and hit the boardwalk running.

Jenna's cries tore at Sophie as she ran into the stable and tripped over Toby's body, lying in the straw. On hands and knees, she stared at the big man, horrified,

until she saw his massive chest move and she knew
he was hurt, but alive.

The solid smack of a slap slashed the silence and
Jenna moaned. Sophie's head whipped around as the
sound pushed her to her feet and she raced to the back
of the livery. Charles had a horse nearly saddled. Jenna
sat in a mound of straw, holding one hand to her face.
She struggled to her feet as Sophie rushed into the
stall.

He made a grab for the girl, but he was too far away
and not nearly quick enough. Sophie snatched at her
little sister and shoved her into the wide center aisle.
"Run, Jenna," she cried frantically. *"Run."*

The girl took off, her short legs pumping wildly as
she made a break for the sunshine beyond the dark
shadows of the stable.

Charles growled furiously, reached out and grabbed
Sophie, shaking her as a lion would its prey. Her hair
fell down around her shoulders, her head snapped back
on her neck, and her gaze locked with his. She saw
the flicker of madness and wondered if it had always
been there or if she'd pushed him into it by denying
him his neatly laid plans.

"This is all your fault, you stupid bitch," he
shouted, shaking her again until she thought her head
might fly right off her shoulders. "The girl is mine.
Mine!"

It's not happening, she thought. This couldn't be
happening. They'd won. They'd beaten Charles and
claimed a life together. They should be safe. They
should be happy.

Terrified, furious at the man who threatened everything that meant a damn to her, Sophie kicked blindly,
slamming the toe of her shoe into his shin. When he

yelped, she pushed at him with all her strength, gaining only a moment's freedom before he grabbed her again. "She'll never be yours," she said, squeezing the words past the knot in her throat. "Even if you kill me, Ridge will protect her. This town will protect her." And that knowledge gave her strength. The kind of strength she'd need to see her through this last battle.

He let go of her long enough to slap her hard. Her eyes rolled and the sharp stinging pain filled her head. And she didn't care. The longer he concerned himself with her, the more time Jenna had to get clear. To reach help.

"Damn you," he muttered and drew his hand back to hit her again.

Sophie braced herself for a blow that didn't come.

"Let her go," a quiet, carefully controlled voice said.

She shot a quick look at the man who stood not ten feet from her. Her husband. His dark blue eyes swirled with an anger so deep, she almost flinched with the hard look of it. He'd tucked the right edge of his jacket behind him. He stood, feet braced wide apart, right hand positioned just above the gun at his hip, his deadly gaze locked on Charles.

Bright sunlight behind him created a golden glow that outlined his body with a shimmering halo and he looked to Sophie like an avenging angel. And she'd never seen anything more beautiful in her life.

"No," Charles said and pulled her to him, her back to his front. She gasped at the sudden movement and looked directly at Ridge. Producing a knife from who knew where, her captor held the tip to her throat, forcing her to arch her neck to avoid the needle-sharp point. "I'm leaving," he said. "And if you don't back off, I'll kill her."

"Oh God, Ridge," she whispered and saw him flinch.

"Hurt her and you're dead in the next second," Ridge said simply. And the easiness of his tone made his threat that much more dangerous.

"Even if you kill me," Charles muttered, "she'll still be dead. And I'll win." As if to prove who was in charge, he pushed the tip of the blade into her throat, and Sophie felt the almost sweet sting of steel piercing her flesh. A drop of blood seeped from the wound and trickled down her throat, to roll beneath the high collar of her green dress.

Short, shallow breaths raced in and out of her lungs and she swallowed heavily, feeling the edge of the knife scrape her skin.

From a distance, she heard raised voices and knew that Jenna had reached safety. And even with the knife at her throat, a strange sort of peace came over her. If she died here, Jenna would be safe. She would have a home, with people who cared about her. With a father who loved her.

But she didn't want to die. She wanted, desperately, to live. To love. To have children. To grow old, looking into pale blue eyes that had offered her a lifetime of riches.

Seconds stretched out as if time were suddenly moving forward in fits and starts. She felt the wind rush down the center aisle of the livery. The scent of horses and fresh straw and fear almost overwhelmed her. She saw the square of sunlight at the edge of the stable and thought it looked like the gateway to paradise. Outside lay safety. Love. Her future.

Here in the shadows there was only death and the end to a dream.

Sophie looked at Ridge and almost didn't recognize him. Her husband—the man she knew, with his kindness and humor—had disappeared. In his place was a hard, unforgiving man whose prowess with a gun had led him into dark and dangerous places too many times to count. And as she recognized the change in him, she knew the end was coming. One way or another, this confrontation was over.

"Walk out," Charles said tightly, grabbing a fistful of Sophie's hair. A small moan of pain slid from her throat as he added, "And maybe I'll let the bitch live."

"I told you once," Ridge said softly, "be careful how you talk about my wife. And I warned you what would happen if you hurt her."

Then his right hand swept up and then down again in a blur of motion. A single gunshot blasted the stillness, a flash of fire from the muzzle of Ridge's pistol nearly blinded her and the knife was gone from Sophie's throat. Staggering, she fell into her husband's outstretched arms. Glancing down at Charles, she caught a brief glimpse of the small, neat hole in the center of his forehead before Ridge turned her face into his shoulder.

"Don't, darlin'," he whispered, "don't look again. It's over."

"Over," she repeated and felt her heart slowly begin to beat again. He'd drawn and fired his pistol so quickly, she'd hardly seen him move. And in an instant, the danger had passed and her world was safe once more. Grateful for his arm around her, for her life and this second chance at love, she leaned into him as he led her from the stall.

People streamed into the stable. Two men bent over Toby and Sophie drew her first easy breath when she saw the blacksmith's eyes flutter open. Concerned faces swam in front of her, but Ridge didn't stop. He kept walking, leading her out of the shadows and into the bright light of day. And when they were clear of the stable, Sophie heard Jenna call, "Mama!"

She looked to her right in time to see Hattie set the child down. The little girl ran to her, wrapped her arms around Sophie's knees and hung on with all her might. "You're all right, Mama. I see'd it. I knew Daddy would save you."

"That's right, sweetie," Sophie said, one hand smoothing Jenna's hair as she looked up into the blue eyes that had captured her from the first. She lifted one hand to stroke his cheek and he turned his face into her touch to kiss her palm. Tears swam in her eyes and Sophie smiled as she told him, "Daddy saved me. He saved us."

Smiling, Ridge shook his head and kissed her. Then bending down, he scooped Jenna up into his arms and planted a loud, smacking kiss on the cheek that still bore a red handprint from the man who had nearly cost them so much.

"Don't you believe it, little squirt," he told Jenna, shifting his gaze to Sophie. "You and your mama are the ones who saved *me*."

"We did?" Jenna asked, clearly amazed. "How?"

"The best way of all," he said, looking deep enough into Sophie's eyes that she was sure he was staring straight into her soul. "By lovin' me."

And together, they walked into the sunlight, leaving the shadows of the past far behind them.

EPILOGUE

TWO YEARS LATER . . .

"Ridge Hawkins," Hattie shouted, "if you don't stop your pacing, I swear I'm gonna shoot you stone dead."

"It's my house," he argued. Hell, he'd built it himself smack in the middle of Foster's meadow—practically on the spot where he and Sophie had made love for the first time. And he'd be damned if anybody was going to throw him out. Especially now. "I'll pace if I want to."

"Durn men," she said. "You ought to go somewhere. I'll tell you when the baby gets here."

He glared at her. "I'm not leaving this house until I know Sophie and the baby are all right."

"Piffle," the woman said with a sniff. "You know durn well they're gonna be fine. Heck, you even know the baby's another girl. Jenna already told you."

But that didn't help, he thought. Nothing did. Not while he knew Sophie was upstairs in their bedroom, in pain.

Ridge shoved both hands through his hair and wondered why in the hell they were doing this again. They already had Jenna and another beautiful little girl, Teresa. Wasn't that enough? Shouldn't they have been satisfied? Grumbling under his breath, he started pacing again, not even noticing the dangerous look Hattie shot him on her way upstairs with a pan of hot water.

He heard a low, deep moan filter down from the bedroom and everything inside him went cold and still. But a moment later, he heard a smack and then a baby's indignant cry and Ridge smiled, taking his first easy breath in hours.

The front door swung open and Jenna came inside, carefully leading her little sister by the hand. "Our baby's here, Daddy!" she crowed.

"She sure is, honey," he said, grinning now as his newest daughter's cries lifted the roof off the house. Crossing to the two little girls, he picked up Teresa, took Jenna's hand, and headed for the stairs. "Let's go see her, huh?"

Teresa's soft reddish-blond hair dusted his cheek as she leaned against him and he heard her voice in his mind. "The baby's name is 'Lizbeth."

He turned his head to look at her. She could hardly speak yet, but her thoughts came through to him loud and clear. He still wasn't entirely comfortable with the way his girls could jump into his mind at will, but he'd learned to live with it. It was, after all, a small price to pay for the happiness he'd found living with his houseful of women. "It is, is it?"

"But we'll call her Bethie," Jenna said matter-of-factly.

"If you say so, darlin'," he told her.

"And she's gonna marry Tall's little boy," Jenna added.

Frowning, he looked down at her. "Tall and Marie's baby isn't even born yet."

Jenna nodded. "I know."

Ridge's eyes rolled and he shook his head. The bedroom door swung open as they approached and he gave Hattie a grateful smile as she slipped out of the room to give the little family some privacy. Then his gaze went directly to Sophie, who was lying against a mound of plumped-up pillows, cradling his brand-new daughter in her arms.

He was a lucky man, he knew, as his heart filled again at just the sight of the woman who was his wife. His love.

"Just look at her," Sophie sighed, holding out one hand to draw them all close. "Isn't she beautiful?"

Ridge eased down on the side of the bed and looked down into the tiny face that already had claimed another piece of his heart. "She is that," he murmured and bent down to place a soft kiss on his daughter's forehead.

Then lifting his head again, he looked at Sophie's tired features, the shadows beneath her eyes, and whispered, "Three daughters are enough, don't you think? I don't want you going through this again."

Sophie reached out and cupped his cheek in her palm. "Don't be silly, Ridge," she said with a shrug. "I promised you a house full of children. And we haven't even started on our sons yet."

"Sons?" he asked. "More than one?"

"Three boys, Daddy," Jenna said, and clambered up onto his lap. She waited until he was looking right at her to add, "But you'll always love me best."

Teresa pushed her big sister, Jenna pushed back, and Ridge set them down on the floor to work out their problems themselves. Stealing one brief minute with his wife, he leaned in close and brushed a kiss across her mouth.

"She's wrong, you know," he whispered, his voice hardly louder than a breath.

"She is?" Sophie asked, her gaze moving over his face.

"Uh-huh," he told her gently. "I love my children, but I'll always love *you* best."

Then he kissed her, oblivious to the new baby's cry or his daughters' giggles. And Ridge Hawkins silently counted his blessings.

Catch a Fallen Angel

KATHLEEN KANE

GABE DONOVAN'S regrets for a life of gambling and drinking come fast and hard when he finds himself hanging from the short end of a rope, framed for a crime he didn't commit. But fate has a little detour on the road to the afterlife, complete with a bargain from Old Scratch himself. The deal: two months of life in exchange for the soul of the scoundrel who should have hung in Gabe's noose.

Maggie Benson realizes that only a desperate woman would hire a dusty, down-on-his-luck stranger with a past, but she has a hotel to run in Regret, Nevada, and handymen aren't exactly lining up at her door. Destiny, however, comes in strange packages, and after one magical kiss, she knows Gabe is hers. Come Hell or high water, she's not about to let go of this fallen angel, even if she has to take on the devil himself . . .

"Ms. Kane writes beautiful stories that will live in the heart forever." —*Bell, Book & Candle*

"Laughter tempered with poignancy is Kathleen Kane's hallmark." —*Romantic Times*

AVAILABLE WHEREVER BOOKS ARE SOLD
FROM ST. MARTIN'S PAPERBACKS

Simply Magic

KATHLEEN KANE

PHOEBE HIGHTOWER is flat broke, burning furniture to survive the St. Louis winter. Cold and desperate, she doesn't pay much heed to the mysterious stranger who grants her four wishes for saving his life. At first, she just wishes out loud to be someplace warm. Overnight, she inherits a saloon in the desert boomtown of Rimshot, Nevada. Unfortunately, wishes don't come cheap. She's also inherited a partner, Riley Burnett, an ex-Federal Marshal with a chip on his shoulder, a three-year-old daughter, and a stubborn streak as wide as Phoebe's. But as her attraction to the devilishly handsome Riley warms her up considerably, Phoebe begins to suspect it's more than simply magic that has landed her in Rimshot . . .

"Kane [has a] remarkable talent for unusual, poignant plots, and captivating characters."
—*Publishers Weekly*

"Nobody can capture the essence of Americana heart and soul quite as well as Kathleen Kane."
—*Affaire de Coeur*

AVAILABLE WHEREVER BOOKS ARE SOLD
FROM ST. MARTIN'S PAPERBACKS

Wish Upon a Cowboy

KATHLEEN KANE

Jonas Mackenzie isn't sure what to make of the beautiful stranger who showed up at his Wyoming ranch with marriage on her mind. While he's trying hard to ignore the sparks flying between them, Hannah Lowell is a woman on a mission with a stubborn streak as wide as his own.

Hannah hadn't been thrilled at the idea of marrying a man she didn't know . . . until she had a good look at the lean and rugged cowboy who was her destiny. But how is she going to convince a man who doesn't believe in magic, that he's got the power to save a town from a terrible fate? And that it all boils down to his belief in his legacy, his heart, and in the most powerful magic of all . . . their love.

"True to her talent, Kane keeps the conflicts lively to the end and fills the plot with many surprises."
—*Publishers Weekly*

AVAILABLE WHEREVER BOOKS ARE SOLD
FROM ST. MARTIN'S PAPERBACKS

KATHLEEN KANE

"[HAS] REMARKABLE TALENT FOR UNUSUAL,
POIGNANT PLOTS AND CAPTIVATING
CHARACTERS."

—*Publishers Weekly*

The Soul Collector

A spirit whose job it was to usher souls into the afterlife, Zach
had angered the powers that be. Sent to Earth to live as a
human for a month, Zach never expected the beautiful
Rebecca to ignite in him such earthly emotions.

This Time for Keeps

After eight disastrous lives, Tracy Hill is determined to get it
right. But Heaven's "Resettlement Committee" has other
plans—to send her to a 19th century cattle ranch, where a
rugged cowboy makes her wonder if the ninth time is finally
the charm.

Still Close to Heaven

No man stood a ghost of a chance in Rachel Morgan's heart,
for the man she loved was an angel who she hadn't seen in
fifteen years. Jackson Tate has one more chance at heaven—if
he finds a good husband for Rachel ... and makes her forget a
love that he himself still holds dear.

AVAILABLE WHEREVER BOOKS ARE SOLD
FROM ST. MARTIN'S PAPERBACKS

KANE 9/98